# THE SIX GUESTS

DIANA WILKINSON

Print ISBN 978-1-913942-91-5

## ALSO BY DIANA WILKINSON

4 Riverside Close

∿

You Are Mine

∿

The Girl Who Turned A Blind Eye

*Dedicated to*
*all our NHS workers who fought*
*on the frontline in the war against Covid...*
*and won.*

*Thank you.*

2020

# WEEK 1

# 1

Annabel, our Zoom host, appears in the centre of my screen, eight o'clock sharp. The complete works of Shakespeare, neatly arrayed a fraction above head height, are clearly visible and look as if they've come from the shelf of an Oxford Don. Perhaps they're one dimensional, wallpaper covering, no shadowed corners, covering up the girly chick-lit.

It's all a stage-set, a theatrical production of West End proportions. I stifle a yawn. Christ, it dawns on me that I'm on camera, that she might have caught the boredom; my face is now bang centre, middle box at the top of the screen. My mouth snaps shut.

Whoosh. Fuzzy leaps across my lap, a furry white bullet whose claws miscue as she cascades down the other side of my swivel chair.

'Shit. Careful. Come here you,' I whisper, leaning to the left as her unsteady legs cling to my arm, and hoist her back up to safety before tucking her neatly under the keyboard shelf. A rhythmic purr vibrates against my thigh, as she slumps heavily into position.

'Hi, Kristi. Just waiting for Barton and the others. Talk

among yourselves, I'll only be a mo.' Annabel screams. I turn the volume down, click, click, click. She doesn't really want us to talk among ourselves, she wants us to watch her, take in every detail from the finely threaded tinted eyebrows to the latest Net-a-Porter outfit. The shapely maroon manicured nails jiggle up and down as she tidies a non-existent mess.

There's no-one else to talk to anyway, but Annabel only feels confident if she's attracted numbers, quantities of people, so she'll not waste energy on the first arrival to the hangout. At the moment she takes up most of the computer screen, main picture, head honcho.

My phone suddenly pings for attention. Holding Fuzzy steady with my left hand, I tap open WhatsApp. It's Logan double-checking we're okay for drinks on Monday. I stroke Fuzzy, disbelieving that lockdown has thrown up both a comforting furry houseguest as well as a handsome online suitor.

As I turn my phone to mute, a third box pops up on the computer screen, as does Annabel again. She's like a tightly sprung jack-in-the-box. But it's not Barton, as she hoped, rather Rihanna who's fluffed up in pink like a cuddly toy, lipstick and nails accessorising her ensemble. But it's the barely concealed cleavage that fronts the screen, draws the eye. The complete works of Shakespeare have been overshadowed and our quiz host will be relieved that the three men are late to the party.

A fourth blurry picture follows; desk, ceiling and laptop images loll around, until Joel's face appears at an angle. 'Fuck,' he says. We weren't meant to hear but I'm a dab hand at lip-reading. I turn the volume back up. 'Hi there,' he says, crisp, clean and confident. That's more Joel, more how he wants us to see him. He's upright now, flaky ceiling paint confined to memory. His face comes closer to the screen, blocking out the sombre backdrop.

'Hi, Joel,' we chirp in harmony, like a group of innocent choristers. The newcomer seems pleased to have arrived, stepped over the threshold into an already buzzing party. His beer glass is half-empty. Perhaps it's half-full but it's hard to tell with Joel. The Peak District seems a long way off, but it's only a few hours up the motorway from London, but he could be in Dubai, Sydney, for all we know. In fact, he could be anywhere. He tells us he's in the Peak District, on a walking trip with a mate, but do we believe him? Do we need to believe him? Who cares? He's not the quizmaster tonight. That's Barton.

Barton likes to be late, keep us all waiting. The casual approach makes him more mysterious, enigmatic. That's what he thinks but I'm not sure the participants would agree. But we all do remember he was the last arrival at Annabel and Clifton's wedding, careering up the festooned garden arbour inches behind the slow-marching bride. How could we forget?

Although I was his plus one, Barton had managed to miss the plane the day before. Annabel's never forgiven him for stealing her thunder as he waved and grinned at the gushing guests who took their eyes off the bride, if only for a few seconds. Yet her festering annoyance is oddly extreme for that one minor misdemeanour.

On a Zoom quiz night Annabel can pretend, showcase her grown-up magnanimity, but the large glass of bubbly (is it in a half pint glass tonight? I peer at the screen, feign interest in the literary tomes) is her crutch of make-believe. Who's she kidding?

The fifth square is soon filled. Declan's forehead appears before the rest of him. It's lined, furrowed with intent and his dark hair has started to recede, an ebbing tide of gentle waves. I wouldn't have noticed if the partial shot hadn't showcased the upper third of his head in isolation. It's weird only being able to catch the top of him, no eyes, no subtle crinkle lines doing their sales pitch, drawing us to invest with their projected honesty. He's not a whole person at the moment.

On reflection, I don't think Declan ever was a whole person. With any luck he'll not use the ten-minute mandatory break (Annabel's too mean to pay for blanket Zoom coverage and disappears for ten minutes while she resets the meeting with new join-up links) to WhatsApp our quiz group and fill us in on the last seven days of misery. He's done this more than once. He likes us to sympathise, tell him that it'll all turn out okay, that he'll get another job. Furlough ended with the sack and although Declan says it was just another lockdown redundancy, we all suspect it might be down to drink. His unhealthy relationship with whisky goes way back.

Our Friday group is made up of the type of friends who say what you want to hear, play along with the charade, and speak anything but the truth. It's easier. It's also easier when Declan is in Bangor, Northern Ireland, staying with his mother. Although the screen tricks us to treat people like they're in the same room, close by, we know they're not.

'Hi, all.' His whole face comes into the square. A distinct red blob, of what looks like dried blood, sits proudly, a mini Vesuvius, at the corner of his lips. He's either been in a fight, cut himself shaving or forgotten to wipe away a rogue blob of ketchup. The latter seems unlikely as he's no slob.

'Let's not panic. Barton will be here any minute.' Annabel's voice has risen a few decibels and the champagne bottle has appeared, label facing us. Dom Perignon. It would make a good quiz question. What did we think each of the others would be drinking? Make and vintage, one point for each. I sip my Sauvignon Blanc. I'm a dry white wine person, with a decent knowledge of vineyards and preferences. Marlborough County, New Zealand, all the way for me.

'Cheers,' I add to help lower the quiz host's anxiety. The five heads, imprisoned in square cells, raise glasses to the screen. A quiz gives us something to do, other than share inane chit-chat about the world's *new normal*, face masks and supermarket understocking of hand sanitisers. It's 8.10. Ooops. Barton is really testing the waters.

Suddenly, his face beams broadly across our screens, momentarily usurping Annabel's place on the main frame. I leave the Zoom setting on Speaker option, giving everyone an equal chance to take centre stage, albeit briefly. Annabel's hard to knock aside.

'Sorry, sorry, sorry,' he repeats. The team feign smiling acceptance of the proffered apologies. Like nodding dogs, we collectively move our heads and listen to the phoney excuses for his tardiness. Everyone pretends to believe Barton, although, speaking from experience, I know he's a compulsive liar. People who keep repeating that they never lie and only ever offer up the truth, are definitely hiding something. Usually a whopper or two.

Annabel flicks back her hair, rechecks the champagne label is square to the camera and pops the end of a gold-plated pen into her mouth, twiddling it provocatively. Her pert, pink-tipped tongue appears every so often through strawberry pouting lips. Jeez. They look as if they've been Botoxed. I squint.

She swore she'd never inject herself with poison, but since our Friday meets, I've noticed quite a few changes. Well, changes since Barton's sudden request to join the party. He asked to be invited, citing boredom, but Annabel thinks he's playing a game to win her back.

Online shopping addiction has certainly adorned our hostess with expensive accessories, but her husband's credit card hasn't stretched to common sense. She still flirts hopelessly, a canary trapped in a gilded cage. I wonder if I'm the only person, apart from Annabel, who suspects ulterior motives for Barton's sudden appearance.

My glance moves to the voluptuous Rihanna. Barton is like a greyhound forever after the unattainable rabbit. A cold shoulder, a sniff of aloofness and he's out of the blocks chasing down his next conquest.

## 2

---

Barton Hinton took me under his wing when I joined the *London Echo,* the Capital's latest newspaper to compete with the Fleet Street giants. He was Grayson Peacock's golden boy. Grayson, the paper's editor, isn't unlike Barton with his loud voice and misogynistic attitudes.

'One *helluva* reporter. If there's any dirt to be found, Barton's your man. Stay close, Kristi, and you'll learn a few tricks of the trade.' Grayson's words stuck, like a needle in an old record groove. Problem was, I got too close.

Two things happened in my first week of employment. Firstly, Barton outed a local MP who was having an affair with a lap dancer from Camden. It hit the headlines, further puffed out my colleague's ego and secondly, I got dragged to the pub in celebration.

Barton is a stereotypical bastard with a capital B; the sort girls fall for, but as easy to tie down as a bucking bronco in a Wild West rodeo. Sharp witted, with charm thick and smooth as double cream. Rippling muscles strain through tailored clothing but give testimony to the hours spent in the company gym.

Dedication to his appearance is showcased by a year-round tan, courtesy of the beauty salon next door.

'What's your poison, honey?' His arm slipped easily round my waist, high enough for etiquette, but low enough to make me shiver.

'White wine, and don't ever call me honey.'

Problem was, my contempt was soon doused, the angry fire extinguished by a healthy dose of caring and genius. Getting to know the other Barton, the side smothered by his public displays of machismo, was a different story. It was a dangerous trip to make, but one which I took in spiky heels and tight dresses because that's how he likes his women.

It wasn't the misogynistic treatment that set my heart racing, but the softer side of his personality coin. He cared about what he did; passion for success and telling the truth flowed through his veins. He was also kind and generous, when he was in the mood.

By the time I let my guard down, opened the gates to let him in, Barton was already moving on. When he told me the problem was his, not mine, it didn't take me long to realise he was telling the truth. Playing the field is Barton's sport. He chases down prey like a big game hunter, shoots them dead and steps across the body, leaving the remains for someone else to pick up.

Seeing him on screen every Friday night reignites the hurt, but Grayson warned me more than once, 'Best not to mix business with pleasure.' A pat on my shoulder, as to an errant daughter, should have warned me off sooner. But Barton has that ability, to suck people into his web, then break their hearts. He decides when and where.

'Hi, guys. Sorry I'm late. Just wanted to go through the question sheets again. Not sure how long it'll take but thought I'd try a few different topics this week.' Typical.

Barton likes to prove he's that bit superior. Not with his brain power, but with his ability to entertain, draw us in and impress by his personality. 'Anyway, pens and paper ready?'

We collectively hold up pens, like soldiers proving their guns are ready to fire, prepared for battle. The instruments wiggle in the air. I wonder where Barton is quizzing from tonight. The room behind him looks like it does every week with clean bland cream walls, but the bedhead looks different. I suspect another Premier Inn but now isn't the time to ask. I'll maybe get a chance during the ten-minute interval break when Barton usually texts to stem his boredom.

Barton reels off the topics before he begins the questions. General knowledge, music (artists and lyrics), geography (he likes us to be impressed by his world travels, the questions usually linked to some far-flung exotic paradise he's personally explored), sport (football, rugby, baseball, boxing and horse racing. Rihanna will doubtless disappear for a toilet break at this point, but Annabel, while bemoaning the male bias, will laugh her way through, joining in as 'one of the lads'. She'll forget, aided by the bubbly, that her Botoxed lips and brightly painted nails mark her out as anything but. Who's she kidding?) and 'the final round of the evening is a surprise one' Barton concludes. 'There'll be six questions about each of us. I've done some research.' Barton coughs, sips his gin and tonic, banging the ice cubes against the glass and swills the contents. He lounges back in his chair. The genius quizmaster.

There's a collective intake of breath. I can see, in my mind's eye, Barton's devil horns. The laden weight of hurt still pulls me down, but I sip my wine, smile and play along. It's been over a year since we split, directly after Annabel's wedding, but at times it feels like yesterday.

'Let's see what we all know about each other. There'll be bonus points on offer in the last round.' His grin seems to be directed at someone, me maybe, but it's hard to tell. The view is very one-dimensional, emotions hard to gauge.

Annabel tucks her blonde bob behind her ears, cheeks distinctly flushed. She's already loaded with champagne. 'But before we start, a little twist. You get the points for the final round next week. You've all got one week to research the answers, and...' he pauses for effect, 'you're not allowed to ask the rest of the group for the answers, and most definitely you can't ask the person who is directly linked to their specific question.'

It all sounds a bit convoluted, and disinterest is painted on the five faces, like sculpted heads in the Uffizi Gallery, that stare back. Shit. What is there to say about this new format, except that it sucks? Muffled words of assent filter out from five screens, imperceptible nods like personality tics.

Whatever. I'm curious as to what the questions might be. Anyway, here goes.

'Okay. First round. General Knowledge. All ready?'

We're off. Horses out of the blocks, pens scribbling on blank sheets, chomping at the bit.

# 3

## MONDAY 7TH SEPTEMBER

To: krisdex1234@hotmail.com
From: bartonupthewrongtree@londonecho.com

**BONUS ROUND**
As promised, extra round. Look forward to
seeing how you all get on. See you again
Friday, 8 o'clock. I think Rihanna's quiz host
next week.
Best
Barton

*Question 1: Who was Joel's first ever serious
girlfriend and (bonus point) how long after
their first date did they sleep together?
(nearest answer gets the point)
Question 2:What's Annabel's tattoo of, and
where exactly (for a bonus point) is it
located?
Question 3:What dating site does Kristi use*

*and what's the name of her current mystery*
***single** lover? (bonus point)*
*Question 4: What was the name of Rihanna's*
*first pet and (bonus point) first fiancé?*
*(although I don't think there's been more than*
*one! Ha ha!)*
*Question 5: What secret society does Declan*
*belong to and (bonus point) what does the*
*induction ceremony entail?*
*Question 6: What's my latest scoop and which TV*
*production giant has commissioned the story?*

What the fuck? Barton can't be serious. These will take some serious googling. Not to mention snooping, digging and muck raking. My stool swivels, a mini merry-go-round, my head veering off in the opposite direction. The empty wine bottle by the sink screams accusation.

Working from home has its upsides. PJs at the breakfast bar, slippers toasting my pinkies. Coffees on tap, not the hot coloured water which stews in the newspaper offices' stained cafetière, but robust seasoned pods from Colombia and Vietnam, India and Bolivia. I'm on my third macchiato of the morning, pod strength ten, with a stain of frothed milk on top. The shakes are usually welcome as they agitate the sluggishness. Habit keeps me going, shot after shot, until the sweats kick in and I'm finally awake.

But today, I set my cup down, nausea gurgling. Barton's sick sense of humour is the spoon stirring my insides. Perhaps I need to dress in my office gear, reread his email in business armour and let my professional hat tell me how to respond.

~

Barton thinks he's funny. He snoops on the office staff and digging has become a hobby where his brain works like a metal detector, unearthing rare, but dirty, golden nuggets. None of us are safe from the *You've Been Framed* moments. I've learnt the hard way, having to bite back knee-jerk replies to seemingly innocent questions. He's a master interviewer, practising his technique on friends and colleagues. He then shares gossip with gay abandon, burying both the teller of secrets and the third party under a pile of guilt.

Lockdown has given Barton too much time on his hands, but social distancing suits him. *Love 'em and leave 'em* has become an easier mantra to follow. We all know that he hasn't brushed sad hands up barriers of frosted windowpanes, waving through the restrictions, but has instead, on more than one occasion, sneaked into a lonely singleton's flat.

'What's a guy to do? We've got needs.' He finds this amusing, but anger simmers amongst the listeners. 'I find it easier to avoid morning-after issues these days. I scuttle home early and am a dab hand at deleting follow-on messages. Not to mention, the chances of bumping into my conquests are pretty slim.'

But a lot is a cover-up. Although Barton sometimes phones me on the pretext of work, the next big headline, I know he wants to talk. Underneath all the bluster, he's needy, insecure. Problem is, I've fallen for the puppy-dog misery around midnight on more than one occasion since we split up. But since lockdown, I've managed to resist.

'Can I come round? Please?' His drunken pleading is hard to ignore.

Okay. So, he's adamant he doesn't want a commitment, but I've found the loneliness of the last few months hard to deal with. It's taken me a long time to realise that Barton is telling the truth in that he really doesn't want to settle down, probably never will.

'I'm like my Uncle Stuart. He never married and lives in Barbados, beach hut by the sea. A rum in one hand, a pretty native girl on his arm.'

Uncle Stuart is ninety-six and this seems to prove to Barton that the single, playboy life could be a long-term ambition. But I'm not sure who he's trying to kid.

# 4

I skip through the questions, fighting back the irritation and embarrassment on rereading number 3. The fact that I've resorted to online dating is no one else's business and the word **single**, written in bold, could be a typing error; but it's unlikely.

I carry on down the list and hover at question 4. How the hell are we meant find out the name of Rihanna's first pet without asking her? Maybe she's posted twee pictures, she's that sort of media poster, of a cute long-haired dachshund or more likely an early cat purchase, all fluff and no substance.

Rihanna, despite her shapely rounded breasts, flawless suntan and squeakily innocent-sounding voice, is someone I can only surmise about. Her appearance might be a cover-up for hidden depths, but it's hard to be certain. She was invited to the group by Joel, and he salivates in her youthful company.

Although the six of our Friday Zoom group were all at Annabel's wedding (was it really a year ago?), we didn't really know each other at that point; still don't. Annabel's drunken brainwave, to set up a regular quiz night for her favourite bunch of besties, was to help us become better acquainted and stem the catatonic boredom of lockdown.

We certainly know a lot more about each other now. Yet, Rihanna, is bizarrely elusive. Maybe it's because I'm a woman, and she only meows for the men. And did anyone know she'd been engaged, or married even? The welcome salutation every Friday is, 'Hi, fellow singletons.' Annabel flaps her hand in disgusted humour and says, 'Whatever. Let's get started.' A couple of hours a week, pretending that she belongs, a singleton enjoying the perks, livens Annabel up. Not sure I believe her happily married crap the rest of the time.

But Rihanna. There's been no mention, ever, of a husband or fiancé. Online dating was the highlight of her social calendar, even before enforced isolation. While the rest of us were out in the real world looking for love, getting sloshed and trying to forget drunken one-night stands, Rihanna was researching potential soulmates from all around the world. But, as far as we knew, she'd never taken it any further.

Although, if Rihanna's been engaged, it might be easier to track down the errant fiancé than finding out what she called a pet hamster or tortoise. Christ. She might even have won a goldfish at the fair.

Emails clog up my inbox, like queuing traffic at roadworks. No let-up. Beep, beep, beep, let me through. The red-light pause is soon followed by a green light that sends through a new set of junk.

I pick through the missives, like sifting stones from dried lentils. Monday mornings are tedious, not helped by my rigid rule to steer clear of work-related matters at the weekend. Although who misses the pre-lockdown stress? Not me, that's for sure. No more paranoia of oversleeping, no slapdash botched make-up regime in the half-light leaving smudged mascara, like chimney soot, under puffy eyes. And what a relief to forgo the ankle-twisting race in my high heels to catch the 7.10 to Kings Cross.

The new work normal suits me. For now, at any rate. Mum's worried that I'll get lonely and sometimes I do, for sure, but who doesn't? Even without lockdown, being single in your thirties is testing.

But on screen company, fake in a manufactured way, has its advantages especially where work is concerned. There's not the same chance of insincerity being picked out by a careless expression, or a fake nuance sensed in a falseness of tone. The screen covers up a mountain of deceit, like carefully applied foundation on a heavily pitted complexion. We're all becoming dab hands at playing the new normal at its own game. Only our head and shoulders need to behave.

It's also good not to have Grayson sitting on my shoulder, like an agitated parrot, reminding me of deadlines. As if I could forget. The lingering stench from his halitosis has joined the stilettos in the corner. Of course, we all like familiar, the comfort of the usual, but I can't think of one co-worker who'll miss Grayson. It's bad enough seeing him on our work TeamViewer meets. The new working regime is becoming scarily homely.

But it's still early days, time will tell. At least Fuzzy keeps me company and doesn't judge.

~

The last round of questions was emailed to us all after the Friday Zoom was over. Annabel was so drunk that she'd lost the ability to organise another forty minutes to finish the quiz. She giggled as she unsuccessfully tried to navigate the system, knocking over the two empty champagne bottles along the way.

The impossibility of Barton's sporting round had

compounded the tedium, even Joel and Declan floundered, so everyone nodded enthusiastically when the quizmaster reached the final round, earmarked for completion at home. Happy snappy collective fingers clicked *Leave Meeting.*

Okay. I'll allot one hour each day until Friday, to try to answer the five questions. My Thursday column for the paper, the *London Echo,* on *Life in Lockdown* is headed up, bullet points numbered and ready to go. As I start to fill in content, I pause. Procrastination isn't possible in the physical office space, when surrounded by ambitious work colleagues, but perched alone on my roost, I decide to cheat the system and click minimise on my column notes.

I set the timer. Sixty minutes. That's my target to find the answers to question number 4. The name of Rihanna's first pet and the name of her first (only?) fiancé. Then it's back to work.

The search engines rev to life, as I pop another espresso capsule in the coffee machine and refill my cup. *Rihanna Conlon, pet's first name, fiancé, Mr Conlon* are entered into Google. I reread the six questions while my provider throws up suggestions.

I wonder if the others will join in or ignore Barton's less than subtle attempts to wind us all up. The questions seem random, but as I digest the content, like hard to chew stewing meat, it seems less likely. Each question requires probing into a secret fact about each of us.

Barton's a journalist, a dirty low-down *hack* as well as a ruthless reporter who chases stories like a fox stalking loosely fenced-in chickens. He's made plenty of enemies along the way but on Friday nights, his handsome smiling face sucks us in, teases us to engage. Everyone knows about his scary reputation, but we don't care. His work has nothing to do with us, so we welcome him with pleasantries, bonhomie and flirtation.

Annabel especially. While she hankers after the company of notoriety, she's not finding it easy to shovel under the carpet her infatuation for Barton's bastardly charms. I like to think I've had much more success in moving on. While my goal is to find love in my thirties, not an easy task, Annabel's reasons for hankering after Barton are something else entirely. She's trapped in a passionless marriage to Clifton, who compared to Barton, is mean and petty-minded. Clifton's got the look of a bulldog, drooling jowls with a barely concealed vicious streak and alas for Annabel, his obscenely huge income can't compete with Barton's sex appeal.

I finish the coffee, push the small cup to one side, and start to browse.

## 5

Midnight. So far, I've spent the last seven hours on the quiz research. Yo-yo googling has tangled me in its twisted string. Barton's questions, a heap of squirming maggots, have eaten their way through the minutes and into my brain. I can't let up. Work on my column has been pushed to one side.

As I go to close the laptop, my mobile screen comes to life, the brightness like a scary 'boo' from behind the sofa. The vibrations, like the drone of a dental drill, set my teeth on edge. Annabel. Again. I switch the phone off. There's no emergency that won't wait six hours till I get up; not even Annabel's suicide threats.

I'm wondering if she's googled all the questions Barton sent, but suspect she ego surfed, concentrating maniacally on question number two for hours, to make sure there were no hidden web clues about her tattoo. However, it's likely that she reached question number four and that's what's causing the hysteria. It's certainly not the name of Rihanna's first pet that will have sent her over the edge. I shut down the laptop, pour myself a long cold glass of water and pull across the curtains.

Of course, I'm curious as to how Barton knew about

Annabel's tattoo. An etching of the Eiffel Tower between the legs, near the crotch, would have been hard to guess at. It was her husband, Clifton's and her little secret. Nudge, nudge, wink, wink. You'll never guess what he bought me as an engagement present? Now we all know. Well, I know because she told me in confidence a while back. I was assured no one else was privy to this juicy piece of information.

I'm a whizz at sneaky delving into the darkest corners. It's part of the job. Barton is the only person I know who's even sneakier, a master muckraker and codebreaker. He could have led the team at Bletchley Park, breaking down the most convoluted Nazi ciphers. Having come to a dead end with googling for snippets about Annabel's tattoo, my mind is tossing like a buoy in the ocean, wondering how Barton found out. But I can guess.

The stairs creak as I climb up to the mezzanine space, my cramped bijou bedroom cell which overlooks the lounge behind a slatted wooden rail. Fuzzy, having once slipped through the gaps, keeps well away but the sofa recently placed directly below will break any careless falls.

I have screen eyes, as if matchsticks are jammed between my lids, forcing them wide apart. They refuse to close. The silence in my little maisonette isn't helping as images whizz back and forth across my brain.

I rip off my clothes, dumping them on top of the pine chest at the foot of the bed, and drag a night shirt over my head.

Fuzzy has beaten me to it, the comforting white ball of fluff purring rhythmically on my pillow. I hump her leaden weight aside, avoiding the irritable claws. Her slit eyes droop shut again as I turn off the overhead light, but the purring rumbles on.

I slither under the rumpled duvet and lie supine, staring up at the ceiling. Pictures, postings, Twitter and Facebook feeds zigzag raggedly round in my head. Sleep isn't going to come. I'd forsaken my rigid two-hour ban on screen time before bed and carried on. And on. And on. I must have only solved question number four moments before Annabel did. It was twenty minutes after I'd discovered the name of Rihanna's fiancé that Annabel rang, sobbing hysterically down the phone.

Yes, Rihanna was engaged as a teenager, for six months give or take. But the bombshell, think Hiroshima for fallout, was that Annabel had no idea it had been to her husband, Clifton.

# 6

Annabel's eyes are black-ringed, panda eyes, but she looks so rough I think tenth round of a boxing bout. She steps into the hall, a wet unsolidified stalactite hanging from her nostril. The screen face of Friday night, the smooth expensive Clarins complexion, has been overlaid by a dry parchment dotted with tiny blood-red broken veins and the white linen shirt looks as if it's been slept in.

'Come in. Are you okay?' Never ask anyone how they are, they might tell you. My mother's voice follows us through to the kitchen. My smile is lacklustre, under my own puffy eyes, but Annabel's concern is flowing down a one-way street.

'Not really. I'm sorry, I know it's only nine, but I couldn't sleep.'

'I would hug you but...'

Annabel pulls back, having been tempted to snap the two-metre invisible barrier, and apologises again. Social distancing plays into my hands, as hugging Annabel is the last thing I want to do.

'Kettle's on. Let's sit here.' I tap a stool jammed in under the breakfast bar, push aside the littered papers strewn across the surface and set out a couple of mugs.

'Excuse the mess. Working from home has taken over the whole house.' I tug my dressing gown tighter, spear my fingers through my straggling hair to shock it back to life while the coffee seeps through the pods.

'Clifton lied,' Annabel begins, like a dog on a lead desperate to be let off. 'He asked Rihanna to our wedding, not Joey from the bank. Joey was Rihanna's plus one, not the other way around. I had no idea Clifton had been engaged to Rihanna. The bastard never told me.'

I stretch my arms above my head, fingers intertwined, and pull out my neck, tipping it from side to side to release the crick.

'I'm sorry,' I say, releasing my locked arms. Annabel's intense stare aims to suck back my full attention.

'He says it doesn't matter, that it meant nothing, and he didn't see the need to tell me as it was all in the past. Can you believe it?' Annabel spits, the bludgeoned eyes wide and sniffs the defrosted stalactite back up her nostril. I lean across and hand her a tissue.

'Maybe he has a point. I doubt it meant anything and it was all in the past.' My yawn is muffled but Annabel glares like an irritable lion, thorn deeply embedded in its paw. Her hoot into the tissue blasts out the toxins and reignites my concentration.

'And why did Rihanna never tell me? I've seen her often enough since the wedding.'

~

That's where our Friday Zoom group met, under the azure paradise of a golden Sorrento sun, enclosed within the walls of ancient baked-terracotta buildings. Sprawling gardens, rich in bloom and heady scent, were handsomely defined by Leylandii trees that towered heavenwards.

Thrilled to be Barton's plus one, it was only when drenched in Chianti and Grappa that he let slip that I was actually his plus three, two predecessors having declined the invitation. His laugh boomed all the way to the Amalfi coast. Annabel, resplendent in puffed meringue, was the centrepiece of a lavishly decorated banquet, part of a feast to fill the senses.

Declan, as best man, threatened the event, sodden with booze and buzzing with energy as the twinkling Irish eyes morphed into red devil pellets. Rihanna's shoulder strap broke loose as Declan swung her round, like a whirling dervish, in the sultry night air to the heady wedding beat. Joey, Rihanna's plus one, finally felled Declan, leaving him for dead under the olive trees. When he finally managed to pick himself up, it was Barton who led Declan to a quiet corner.

Joel stuck close to Rose, the sixteen-year-old bridesmaid, and embraced the selfie-taking as well as the young woman's burgeoning body, his arms like jellyfish tentacles. Funny what you remember. I had all the time in the world to people watch while Barton roamed the terrazzo plains.

No one batted an eyelid when Rihanna kissed Clifton at midnight over the starlit breakfast. Annabel was close by and immediately ducked in to hug them both, pulling her husband and guest tight, for one more photoshoot opportunity. But standing behind Clifton, I'd noted the groom's white freckled hands slither over Rihanna's bottom, out of range of the camera lens.

As guests took to the dance floor, I watched Clifton's fingers slide across the flimsy, silk material of Rihanna's dress and the lingering kiss he planted on her lips.

'Cheese,' I said, smile like a sunbeam, as I broke their trance but not before I'd captured their glassy expressions as they turned. I often wonder what happened to all the snaps taken by guests on disposable cameras, the snaps that no one ever saw.

~

'What did you make of Barton's questions?' I change tack, derailing Annabel's train of thought.

'He's a real git but I suppose if he hadn't asked them, I'd never have found out about Rihanna and Clifton.'

'What about your tattoo? Does anyone else know? I doubt they'll be able to find out anything on the internet.' The coffee is bitter, bittersweet. I cut up a crusty croissant and pop it in the microwave.

'Oh that. Everyone knows it's a tattoo of the Eiffel Tower,' Annabel announces a bit too loudly, clearing her throat in the aftermath. 'And what about your dating site?' Tit for tat. She raises a questioning eyebrow, one of a pair of thick black pencil brackets turned on their side.

'Okay. I may as well own up. *Suave Singletons*. There's no other way to meet guys at the moment, except remotely.' The microwave pings and I offer up the squidgy pieces of flaky pastry. 'It'll sweeten the taste.'

'I won't ask which way your tattoo is pointing.' My smile aims at conspiratorial sisterhood.

'And I won't ask who your latest date is.' Touché.

Annabel gets up, wipes her mouth with a fresh tissue ripped from the box, and drips small pastry flakes onto the floor in the process.

'I'd better get going, but hey, thanks for listening. Sorry I've been such a bore. Looks like I'll have to let it go as it's not really a divorceable offence and anyway, it's nice to talk.' A sigh, mingled with a sharp tinny laugh, puffs out.

'Anytime. I'm always here.'

It's good not to have to do the insincere air-kissing routine, certainly not at ten thirty in the morning, hung-over and queasy.

I open the front door and as icy air rushes in, I tighten the cord of my dressing gown. Annabel steps past me and slips back on her fine leather gloves.

'Bye, Kristi. See you Friday at eight.' Annabel digs in her handbag for her car key and wanders down the path. She'll carry on as if nothing's happened, her glasshouse intact, and have us all believe Barton's questioning shots only glanced the sides.

'Definitely. I'll be there.' I wave her off, shivering in the cool morning air as she slides into her red two-seater Audi TT roadster which mocks my modest Mini Clubman. Annabel's sports car is her run-around vehicle, the Range Rover saved for longer journeys.

Marriage certainly has its upsides.

# 7

Patio heaters, evil polluting guards, tower over the physically distanced drinkers, baking us in $CO_2$ emissions. Who cares? We're like convicts out on bail, relief and excitement pumping through our veins. A growing number of rowdy guys hover, like wild animals freed from cages, and pump up the volume. The steaks on the BBQ have us salivating.

Random punters test the two-meter rule, alcohol vacuuming up the space as measurements become vague. At least I don't need to worry about Joel. Flouting authority isn't a pastime of his.

'Yoo hoo, over here. Joel.' My scream gets swallowed up by the deafening high-octane chatter. I know it's a pretty shitty artificially grassed pub garden, but it's a start, and boy, is it good to be out.

I shake my hair from under the bright-red hood, flipping it away, and turn my face up to the heat. My bright outfit gets Joel's attention, and he strolls over, skinny jeans sprayed on to spindly legs. A puffer jacket bulks up his chest which makes him a man of two halves. I think puffed-up pigeon, keeping warm on top with scrawny chicken legs attached below.

'Hi, gorgeous. How the hell are you?' Social distancing keeps him well away as he'd rather yell, burst his vocal cords, than be caught getting too close. His respect for authority might be why he became a schoolteacher. He's mentioned more than once how he likes when pupils call him 'Sir'.

I break the rules for him when I stand up and lean across, landing a slobbery kiss on his cheek. I dare him to step back, admonish me, and turn his head away. It's very tempting to poke around in his pocket to find the face mask.

'What are you drinking? Lager? Crisps?' My finger hovers over a small electronic tablet menu which is neatly inserted into the top of the rickety table. 'We order and pay here, and they bring it all to the table. How cool is that?'

'Brilliant. Saves queuing. A pint please.' Joel slips off his jacket, reducing his upper-body mass by half and rubs his hands under the hot glowing filaments. My fingers tap in the order and I present my card and hey presto, it's done. The new normal has thrown up rare advantages as slickly designed technology races ahead.

Joel fills me in on his drive down the previous night from the Peak District, where he's been sightseeing, sneaking off for some excitement. He overdoes the chat about the Peak District, the scenery, the weather and lack of traffic and it crosses my mind that he mightn't have been away at all.

Before lockdown, he never went anywhere, didn't see the point. Born and bred in Barnet, Joel boasts he lives in north London in a bedsit near the station, less than a mile from his parents'. His living quarters are spartan and dull but no matter, he's the proud owner of his very own slice of suburban mediocrity. On the group's first-ever Friday night Zoom, we asked him to give us a virtual guided tour of his premises, but unsurprisingly he declined.

'Have you started on Barton's questions?' We're twenty

minutes into the small talk, foamy lager creaming our lips, when Joel brings up the subject.

'Oh my God. What's he playing at? I checked out the questions yesterday. What about you?' I ask. I don't mention the seven hours of riveting online snooping nor Annabel's tearful, suicidal visit earlier.

'Are you going to bother?' He shrugs, sips his beer.

'Not sure I've got much time and the questions are pretty personal. It'll take some serious digging.' My reply gets swallowed up as I crunch the crisps and open out the packet. 'Help yourself.'

'I can't see the point. Barton's just being nosey, trying to wind us all up. God knows why.' Joel ignores the crisps and rubs his hands together.

'What was the question about you? I can't remember.'

'Something about my first girlfriend and when I slept with her.' Joel blows into his bluing hands, the fingertips white and bloodless. His long skinny legs stretch out to the side of the table. 'Everyone knows it was Olivia, freshers' week. Vicars and tarts, and I was the tart.' A flat laugh plonks onto the table between us as Joel recoils his legs and knocks back his drink.

Tinny speakers attached to a sturdy wooden fence suddenly burst into life and spew out loud unrecognisable songs. The guys in the corner start cavemen routines of arm swinging and hip gyrating, the two-meter rule reduced to a six-inch crack. Joel covers his ears with his hands, and mouths silent exaggerated movements in an attempt to make me understand that conversation is futile. He lifts his jacket from the back of the chair, turns his head, and waves his hand in the direction of the exit.

'Walk?' He mimes, lifting his feet up and down on the spot.

I pick up my bag, throw my hoodie back over my head and

follow Joel to the gate. I glance backwards at the politically incorrect crowded garden. Who can blame them? It's been a long-dreamt of pleasure, meeting friends for a few beers.

## 8

After work, Barton and I would end up gripping cold frothy lagers on the decking of a riverside pub not far from the office. The Thames meandered alongside, its murky water dotted with barges, and kept us company.

I used to live for those moments, willing the working hours to pass, so I'd get Barton to myself. From early morning until six, Barton was pumped, energy fizzing through his veins as he chased the scoops, the next big headline. But he would slowly descend from the heights of adrenaline-fuelled mania, tear off his tie and stuff it in a pocket, as the offices emptied. Exhaustion forced him to a reluctant slowdown.

When Annabel invited me to join Friday Hangouts, the nickname for our Friday quiz night, I was curious to find out more about the other members. Although I'd met them all at Annabel's wedding, their personal relationships with Barton were vague. I knew little about any of the group. Although Barton didn't ask much about my life, I dug around in the archives of his.

'How well do you know Joel?' Asking about the youngest

male member of the group seemed the safest, least threatening, place to start.

Barton and I sat outside in all weathers, relieved to be away from the office sauna. I'd pull my coat collar up, shiver and brace myself as I delved. Lovers' pasts were a dangerous zone; innocent probing could lead to explosive discoveries and my stomach would knot, like twisted yarn, when I dared to ask.

'Joel was at uni with Annabel and me. His was in the room next door to mine in halls, first term. The only thing we had in common was a paper-thin dividing wall. That and a love of chocolate biscuits.'

'Why did you stay friends?'

'Friends is a bit strong. He hung around like a stray mongrel, even after a good kicking or two. I couldn't shake him off. Problem with Joel is he seems harmless enough, but his insipidness disguises a dogged, yappy determination to prove himself. Also, Annabel was a sucker for a lost cause. Still is.'

It hurt to ask, but I had to know. 'Did you and Annabel go out for long?'

Barton's phone would constantly vibrate with messages whenever I had him to myself. He vetted every call, dithering before accepting or deleting. His eyes lit up when the interrogation on this particular evening got interrupted and he quickly slotted the phone to his ear.

'Ha. Talk of the devil. Annabel, how the hell are you? Your ears must have been burning.' Barton's egotism thrives on flouting conquests, especially in the faces of current girlfriends who might be getting too close. I suspected he was scared of losing control.

I watched him get up, pace the empty decking and laugh with guttural huskiness at whatever was being said; then he'd smile over, make sure I was taking it all in. In hindsight, I think he'd started to care for me. Perhaps too much. He thought my jealousy might help rebuild his challenged ego.

'Back to your question,' he said, scraping the cold metal chair closer to mine as he sat down again. 'We went out, off and on, for a couple of terms. Annabel was my first real girlfriend.' He finished his drink and plonked the glass down on the slatted table, the surface of which glistened with a damp sheen of spilt beer.

'We got on really well, until Joel stuck his oar in.'

'Joel? Where does he come into it?'

'He's a jealous little git, always has been. You see, he knew that I wasn't a one-woman type of guy and I suspect he used his coffee mug to listen through the plaster wall at what was happening on the other side. Get my drift?'

'Is that why you still don't like him? Did he tell Annabel?'

'Yes. Is it that obvious that I can't stand him?' Barton turned his head, looked out across the Thames, and closed his eyes.

I nodded. 'Yes. It is. Very.'

# 9

---

Joel and I stroll through Hitchin and follow the precinct past the empty market stalls and St Mary's church. The silence of the graveyard mirrors the eerie stillness of the night.

Our conversation is stilted because, although it's good to be out, Joel and I don't have much in common except a few Friday night acquaintances. But when he called, it was too tempting not to escape the house for a couple of hours.

I jump over a barrier into the town's main car park which overlooks the River Hiz as it meanders past the medieval church buildings. A stray duck waddles by.

'Listen, let's tell Barton we didn't have time to answer the questions. He'll not mind.' Joel, eyes forward, stuffs his hands into the puffer but his voice is clear and clipped as it echoes in the crisp night air.

'Do you think? At least we all know the name of your first girlfriend and when you slept together. It's been tossed around like pass the parcel.' I force a giggle.

Joel clears his throat, struts ahead.

'Whatever.' Even in the dull artificial yellow lighting, it's hard to miss the thick flush of red which floods his cheeks.

'At least no one knows what dating website I've been using but how the hell did Barton know I was using one at all?' I know I let it slip, but I'm not keen to share my stupidity with the others, certainly not with Joel.

The market car park, usually crammed full of traders' and shoppers' vehicles, is deserted. The sombre silence has the timbre of a battlefield, soldiers having fled the approaching enemy. I count a mere six cars, irritation at manoeuvring into tight spaces a distant memory.

'Even if Barton does know what website I've been using, there's no way he could know who I've hooked up with.'

'Don't be too sure. Barton must know, why else ask the question? Perhaps he's waiting to spill the beans. What I don't get, is why he wants us all to know each other's dirty little secrets.'

Joel zaps open his Mazda MX-5 Miata and zips his pipe cleaner legs into the cramped space. He rolls down the window, nonchalantly spreading his arm along the sill. It's a showy car for someone with such an outward lack of dynamism.

I inch back from the vehicle and my voice clips through the awkward silence.

'Thanks for calling. It was good to meet up, do something normal. I miss getting out and can't wait for a wild party or two.' The latter is definitely true. 'Anyway, take care and see you Friday.' I beat the bonnet and step away.

Joel's finger hovers on the ignition. 'Friday?'

'The quiz, you idiot.'

'Oh that.' He starts the engine, revs the accelerator, and trills his bony fingers. 'Yep. See you Friday.' He blows me a kiss before the car speeds off through the car park, thick fumes billowing from the exhaust pipe.

'See you,' I yell after him.

But he's already closed up the window.

# 10

After Joel's car disappears from view, I walk slowly towards the main road that joins Hitchin Hill. My mind is buzzing from today's events. First Annabel and now Joel.

The name of Joel's first girlfriend, Olivia, and the fact they slept together in freshers' week aren't dirty little secrets but as my pace increases up the steep incline, seeds of concern are planted. As a light jog throws me back onto the flat, I try to rationalise events.

Perhaps the five questions aren't completely random and the answers not so innocent. Joel's agitation was at odds with his trademark calmness. Our little group is too selfish, disinterested, to dig below Joel's surface. Annabel insists on inviting him to make up numbers, a sense of magnanimity coating the rest of us with a phoney selflessness. But he's a link from university days, when he hung around with Annabel and Barton. He's a reminder of days when the decency of youth wasn't tainted by background snobbery and size of income.

Olivia and freshers' week are the answers Joel's happy for us to put down, one point for each. But are these the right answers? The doubts are creeping in.

My head is buzzing when I reach the front door, my thumping heartbeat the echo of my brain. As I slide my key into the lock, I glance up at the waxing crescent moon; a familiar slice of something permanent. I wonder if the man in the moon is watching.

~

I peel off my damp clothes and slip on my fleecy grey-zipped onesie. I decide to allow myself one more hour, tops, to do a bit more digging. It's become addictive, usurping Facebook for time-wasting.

Joel. He's hiding something, and I'll not be able to sleep until I've opened up the laptop. I blame the journalist in me. Barton calls me a nosey bitch and perhaps he's right.

I settle in the lounge with a glass of neat whisky, an eighteen-year-old Glenfiddich malt. It's the only medicinal nightcap that helps when restlessness and anxiety threaten insomnia. Since March, night-time has become a new enemy. Macabre imaginings and morbid fears are playing havoc with sleep patterns around the world; it's a global phenomenon.

Perhaps tonight I'll sleep on the sofa, try to give the nightmares the slip.

I've found out the answer to the Annabel question, have more work to do in finding out the name of Rihanna's first pet (seriously though – who cares?) and also to find out what Joel is hiding.

But instead, I click on the name Declan Mooney. He's more elusive than the others, ensconced in Bangor with his mother (or so he says) and I fancy a new challenge. I type in *secret societies, initiation ceremonies, Belfast* and wait for the search to begin.

Once again, I set the timer on my phone. Here we go.

# 11

Declan shook the bottle, swivelling it round to the light, peering through the empty opaque glass. He held out his hands and like a nauseous spectator at a bullfight, watched them tremble.

Outside, the rain blocked out the dying embers of daylight, the thick grey blanket a mirror to his mood. Since he'd got back to Bangor on the coast of County Down, there'd been no let-up in the weather, and he'd polished off the only comfort against the dullness.

Clifton was ignoring Declan's calls, his boss's secretary panning him off with creative excuses. But Declan was desperate for the bank reference, before Barton's muck spreading escalated out of control. A positive reference might be Declan's only chance of another job as he had no idea how much Barton knew. The Friday quiz questions had been like a round of machine-gun fire, piercing his rusty armour and had sent Declan back to find solace in the bottle.

'Once an alcoholic, always an alcoholic.' His mother had greeted him by stuffing the key to the sherry cabinet down her cleavage.

Since he'd read through Barton's questions over the weekend, Declan's stomach had been in knots. He'd spent the last few days navigating the web, ego surfing, trying to see what bits of his life were floating around in the ether. Barton could be bluffing, or else harvesting for a major scoop, in which case Declan's life was all but over.

~

The windswept coast road which skirted Bangor was deserted. Declan pulled his collar high, rubbed his frozen hands together and gathered up pace. The angry waves from the ocean crashed against the sea wall, catapulting spumes of surf into the air and across his path. Declan bent his head and tugged a woollen beanie down over his ears.

McGinty's pub, half a mile round the headland, was hewn into the rock face, and a rusty red metal sign at the entrance creaked back and forth. Declan slowed his step as he approached and hovered outside for a few minutes. He glanced up at the clear starlit sky, did the sign of the cross, and took a deep breath before he stepped inside. His head ducked under the low entrance beam, the painted warning a dirty yellow and barely visible: *Duck or Grouse.*

Bill McGinty pulled the lever of a beer tap with one hand and sipped from a frothy pint of Guinness which he held in the other. Clear white foam, like lightly beaten soufflé, lathered his thick grey moustache.

'Christ, look what the cat's dragged in. Jesus. Declan Mooney. How the hell are you?' Bill wiped his large, calloused hands on a dishcloth and thrust a dried palm over the counter.

Declan yanked off his hat, ruffled his flattened hair and extended a hand.

'Grand thanks. Good to see you.' Bill's steel grip crunched through Declan's bones.

'What'll it be lad?' The barman lifted a tumbler to the whisky optic and raised a questioning eyebrow.

'Yes, Scotch on the rocks please, and have one yourself.'

The smell of stale beer and damp towels mingled with the fishy smell from the harbour. A plate of unfinished chips, smothered in bloodied congealed ketchup, sat atop the counter. Declan swallowed hard as the acid stench of vinegar hit his nostrils.

'Here you are, lad. Tell me how you've been. And why are you back in this godforsaken hole?' Bill's palms plonked heavily on the counter, his eyes wide, ears twitching for gossip.

Declan at first didn't recognise his own reflection in the mirror that extended the full length of the bar behind the optics. The straggly hair and peppered stubble reminded him of Robinson Crusoe. He scratched his chin, his fingers picking up grease and sea salt. He threw back his head and downed the glass, wiping his lips with the back of his hand.

'Same again please.' Declan slid his glass forward as Bill clicked a button on a music deck, letting Irish country music flood the room.

'Another whisky coming up.'

Slowly, Declan turned. Two men who were slumped heavily at the bar looked away, swivelling their glazed eyes towards the small TV screen pinned up near the ceiling. The graphics were like those of a blurry CCTV system.

Sixth sense, and history, told him Sean Ferran would be sitting behind him in the corner on the hard wooden bench, engraved *To Aisling, Fighter for the Cause*. He wasn't wrong. Declan held his glass to his lips, took a gulp and inched away from the bar.

The worn, black felt fedora hat was pitched over Ferran's

forehead. The elderly gentleman's shoulders were stooped as he leant forward, arms stretched out on the table. A cough, ragged and chesty, pitched towards Declan as he approached and set his drink down. Violins screeched through the sound system; boisterous Irish jigs inflamed with patriotism.

'Declan. What a surprise! Here, have a seat and welcome home, son.' Sean pinched the fedora along the centre pleat and tipped it off his head. Strands of white hair, fine woollen fibres, criss-crossed his liver-spotted pate. A cold, damp handshake made Declan squirm.

'Sean, I need to talk to you.' Declan lowered himself down opposite Sean, keeping his eyes locked on the old man's face.

'Okay, but let's have a bloody drink first. Sláinte. Cheers.'

## 12

Declan first met Barton at Annabel's wedding. A competition to see who could hold their drink was a close-run event. Barton had body mass, muscle and determination but seriously underestimated Declan's Irish ancestry and an inherent ability to drink most people under the table. 'Hollow legs, as my ma would say.'

It was well past midnight, and slumped alongside each other in the balmy night air, soft music the backdrop to a fading affair, Barton began to ask questions.

'That's what I do. Ask people questions. You'd be surprised the stories I hear.'

'What is it you do?' Declan asked.

'I'm a reporter. *London Echo*. I'm working on a story about a guy from your part of the world, as it happens.'

'Oh. Would I know him?'

'Are you a protestant or catholic?'

Declan's eyes glazed over as his head began to spin. He pulled himself up.

'Why?'

'I'm doing a piece on an IRA informer. The guy brought

down many hard-line terrorists in his time. Just thought you might have heard of him. Patrick O'Halloran?'

Even under the warm, clear starlit Italian heaven, the flames of hell still raged in Declan's soul. He staggered from his chair, clutching the sides and put a hand on his stomach.

'No. Never heard of him. Sorry, I need the boy's room.' A choking sound erupted from his throat.

'Looks as if I've won the drinking contest.' Barton laughed and slapped his glass down. He got up and pushed his own chair to one side before thumping Declan on the back.

'You'll be okay, mate. Look, there's a flower bed over there by the statue of Venus.'

Patrick O'Halloran had been there that night. Sean Ferran, weasel in the wings, had given the orders and Patrick had been sent to the frontline with Declan and his brothers.

'There's no need to do this, Declan.' Patrick's soft, lilting Irish accent, still rang in his ears. 'You don't have to.'

'I've no choice. Sean says it's them or us. If I don't, Sean says things will get worse for my family.'

Patrick had watched on as Declan kneecapped the entire protestant family but when Patrick disappeared from the scene a few months later, Declan tried to forget him.

Now as he hung his head over the flower bed, gripping the bricked edge with both hands, it all flooded back. Soon he was rocking as his insides lost their battle.

Declan wound his way back from McGinty's pub, wandering through the back streets of Bangor. His teeth chattered as he clapped his blue hands together and blew into the palms, vapour clouds puffing out through frozen lips. He sat down on a low garden wall, and replayed Sean's words.

'Listen, Declan. It was years ago. No one will remember you. If that bastard O'Halloran dares throw up our names, we'll be gunning for him. We know where he is. You've nothing to worry about. Anyway, I thought O'Halloran's story ran in the papers a few years ago?'

'It did, but someone from the press is now hinting that they know what I got up to. O'Halloran or someone else might have grassed us up more recently.'

'What makes you say that?' Sean's wry smile, arrogance writ large, and his black eyes like hardened coals sent a chill through Declan.

Declan ignored the question. 'I'm thinking of owning up, Sean, before they come for me. The nightmare's never gone away. The guilt, knowing what I did. Doing time seems the only way forward.'

Sean crashed down his beer tankard. Customers' heads turned in unison, like spectators at a tennis match, as the glass shattered, spewing lethal fragments through the air. Golden liquid sloshed over the sides of the table.

'Once a member, always a member. You don't get to confess. Where's your fucking pride, man?' Sean spat in Declan's face, leant forward and hissed. He grabbed both sides of Declan's coat and yanked. 'And don't ever forget that. Or you'll be sorry.'

Declan had breathed more easily when the media ran the story on O'Halloran. Declan's name hadn't been mentioned, although he doubted O'Halloran had forgotten him. Sean Ferran had always managed to evade capture as he was never present during atrocities. He was the Mafia boss of a small-time provincial operation, basking in being the big fish in a small pond. He gave the commands but as a coward hiding in the wings.

A cat suddenly appeared and wandered up to Declan, rubbing up against the man's legs and purring loudly. Declan stretched his fingers out and patted his thighs for the animal to jump onto his lap. He opened his coat, nudged the furry stranger inside and rubbed its back with a chilly hand.

The guilt had never really gone away, and Barton's bloody questions had brought it all back. Declan had only two options and handing himself in to the police was starting to look the least likely.

There was only one other thing for him to do.

# 13

*Suave Singletons* blossomed during lockdown as an exclusive London dating site for professional people. New members had to agree terms and conditions. Most importantly, those looking for romance on the slickly worded website had to be single, as in not married, and secondly earn a salary in excess of £50k a year. Logan and I had laughed, wondering who was likely to check and if we'd be sent to prison for lying.

Having wasted months on Barton, think Daniel Cleaver in Bridget Jones, my tummy is finally somersaulting in anticipation of a proper date. Logan has bombarded me with messages and texts since our first casual meet-up in Starbucks near Kings Cross; a little less than a week ago. Lockdown isolation has helped dampen my usual critical eye and has coated Logan in glossy hues. I've never gone looking for dates, in no hurry to settle down, but five months with only Fuzzy for company, has drawn a scary picture of what a permanent single future might really feel like. It's as if I've been locked in solitary confinement and the warder has thrown away the key.

As I stroll through Hyde Park towards the bandstand, which is randomly placed in a wide-open space, I wonder where Logan lives. Surnames and home addresses are not recommended to be shared by *Suave Singleton* members and the website's terms and conditions stress that users do so at their peril. Disclaimers are written bold. Public meeting places are recommended, at least for the first few dates.

Logan is standing up ahead, by the steps up into the bandstand. I raise my hand from about a hundred yards away and jiggle my fingers. His *Suave Singleton* head-and-shoulders profile doesn't do him justice. Now that his black sculpted head is attached to the rest of his body, it's the muscled torso that defines him. Press-ups, ab work, weights, marathons, tennis and cycling have turned him into a one-man decathlete. These are the pastimes he's owned up to, but I suspect they're the tip of the iceberg. He's not unlike Barton in attention to physical detail. Hopefully though, he'll not be another commitment-phobe.

When we met for the first time in Starbucks, Logan had been covered up against a heavy downpour and his wavy black hair had dripped wet globules onto an oily raincoat. When he stripped off a layer, a loose cashmere jumper camouflaged the ripping muscles.

Today, the beautiful Indian summer afternoon has put paid to extra clothing and an open-necked pink shirt leaves little to my imagination. As I get closer, my step falters. Why is this guy doing online dating? Perhaps lockdown has left him starved of female attention. Yet I can't imagine him suffering the same dark melancholy that has clung to me like a pesky limpet.

'Hi,' I say.

'Hi. What a lovely day.' He smiles, leaning in to brush his lips against my cheek. He smells of fresh air and woodland, no subtle hint of aftershave.

'Yes, fabulous.' I look up at the cloudless sky and fiddle with my hair, tousling it from side to side. 'You been here long?'

'Ten minutes or so. That's all. I'm working nearby, not far from Hyde Park tube station.' He pats a small Gladstone bag, smooth tan grained leather. 'Have you eaten? I've brought some food, if you're hungry.'

My stomach gurgles, butterflies battering against the vacuum. He pats the bag a second time. 'White wine too, if you fancy it.'

'Now you're talking.' My smile erupts.

Logan leads the way, deeper into the park, until we reach a large sweet chestnut tree, its foliage reluctantly shedding the deep rich greenness of early summer. A sadder hue shades the grass beneath.

'What about here?' His eyes scan the area which is strangely forlorn except for a dog chasing after a lone cyclist in the distance.

He opens his bag, the sort that used to accompany doctors on house visits, think *Call the Midwife*, and magics a rug, red and green tartan, a bottle of Sauvignon Blanc, a couple of plastic glasses and an array of sandwiches in a sealed container.

My cheeks flush. 'Wow. This looks fantastic,' I gush, slipping awkwardly down onto the rug beside him. I peel my pumps off and push them to one side.

'My pleasure.' He produces a bottle opener, pulls out the wine cork and fills the glasses. 'Not a fan of screw tops,' he says, reading my thoughts. 'Cheers.'

'Cheers. And thanks.'

The wine weaves its magic, loosening my limbs and tongue. Logan leans back against the gnarled trunk and asks me about my work.

'I'm working on a column for the paper, the *London Echo*. *Life in Lockdown*. I'm concentrating on the effects of the pandemic on single people, late twenties, early thirties. But my boss is keen on a more dynamic angle than one based purely on loneliness and remote dating. At the moment I'm trying to come up with new ideas. What about you?'

'Currently? Installing a new computer system for a small investment company not far from here. Pretty boring stuff really.' Logan's smile is broad, effortless. His left palm rests flat against the rug, and my eyes are drawn to the small soft hairs coating the back of his tanned hand as it inches closer.

'Another sandwich? Go on. There's plenty.'

I nibble the end, grateful for the lack of crusts and wonder at the effort he's gone to. He leans across, pushes a lock of hair back from my forehead and gently brushes his lips against mine.

'I've been wanting to do that since we got here.'

He puts his hand behind my head and pulls me down beside him onto the rug. There's not a soul in sight as we lie alone in the warm sunshine, the wide-open surroundings deserted. Avoiding empty spaces was top on the list of considerations when arranging dates, but that's not what's causing me concern.

Rather, it's the beating of my heart and the thrill of Logan's warm soft lips that signal danger.

# WEEK 2

## 14

F ive past eight and there's no sign of our host, Annabel. I keep myself company, checking my face on screen, the camera turned on. Fuzzy is doing her fast-asleep act, slumped tight in the crack of my thighs. Tonight, if Declan quips again about spinsters and cats, I'll laugh it off. Lunch with Logan yesterday has left me on a high.

I fiddle with my hair, using the screen as a mirror and run a moist finger along my burgeoning eyebrows, caterpillars crawling slowly across my pale Celtic skin. I make a mental note to locate the tweezers.

'Hi. Sorry I'm late. Looks as if the others are too. How's things?' Annabel's sharp voice breaks my reverie as she pops into view.

Of course, we all judge books by covers and Annabel is definitely an expensive hardback tome with gold lame edging and a glossy veneer but with a distinct absence of heavily thumbed pages, the richness of the cover a camouflage for unread content. She's a clean crisp bookmark type of woman, editions for show rather than reading.

I smile as my face appears in the centre, the diva of the moment. 'I'm good. You?'

The door behind Annabel opens and Clifton, think Cliff Barnes from *Dallas*, pokes his head round. He's carrying the glasses, not on a silver salver, more Aussie beach bum style in his unbuttoned-to-the-waist Hawaiian short-sleeved shirt and unkempt hairstyle; fringe swept across to veil the thinning. He slips up behind Annabel, half his face appearing alongside his wife's more-bouffant-than-usual head of hair and kisses her on the crown as he sets down the glasses. I smirk, thinking of patting my head and rubbing my tummy at the same time but Clifton manages not to dribble liquid from the top-heavy glasses. An overflowing champagne flute for his wife, a lager for him.

'Hope it's okay for me to join in? Help with sport and history.'

Annabel's hand nudges him to the side, off centre.

'Of course. The more the merrier,' I chirp. He's here for moral support, or perhaps it's the other way round. Not sure which one is more obviously standing by their man.

Over the happy couple's shoulders a photograph has been plonked in front of the Shakespeare tomes. It's the pair on their wedding day and it definitely wasn't there last week.

Rihanna and Joel appear simultaneously.

Rihanna's bright sparkly top is toned down by her cottage's bleak background. The usual fluorescent desk light is turned off. Heavy low-level beams appear to be resting inches from her head, the view like an optical illusion. Think Penrose staircase, when what we're looking at is an impossibility.

Joel's intense face is very close up, his complexion pasty, similar in tone to the pale creamy walls behind. A faint line of acne runs down from his forehead, a tributary emptying into an angry contusion on the tip of his nose. It must be a recent outbreak.

If I stick with book cover analogies, Rihanna is Enid Blyton and Joel more Dan Brown. Rihanna appears uncomplicated simplicity, a likeable member of the famous five, Joel mysterious, clever but exceedingly dull; think Tom Hanks in the *Da Vinci Code*, the cryptologist genius always one step ahead of his pursuers, although Joel is definitely more Einstein in the looks department. That's the Zoom portrayal covers. Like the Shakespeare volumes, they're a cover up, a false front.

A week of googling has thrown completely different storylines from the ones being displayed in front of me. I've since learned that the pink kitten is more Fifty Shades and the mastermind more an In-betweener.

Declan is next in the queue for pleasantries. 'Hi, all,' he says.

Clifton's head jiggles in from the side of the screen again and he's soon waving a hand up and down like an artificial prosthetic.

'Evening, Declan. Good to see you.' Clifton's voice peters away as Annabel's elbow forces his face to disappear. He's the support cast, nothing more. I wonder how many of our merry little band of quizzers know why he's turned up tonight.

Declan is fronting up a room decorated in 1950s post-war style. Perhaps his secret society is linked to a weird group of people who like to live in another period behind closed doors, like the medieval peasant groups living out fantasies in dark corners of the Yorkshire Dales, raking out pig sties and chucking rotten tomatoes at heads in stocks. I haven't been able to get to the bottom of Declan's mystery yet; but give it time.

Declan is swilling ice cubes round in a thick glass tumbler and to the right of his shoulder there's a hearth and mantelpiece, ornate with white alabaster moulding. Small picture frames with tarnished silver-plate surrounds, crowd the surface. Dull dark green wallpaper, dotted with yellow and pink flowery patterns, makes Declan's wholesome appearance look exciting.

His skin is pale, Irish pale as opposed to Joel's sickly pallor, and more strikingly so because of the dark hair and thick eyebrows. I think I'd have guessed he was Irish if I hadn't been told.

'I'm still at my mum's,' he offers, raising his eyebrows and letting slip a faint tutting noise.

'Who are we waiting for?' Rihanna's voice squeaks over the scene but Annabel doesn't reply straight away. It's an awkward moment, but at least Clifton is well out of the picture.

'Barton. That's all. He'll be here any moment.' Annabel's voice is quiet, stifled.

It's 8.15. Even for Barton this is late. Rihanna suggests we start without him.

A sudden minor explosion sends a cork flying past Annabel who momentarily mutes the volume. I can guess the grief Clifton will be getting.

'Five minutes.' Annabel's sound is soon back on. She lifts her glass as Clifton's bony Rolex-bedecked wrist, appearing on screen minus the rest of him, tops her up. The glass is three-quarters full when a sixth screen comes to life, ceiling first with, heaven help us, a mirror in the centre. Barton's at home, must be, unless he's staying away at a kinkier hotel than usual. His moniker announces B J Hinton.

'Hi. Sorry I'm late. Alex, by the way. Barton asked me to take his place as he's having to work again. Hope that's okay?'

## 15

Alex Allard and Barton Hinton were old school friends. An unconfident teenager, Alex was drawn to Barton's charisma and sure footedness, but competition between them soon became fierce, especially when dating girls replaced rugby as the game of choice.

Barton, the handsome in-your-face bounder, was the bait that hooked the princesses, Alex the shark that circled. When Barton cocked up, Alex snapped up the prize and he never had long to wait.

During lockdown, they'd kept in touch, facetiming to quell the boredom and as soon as restrictions were eased Barton invited Alex for coffee at the new *London Echo* offices in Canary Wharf.

Alex wandered around one step behind Barton, the proverbial strutting peacock, and tried to swallow back the envious lump that had lodged. The state-of-the-art premises afforded panoramic views of Docklands and Barton's personal glass-encased sanctum made Alex think Wolf of Wall Street.

Their friendship hadn't changed much over the years. Alex still followed in Barton's wake, easily cajoled into actions that instinct otherwise told him to avoid. Problem was, Barton was hard to ignore. His magnetism drew you in and wouldn't let go. Alex still hadn't learnt his lesson.

'If you're that bored with Elisa, why not try a bit of online dating?' Barton suggested, tongue-in-cheek, but with enough subliminal suggestion to hit his target.

'Don't be stupid. Single girls aren't looking for married guys and I've no intention of leaving Elisa. Boredom is one thing, cheating another.'

Barton strolled across to the coffee machine in the corner and refilled their mugs, handing one back to Alex before he took up position by the floor-to-ceiling triple-glazed window.

'Brilliant views,' Alex said as he came alongside.

'There's a girl works here. Kristi. I took her out a few times. She might be up for some fun.' Barton's brown heavy-lidded eyes stared out over the top of his mug, the rim resting on his lips.

'I'm not looking for you to fix me up with a blind date, for God's sake.'

'She's been using a dating site called *Suave Singletons* during lockdown but not getting very far. Go on, it'd be fun. I'll give you her details.'

'I don't know, mate. What's wrong with her if you're passing her my way?'

Barton set his drink down, licked his fingertip and wiped at a smudge on the glass. With a clean handkerchief, he polished the result.

'Nothing. She's a real doll but, you know me; shy of commitment.'

Barton wandered back to his chair, sat down and splayed his legs across the desk.

'What was it called? *Suave Singletons*?' Alex lifted his jacket off the back of a chair, slipped it on over his muscled torso and slid his hands into his trouser pockets.

'That's it. You know it makes sense.' Barton laughed. 'Go and have some fun. Try to remember what it felt like.'

Oh my God. It's one of those weird, scary moments as if you've suddenly spotted a terrorist depositing a ticking time bomb and you're not far enough away to avoid the explosion.

Fuzzy squeals as I pinch her fur while grabbing for my wine. Blood drains from my face, as if a syringe is sucking out a pint or two. Alex is wearing an open-necked flowery shirt with a thin gold chain circling his thick pulsing neck. Something is dangling from the chain, but I can't make it out. I blink furiously to clear my vision, screen dryness on the early attack. Why the hell is Logan calling himself Alex? Or did Alex call himself Logan? Who the hell is this guy? And why is he taking Barton's space? How does he know Barton?

'Hi, Alex. Welcome to the quiz.' Clifton's face pokes round, and Annabel hisses, think rattle snake, to move his chair back again.

'No problem. Welcome, Alex.' Annabel's tone is like a flattened pancake. 'Did Barton tell you how it works? Rihanna's our quiz host tonight so it'll not take too long.' Her lips snarl at the edges, her voice laden with sarcasm but laced with disappointment.

'Thanks,' says Alex, deep-throat, Rod Stewart husky. His eyes move but it's hard to tell if he's checking out the members, but he doesn't seem to know them. I stare at the screen, waiting to catch the moment he picks me out of the line-up. We're like a row of convicts without the numbers.

'Kristi works with Barton on the newspaper,' says Annabel.

A tickle catches my throat and a dribble of wine slithers over the top of my glass as I tilt it back.

'Hi. Alex did you say? Sorry, I thought you were someone else. I must have got it wrong.'

He squints as his neck stretches forward. He takes a second too long, not certain if it's really me. Relief brings trickles of blood back to my face.

'That's right. Alex. Good to meet you, Kristi; nice name by the way.' He smiles, big dental-advert teeth, the all-American preppy. Think JFK, ladies' man, once a cheater, always a cheater. What is he doing here? He obviously knows Barton and now question number three on the quiz sheet seems loaded, like a smoking gun.

Barton knows I use *Suave Singletons*, but how the hell is he linked to Alex, or Logan, or whatever his name is.

## 16

A snippet of a recent conversation with Barton, standing by the coffee machine, pops into my mind. It was during a rare trip into the office, for a strategy meeting on working from home.

'Go on. Tell me what he's called. You're surely not seeing him on a weekend? Jeez. This guy could really be single.' Barton had nudged the plastic cup from my grasp, his smutty laugh bouncing off the glass walls. 'Shit, sorry,' he said, bending down and mopping up the brown sugary mess from my shoes with a clean tea towel. Social distancing isn't Barton's style, not even in the face of a world pandemic.

That was two weeks ago, the first day the whole second floor staff of the *London Echo* had got together since the easing of lockdown and a few days after I'd first met Logan for coffee.

But Barton has been keeping up the snide little innuendoes whenever we Facetime, digging around with his sharp tool of a brain for graphic details of my *Suave Singleton* hook-ups.

However, I'm certain I've never shared individuals' names.

~

'Shall we start?' Rihanna makes a polite, ladylike cough and holds up a sheet of A4 paper which covers her chin and mouth.

'Yes. We're ready.' Six voices, seven including the invisible Clifton, crackle assent.

'By the way,' Alex/Logan interrupts, now centre on my screen. 'Barton has instructed me to collect the answers for his bonus round from last week. He's got a nice surprise for the winner.' Alex's white teeth bare for the audience, a savage twinkle in his eye. A warning heartbeat picks up a similarity to Barton.

I use the interruption to take a few screenshots, assuming the clicks won't resonate but the assembly's silent attention is rapt, like at a funeral gathering as the spouse of a dead partner takes to the rostrum.

'Whatever,' Joel says into the silence. 'Can we get started. It's nearly 8.30 and there's football on at 10.00.' Good old Joel.

'Okay. Five rounds this week, one each on our individual specialist university subjects.' Did Rihanna go to university? Logan disappears momentarily from view, his screen a black box. 'Here we go. First round: geography.'

## 17

Declan teetered at the water's edge, hands and feet numb and bloodless, and stared out across the Irish Sea. The ghostly outline of the Scottish mainland appeared and disappeared from view, keeping rhythm with the sun as it popped back and forth behind the fluffy clouds. Half an hour and the dullness would return, but he'd be long gone.

As he stood for a few minutes, his life flashed before him like a condensed film reel, scenes from childhood merging raggedly with teenage nightmares. Everything was in black and white, no colourful shades to brighten the images. He raised his hands to his ears as bursts of exploding gunfire, imagined fireworks in his brain, riddled his thoughts.

He opened his eyes and looked down at his toes, shrunken nibs of icy blue, which curled around the dark smooth glassy pebbles. He wiped the back of his hand against his eye sockets to clear the steadily dripping rivulets of water weeping down his cheeks. With his other hand he shielded his forehead and one last time scanned Ballyholme beach. It must be nearly four.

The only sign of life was a couple walking in the opposite direction away from a small grey car parked further up along the beach. He smacked his hands together tempting the circulation to return before he stepped forward. Whisky had anaesthetised his mind, but not his body. Inch by inch he slithered over the pebbles until water finally lapped his calves.

'Fuck, fuck, fuck, fuck, fuck.' His voice quietened with each expletive, a diminuendo announcing the end of a funeral march, as he inched through the shallow gently gurgling waves. A seagull swooped, a loud squeal piercing the silence. Another few steps and he'd slip under the glass ceiling towards oblivion. His mother's voice rang out. 'You'll be going to hell, young man, for what you've done.'

But he no longer cared.

∽

'Our Father, which art in heaven, hallowed be...' Declan's voice shrunk to a whispered waft of air, the gabbled Lord's Prayer dissipating in the wind. He locked his eyes and sprinkled icy salt water over his head.

'The Lord calls us when our time is up.' Father Padraig's words came back, in the split second as Declan prepared to take his final step.

A blurry noise all at once bubbled through the air as a pulse vibrated in the pocket of his jeans. The Lord was calling.

'Fucking hell.' Declan let out an ear-piercing scream and covered his ears against the onslaught. The vibration continued, faint but steady. 'Piss off,' he yelled. But instead of slipping on down towards the seabed and his maker, he pushed a hand into his trousers and scraped out his phone. The world was calling him back.

*Kristi*. Her name lit up the screen. For a moment he thought he might be dreaming, the other side ushering him in with an eerie welcome. He managed to take several steps backwards, clinging to his mobile as if to a deflating rubber ring.

'Why the hell would I need a waterproof phone?' he'd yelled at Clifton's suggestion.

'You never know. It might save you when you're drowning in alcohol.' Clifton's sarcastic advice might have saved his life.

A couple of yards from the shallows, and his deadened forefinger made a connection.

'Declan?' Kristi's voice was faint, far away.

'Kristi.' The phone slithered in his grasp and he placed his left hand on top of his right to find purchase.

'I wanted to see how you were. Annabel says you're pretty down since losing your job at the bank.' A few seconds lapsed. 'Declan. Can you hear me? The line's dreadful.'

'I can hear you.' His teeth chattered a chorus, tapping together like castanets, the beat hard but rhythmical.

'Where are you? It sounds as if you're in water. Declan, are you okay?'

Then the screen went black.

Christ. Declan had fancied Kristi since they'd met at Annabel's wedding. But this was the first time she'd phoned, communication between them limited to occasional emails and Friday night banter. He kept putting off asking her for a drink, lockdown providing the perfect excuse to procrastinate.

He put the phone back in his pocket and slapped both arms around his chest, banging his palms hard up and down. He began to inch back towards the beach, and as he glanced down, he noticed blood poured from his dead feet, which had reached Hell before him. Razor shells with sharp serrated edges, like lethal shards of broken glass, ripped at his soles as he wended his way haphazardly through the shallows.

'Bit nippy for a swim, mate.'

Declan heard a man's voice before he noticed the fat slobbery hound bounding towards him. The Labrador's cushioned paws careered onto Declan's chest and catapulted him backwards into the foaming lips of the saltwater.

'Jesus Christ. Can't a man drown in peace?' Declan's scream shocked the animal off his defeated body.

'Buster. Buster. Bloody hell. Come here. Buster!' A skinny man with a flat cap and heavy Ulster great coat raised his walking stick and marched towards the spume. 'Jesus. I'm so sorry. Buster, get over here now!'

The heavy-coated black dog, tail skulking between shaky hind legs, shook its body violently and showered his dapper owner with slime. A piece of seaweed had stuck in the animal's paw which he worried over with his teeth.

Declan's phone dislodged in the fracas and as he reached down into the water to pick it up, his fingers caught in the tentacles of an opalescent jellyfish. 'Christ. That's all I need.'

'You don't look so good, mate. Listen, I live across the road. Come and get dried off, have a hot shower and I'll lend you some clothes before we pop to the pub next door. It's the least I can do. The name's Gerry, by the way.'

Buster wagged his tail again, the bubble wrap of slimy algae proudly deposited at his owner's feet.

Declan smiled. 'You know what. That sounds like a plan. I could certainly do with a drink.'

## 18

I hover by the door of the pub. With the doors flung wide, the noise from inside can be heard up and down the street. Frothing beer and volcanic chatter have buried social spacing, relief and merriment on the syllabus rather than cautionary tales about the spread of the Black Death.

When a guy in a hi-vis jacket indicates for me to enter, I slip my phone away and follow the directional arrows towards the bar.

By midnight on Friday evening, I had a few answers to the name conundrum of *Alex versus Logan*, but my fury didn't abate until this morning when lack of sleep and battle weary, I capitulated and gave in to sadness and disappointment. My stomach behaving as if I've been jilted by a long-term lover. Feeling squeamish and nauseous, my healthy breakfast routine of muesli, semi-skimmed milk and blueberries has been replaced for the last few days by strong black coffee and dry toast.

Eight texts, a couple of voicemails and a long-garbled

explanation on the *Suave Singleton* message link went some way in clearing up the 'misunderstanding', as Alex called it. Logan is his middle name, and he chose it, rather than Alex, to maintain some anonymity while online dating. I got that, surely? Perhaps, but why hadn't he told me when we'd picnicked in the park?

Wandering round in my PJs for the last few days hasn't help lift my mood. It's as if I've woken up, heavily hung-over, from an overzealous attempt at snaring the most available single guy for miles. Desperation with a capital D is tattooed large across my forehead. I bet Barton has had a good laugh, the bastard.

Alex's zealous explanations, to which I was tempted to respond with some venomous retort, haven't gone far enough in explaining his relationship with Barton. Apparently, Alex would prefer to meet up again and go through things face to face.

Please? I'd really like to see you and explain.

His text sat unanswered for a couple of days.

Problem is, reaching my thirties has been accompanied by bitter lessons in love which have been carefully archived, meticulously labelled and definitely not shredded. Knee-jerk reactions, sexual lust and eagerness to couple have been reined in, the need for control nervously masking fear of rejection.

Okay. One chance. Where?

It was Monday early evening when I finally replied, and a text bounced back five minutes later.

Covent Garden. The Flounder Pub. I'll text the details. Thanks.

~

'Hi,' I say. Alex is standing at the bar, beer glass in hand, when I approach but I stick rigidly to the two-meter rule.

'Hi,' he replies, his cheeks flushed from alcohol, embarrassment or a combination of the two; it's hard to tell which. But I suspect he got here early. The determined set of my lips discourages the kissing ritual, but instead he hands me a large glass of white wine. Churlish I know, but instead of accepting it I take the top off my plastic bottle of mineral water and take a swig.

'I've booked a table. It's over here, number six. They're trying to control numbers, but people are pushing in from the street.' For some weird reason, I feel like a child being led to the naughty step, yet I've done nothing wrong. The enthusiastic, energetic atmosphere is starting to nudge doubts about my companion under the carpet. I'm not sure whether it's my insecurities or Alex's chiselled machismo, that makes me ready to dispel the concerns. Or perhaps lockdown loneliness is catapulting me back to recklessness.

I peer round the eating area, customers at the tables like exam-takers, spaced apart to avoid cheating. The clinical atmosphere away from the crowded bar isn't quashed by the dim lighting; and the sterile tabletops remind everyone that there's a lingering problem. Perched on the edge of each table is a container of hand sanitiser, disinfecting the romance. I sneeze, too slow to cover my nose.

'Bless you.'

'Thanks.' I dig in my bag for a tissue, sopping up invisible rogue germs like a guilty child guzzling a sweet after its errant hand has stolen the treat.

A number 6 is etched into the small square wooden table and two hard chairs face each other. It's like a speed dating set-up; but then again, perhaps that's what it is. I take off my jacket and hang it on the back of my chair and sit facing Alex. He seems even taller sitting down, which is a conundrum, but his head sits a whole skull higher than mine. The table wobbles, one of the legs floating randomly off the ground and Alex looks for inspiration.

'No beer mats to steady it,' he says. 'Covid has dispensed with all non-essentials.' He jiggles the table from side to side as his lager swills in the glass. I dip back into my bag and bring out a healthy wad of tissues.

'Try these. Should do the trick.' I lift the wine glass, accepting ownership, and grip it tightly.

'Voila. Steady as a rock!' Alex whoops, teasing my lips to upturn as he places his palms firmly on the tabletop, confident in the seaworthiness of the steadied vessel.

'Right. Shoot. What's the story?' The cold white wine slithers down, lifting my confidence and determination. On hearing my question, Alex sets his glass aside, preparing to recant a carefully rehearsed speech. It's the deep intake of breath that gives him away.

'Are you a spy?' I help him along.

He laughs. 'No, I'm not a spy.' He leans across to take my hands but I'm too quick. Instead, I sit on them, a dull cramp preferable to his blackmailing fingers. 'I hope you're not in a hurry. It's rather a long story,' he says.

'Go on. I'm not in any hurry.'

## 19

A lex is married, no kids, works in IT running his own company and does freelance work for large London finance firms and banks, installing and helping to maintain their computer systems. He lives in St Albans. A pretty ordinary CV, not quite matching the intrigue of his concocted *Suave Singleton* profile which showcases the healthy salary and jet-set lifestyle. His wife doesn't understand him, they're not suitably matched and a divorce is pending, solicitors standing by.

Alex's eyes, dark and intense, will me to buy into his story. He's trying to draw out comments, like poison from a snake bite but I let him talk, wondering if he'll hang himself with his own noose. So far, he's doing quite the sales pitch.

'How do you know Barton?' I ask.

'School. I banged into him in London a couple of years ago and we've since kept in touch. Sometimes, he lets me use his flat when he's away.'

'Oh, is that where you were last night? Loved the mirrored ceiling.'

'Sorry?' A questioning eyebrow shoots up. For the first time I notice his eyes are surprisingly close together, although still hooded and dangerous. I let my perception take off the blinkers, my observations no longer clouded by starry-eyed notions of an immediate future together.

Alex peels off his suit jacket and wipes a hand across his forehead. 'Christ, it's hot in here.'

'The mirror on the ceiling. So typical Barton.' I keep at it; a dog with a bone.

Alex loosens his thin blue tie and threads it over his head. His hair sticks out from the attention and I smother a giggle.

'Where's he off to now?' I continue. 'Barton.'

'I'm not sure. He talked about going to Paris, or possibly Spain. Some scoop or other, but I haven't heard from him for a few days. He also mentioned going up to Durham to do a piece on student life, but I'm not certain. I've got a key to his flat. It's just around the corner.'

Alex as a whole is attractive, but considered in parts, dissected down into individual components, he's asymmetrical, his features random. His grin is lopsided, which is a bonus on some people, a cheeky sexy attribute but looking head-on the up-tilted corner reveals a ragged filling, off-white. It's like the Zoom views, which give you less to go on when making judgements. I'm studying his head for clues about his character, one trait at a time.

'People at work don't seem to know where he's got to. By the way, did you see the questions he sent our group?' I ask.

'No. He just told me to ask for the answers. What were they about?' He knocks back his lager and looks round for a waiter. 'Another glass before we order?'

'Yes please. Oh, the questions were about nothing really. Nothing important,' I add. I'm not sure he's telling the truth, that he didn't know what the questions were about, but it doesn't seem to matter as he ignores the thread.

A waiter appears and drops spotlessly clean menus in front

of us. Alex orders more drinks and indicates that we'll be ready to order the food in five minutes.

Alex does the ordering, picking favourites from previous visits and we share a medley of tapas. Conversation eases into small talk about the virus, cancelled holiday plans and prospects of successful vaccinations. He's easy company and I'm soon enjoying the casual patter, increasingly tempted to trust the answers from my dangled carrot.

As we share jokes and observations about the state of the world, it feels good to be face-to-face with male company again, in the real world, rather than on screen.

After he's paid the bill, Alex places both his hands firmly over mine. This time I don't object.

'Listen, it's less than half a mile to Barton's flat. Why don't we walk back there and have a nightcap? I'm staying there for a few days. It's quite a pad, and well worth a look if you haven't already been there.' He watches me.

'Okay. Why not. I've never been there as Barton only moved in at Easter time.'

I don't mention the numerous invitations from Barton to break lockdown and sneak round and see him in the dead of night. Loneliness had made it tempting to break the rules, but I wouldn't for Barton.

'Great.' Alex is on his feet, hand outstretched to pull me up. 'Let's go.'

# 20

We stroll along side-by-side and I keep my hands stuffed in my pockets. Assaulted by the cold night air, handholding still seems out of sync with the evening's revelations. The teasing atmosphere of the dimly lit restaurant fades further into the distance as we walk.

'I've always wondered what his new flat was like,' I say. 'I've never been there, and he doesn't talk about it much.'

'He mentioned you'd gone out with him a few times.'

'Did he? I went with him to Annabel and Clifton's wedding last summer, as his plus one, nothing more. Not all ladies love a bastard.'

Alex laughs, a guttural chortle, relief flooding out like water from a burst pipe. 'He's not all bad.'

I snort. 'That's a man's perspective.'

Barton's flat is in a small mews about half a mile from the centre of Covent Garden. A bright red door, with a heavy brass knocker and a gold polished number 2, welcomes us. Alex fumbles in his pocket and produces a large collection of keys on a BMW key ring. They rattle like a gaoler's bunch.

My tread is tentative as we climb the stairs to the first floor. Alex, up ahead, walks with more purpose and I'm tempted to turn back until he throws open the door to Barton's apartment. A few steps and we're in the living room.

'Wow,' pops out.

'Told you.' Alex smiles and pushes the door gently shut behind us.

Sleek black and white lines define the room, luxury with a capital L. A twinkling line of inbuilt lighting runs all the way round the perimeter of the black shiny marbled flooring and glass windows run up to the ceiling and reveal the glittering lights of London through spotless panes. The furniture is white leather, and the only colour comes from a large red oil canvas, decorated with thick black lines and white circle blobs.

'Jeez, it's fabulous,' I say.

'I know. I'm bloody jealous.'

'He must be paid a lot more than me. That's for sure.'

'There's definitely more to Barton than meets the eye.'

Alex shows me round, like an owner trying to impress a potential purchaser. Off the living room, he leads me down a wide bright corridor.

'Is this where you did the Zoom quiz from?' I ask.

A desk sits in a small square-shaped niche about halfway along; an Apple iMac perched on top. It's like a cubicle study; think Japanese design, square simplistic origami perfection. The user faces out towards the corridor and on the wall behind the computer is another modern canvas, bright azure blue with a ragged yellow sun plopped in the centre. I have it on screenshot. I look up and check out the mirrored ceiling which had announced Alex's off-kilter arrival to the quiz. He must have been moving the computer when we were all given a glimpse of the gleaming glass.

'Yep. Cool, isn't it?'

As we walk on to the end of the corridor, Alex pauses, takes a theatrical intake of breath and flings his arms wide as he opens another door.

'Voila.'

A huge circular bed takes up the centre of Barton's bedroom, where the black and white theme continues. Black satin sheets are in stark contrast to the blinding white glaze of a free-standing bath.

Before I've time to react, Alex reaches for my hand, nods towards the bed and puts a finger to his lips. 'Shhh. Say no more. Come here, you.'

## 21

Rihanna felt the cramp tighten her right calf, wincing as a sudden searing spasm shot up her leg. She undid the top of her water bottle and gulped greedily before sitting down on the grass verge. She let her fingers knead furiously at the rigid knotted muscles to release the pain.

The empty fields, flat and barren, were sympathetic onlookers. The fading summer landscape whose auburn and burnt sienna hues had nudged away the verdant greens, kept her company. A lone horse stuck his head out through a wire fence and whinnied.

Pounding the country lanes helped to numb the loneliness, but the heightened feelings, brought on by the increased endorphins which lifted her mood, soon dissipated and left an aching sadness in their wake.

∾

Clifton had phoned, texted and emailed her all manner of messages during lockdown. He wouldn't let go. Now Barton had unscrewed the lid off their past, Rihanna was swamped by fear and panic. It was as if she'd stepped into quicksand which was sucking her downwards.

Annabel had stormed round after she'd solved Barton's riddle about Rihanna's first fiancé, turning over the past with a gravedigger's spade, eager to bury the remains and Rihanna with them.

'It was in the past, Annabel. I'm really sorry.' The lie had hung in the air.

'Why the hell didn't you tell me? I mean you came to our wedding, for Christ's sake and I had no idea.' Annabel spat, wet vitriolic spurts that landed on Rihanna's cheeks.

'I thought you knew, and that Clifton would have told you. I'm really sorry.'

'What I don't get is why he invited you to our wedding.'

Rihanna met Joey on the rebound from Clifton. Joey was young, penniless and free-spirited, the polar opposite to Clifton. Rihanna decided, after the heartache of being given the elbow by her soon-to-be married lover, that Joey might help heal the wounds; lighten her life.

She should have guessed, perhaps did on some level, that moving on so quickly would spur Clifton to regrets. His ego and competitiveness wouldn't let her walk away and certainly not with a single, good-looking younger man.

'Bring him to the wedding,' Clifton suggested one night by phone.

'What about Annabel?'

'What about Annabel? She doesn't know about us. I'll add Joey to the guest list, and you can be his plus one. Annabel will be none the wiser.'

'But you've never met Joey.'

'Doesn't matter. I'll just say he's an old friend.'

Rihanna could easily have said *no* but the crumbs were hard to ignore. Her and Clifton had too much history. But with Clifton getting married and the lack of spark in her new relationship with Joey, she felt lonelier than ever. Rihanna decided that, after the wedding in Italy, she'd end it with Joey. She needed time out from dating and to put herself first again.

When Barton Hinton bowled up at the reception, the first question he directed at Rihanna was how Joey knew Clifton. Rihanna had squirmed but Joey was too centred on the present to care much about Rihanna's past and, after a few drinks, owned up to Barton that he'd never met the groom before.

'Oh. That's weird. Annabel told me you were an old friend of Clifton's,' Barton said.

When Joey disappeared off to the free bar, Barton slid his arm round Rihanna's waist.

'So, you're a friend of Clifton's, are you? What a dark horse he is.' Barton laughed, as the palm of his hand caressed her bottom.

'Can you move your hand,' Rihanna snapped, swatting his arm away.

'What's Clifton got that I don't?'

Barton's sneer followed her round. She could feel him watching when Clifton swirled her across the midnight dance floor.

It was only at the airport the following day, that Rihanna picked up on Barton's dislike of Clifton.

'The bastard's got what he deserves. Good luck to the pair of them. Bye, everyone.'

Barton had sloped to the back of the plane with Kristi, and

Rihanna hadn't seen him again until the Friday quiz nights. Annabel's invitations seemed harmless.

It was five more kilometres, uphill most of the way, to Welton village. The country lane twisted and turned, like a meandering riverbed, through wooded copses thick with darkened foliage. As her muscles loosened, Rihanna pushed harder and harder, her arms soon in steady rhythm with her legs until the pounding in her head lessened and the wind wafted effortlessly past her ears.

When she rounded the final bend, the triangle of village green teased with the homely pull of country living. Low freshly painted wooden fencing circled the grass perimeter and a bold white metal sign bellowed 'keep off the grass'. The villagers were at war over community matters, a nuclear fallout brewing over policing the green; fractious parties choosing sides. The pub landlord fed his customers regular updates.

Rihanna skirted past the front entrance to the Red Lion and headed for the small adjacent car park. It was almost midday, a couple of minutes to go. But the dark-blue two-seater Mercedes SL was already there, parked in the far corner.

She freed her hair from its headband, untied the ponytail and shook her long blonde hair loose. She counted to ten and entered through the back door. When he saw her, he waved from another dark corner.

'Clifton. You're early.'

'Aren't I always? What do you fancy? Usual?'

## 22

It's hard to concentrate. The *Lockdown Life of a Singleton* column has definitely drawn in the readers, but Grayson, the editor, is closing it down in two weeks. I need to come up with a more novel, fresh-angled, idea. My black pen doodles on a blank sheet.

*Dating During Lockdown. Loosening of Lockdown. Lies and Lockdown.* My pen hovers over the last heading.

~

I had knocked Alex's hand away, laughing in the face of his supposedly seductive 'Shhh'. What a prick! But recall of the evening when Alex and I had walked back to Barton's flat pushes me to head up a tentative bullet-point list with pithy loaded headings for *Lies and Lockdown*.

There's no Barton to run through the ideas with, still no sighting, but perhaps it's just as well. He's unlikely to condone a column that might touch on subjects like renting out bachelor pads to mates as knocking shops.

- **Zoom meets.** *Where are the participants?* Like Barton's hotel suites, they could be located anywhere in the world. The only time our Friday group got a peek into Barton's actual home was when Alex took his place on Friday. Although Barton never joins the Friday quiz from his flat, I can imagine him using the origami cubicle as an interrogation hub for carrying out Skype calls with unsuspecting members of the public who crave press time in the spotlight. They'll be unaware that Barton Hinton, *London Echo's* most senior reporter, only wants shit as he pokes and prods like a chiropodist at stubborn corns. By the time the interviewees twig, it's all down on paper.

- **Dating sites.** *Plenty of lies there.* Married, single, rich or poor? *Suave Singletons* has thrown me up my own piece of dirt which I could use. That would put Alex and Barton both in the limelight. Ha ha. Comeuppance with a capital C.

- **Quiz night cheats.** Okay, it's a pretty tame storyline but perhaps tagged at the end of a piece it would provide light relief and smiles of recognition. Joel claims to win our group quiz every week but we all know he googles the answers on his phone. Let's face it though, who cares? It's something to do for a couple of hours on a Friday night and, Annabel certainly doesn't turn up for the cerebral challenge. Quiz nights have been a distraction from the pandemic, the regular invitation helping to battle the crippling fear and ennui. Now a sense of loyalty brings us back to the screens on Friday, each of us as yet unwilling to cite the reopening of pubs and clubs as a reason not to participate.

- **Two-dimensional stage sets versus three-**

**dimensional reality.** The showcased bookcases plucked fresh from the Bodleian Library, original oil-on-canvas paintings with their gaudily bright splodges and the strategically placed photographs, competing for the eye, have been the two-dimensional props of all our weekly hangouts. Hard to decipher three-dimensional reality in a two-dimensional world. The lies of lockdown are there for all to see, for those who look.

I swivel on my stool, rereading the notes, the end of my pen jigging up and down against my teeth.

'Yes,' pops out. 'Yes, yes, yes. *Lies and Lockdown*.' I toss my pen to one side, stretch my arms wide and flop back. Five on the dot.

Fuzzy rubs up against my leg, purring loudly, persistently. She's after more of the fish stew left over from the weekend. A bowl each, side salad for me, milk for Fuzzy.

Yes, I'm quite content, for now, working in my purple leggings and furry moccasins with only my ball of fluff for company. I take a snap of my legs from knee down and post on Instagram. *New Working Outfit!* A couple of likes bounce straight back.

Alex is there if I want to work on him. For now, I've got the upper hand but I'm not in any hurry to push things along. He's got far too much baggage, but some things never change. The more challenging the chase, the stronger a suitor's determination. Alex is no different if the number of texts is anything to go by, but he's got a lot of work to do to convince me he's serious. I need to be certain he's getting divorced as I'm in no rush to repeat past mistakes. Age isn't on my side to waste on vacuous promises. I'm ready for commitment, with someone who wants it.

I get up and wander into the kitchen, lifting the wine out from the fridge. Okay. A couple of hours earlier than usual, but the treat's too tempting and I'm feeling due a reward for the progress on my column content. As I struggle with the cork, my phone beeps.

Hi. Fancy a drink tonight? Happy to drive over again. Joel x

Before I've time to reply, he sends through a second message.

BTW, have you heard from Barton?

No one's heard from Barton, and this is the third time I've been asked that question this week. I set the phone down and pour out the wine, unsure if Joel has been encouraged to contact me since Barton flagged up that I use dating sites and wants to save me the expense. Or perhaps it's something else. Barton's sudden disappearance from the scene has thrown up more than the six questions he asked, and there's a definite uneasiness in the air.

I dig out the congealed cod and monkfish stew and heat it through in the microwave. Fuzzy sticks fast to my legs, weaving in and out like a performing show dog. I divide the food equally, stroking her on the head as I set down a bowl. A sliver of pink tongue scoots out through the whiskers and starts to lap.

Carrying my own bowl through to the lounge, I chuck off my moccasins, wiggle my toes and wander over to the sofa. Joel will have to wait. My entertainment this evening will be a bit more googling, curling up on the sofa with Fuzzy, and settling down to watch the latest Netflix box set.

Lockdown life as a singleton isn't all bad.

# WEEK 3

# 23

Haircuts, tints and blow-dries have definitely smartened up the screenshots, except for Declan. His hair still hangs lank, unshorn, and a rough five o'clock shadow coats his chin. He's swivelled his laptop and there's the thrum of rainwater against the windowpanes behind him.

A delicate white arthritic hand, fingers like bird claws, appears accompanied by the rattle of a cup and saucer. 'Thanks, Ma,' Declan whispers to the ghost over his shoulder. Before the door has clicked shut behind his mother, a full tumbler of something stronger has appeared alongside the delicate china.

I've tried to call Declan several times since Monday but got no response. It's as if his phone is turned off. His sarcastic sparkle seems to have got washed away by the rain. I still don't know what happened after our brief talk on Monday but he's definitely not himself.

'All okay, Declan?' I ask. He doesn't answer straight away, the screen now showing a close up of his back and hunched shoulders with a small hole in his T-shirt near the right blade. He swivels back.

'Sorry?' he asks, proffering a weak milky-white-tea smile.

'Hi, Declan. All okay?' I repeat.

'Fine thanks, Kristi. Catch up soon.'

'Hi, everyone.' Our host pipes up, the champagne flute already fizzing. Annabel's recent highlights and generously moussed blow-dry make me think Dolly Parton. But apart from Annabel's bubbly demeanour, the atmosphere is leaden, burring through the screen like a dentist's drill, and the wet swoosh of water that is Declan's backdrop isn't helping with its sodden beat.

'No Clifton tonight?'

'No, he's gone to the pub. Oh. Here comes Rihanna.'

'Hi.' The squeaky mouse appears, dressed in pink but the elephants should tread carefully. 'Hope I'm not last.'

Behind Rihanna the scene is even darker than usual, the bright light beside her computer still turned off. With only a dimmed warmth from the wall lights, there's an eerie feel to her setting. It matches tonight's general chorus which definitely isn't so chirpy.

'Just waiting for Joel and Barton. Anyone seen or heard from Barton?' Annabel sips through plumper-than-usual red lips, a curling sliver of tongue lapping up the alcohol, reminding me of Fuzzy's delicate milk sipping. But the likeness ends there. I stroke my warm and comforting housemate, who is squirrelled away out of sight.

'No, nothing. He's not been at work either,' I say, but Joel's sudden appearance grabs the attention and puts a loose lid on the concerns. He's in the kitchen tonight, dishes stacked on a draining board over his shoulder. He moves in closer to the screen, his head and shoulders soon blocking out the mess.

I leave my seat and pop back to the fridge for a top-up. Wine will be the only way through. It's as if we're all part of a marathon, no one willing to lay down their shoes. But the finishing line for the Friday night quiz party is definitely in sight. Another week or two and someone will make their excuses, citing new commitments, fresh invitations. Maybe Barton's got there first. It's been a regular date now for three months, every Friday, 8pm, but parole is pending.

As I return and reconnect with the flat faces, I think that perhaps I'll be the first to leave the party. I scoop Fuzzy back up and wonder what excuse I'll use to jump ship.

The sixth screen jitters into focus. Christ. It is Barton. He's back. The black square soon presents its image. But it's Alex again.

'Hi, guys.' Alex's face, large, chisel-jawed and dark, centres the box.

'Shit,' I say, as wine spills onto my iPad.

The blue and yellow canvas behind Alex seems brighter than usual, but his smile duller. His face, like Joel's, is closer to the screen than last week and he's managed to avoid his previous undignified entrance which showcased Barton's tacky ceiling mirror. His flattened damp-looking hair suggests he's showered for the occasion.

'Where's Barton?' Annabel's question snaps accusation.

'Sorry, guys. No idea. I thought I might as well join in again as I'm back at his flat. He must still be away as there's not even milk in the fridge.'

Perhaps that's part of the package. I wonder what Alex gives Barton in return for milk, cereal and hospitality. Money? Computer repairs on tap? Barton will have some agenda though, that's for sure. He doesn't do largesse.

'Anyway, let's get started. It's all general knowledge tonight, fifty questions.' Joel's lack of inventiveness as quizmaster and speed of speech hints that he's out of here as soon as he's done his bit. The end's definitely not far off for us all.

'I'm ready.'
'Me too.'
'Yes, got my pen.'
'Right. First question.'

## 24

Being a journalist, albeit a lowly columnist, teaches you observation skills. All part of the job. People watching takes on a whole new dimension, as the small, seemingly insignificant, personality traits and actions get dissected into minute pieces and assigned to long-term memory and insightful features.

It was the evening of Annabel and Clifton's wedding, long before the riotous midnight breakfast, that I recall a scene in the vibrant sprawling gardens. The red-tipped ends of cigarettes glowed, one attached to the smooth fake-tanned arm of the sugar-coated bride and the other an extension of the finely dark-haired muscular arm of Barton Hinton.

I sat out of sight on a stone bench under an arbour which trailed bougainvillea, my shoes discarded by my feet as I craved ten minutes respite from the pain of wedding heels. I was just within earshot.

'One last kiss. Go on. Married women are much more

exciting than single ones.' In the dark I imagined Barton's wolfish grin, his smoky breath, and I watched in horror as my escort circled the bride's waist, pulled her in and sought her lips. Oh my God. They'd done this before.

Unable to move, I shivered in the balmy night air. This was one secret I'd have to keep. Barton's slim manicured fingers slid down the front of Annabel's dress, and squeezed her breasts.

'Get off me. For Christ's sake.' Annabel yanked her dress back up, flapped his hands away and with tears streaming down her face, flounced back the length of the garden towards the reception. Clifton was watching, legs planted firmly apart and arms wide to welcome her back.

'Shit. I thought I'd lost you already.' Clifton's imperious voice carried for all to hear. 'Come on. One last dance before we go.' With that he took his new bride's hand, raised it to his lips and whispered something in her ear. I can only guess at what he said.

'Last question. Where's Barton?' Joel's staring face doesn't blink as he fires the gunshot question.

Silence is followed by a tinny group laugh. Where's Wally indeed, snaking in and out the crowds, having rattled all our cages. He's out there somewhere, watching us sweat but the question is where, and more importantly, why has he not shown up?

'No idea.'

'Haven't heard from him.'

'He hasn't been at work either.'

We all dutifully offer knee-jerk responses to the sudden off-kilter question.

'Come on, Joel. Let's have the answers, put us out of our misery.' Declan's interruption dilutes the awkwardness.

Joel fumbles with his answer sheet and holds it up in front of his face as he reads out the answers at speed, brushing aside queries as to the correctness of certain ones.

'Rationing didn't end till 1954. It ended in 1953 for sugar and sweets only. The question was "when did rationing end?" All rationing didn't end till 1954, not 1953.' Declan corrects, his pride at outwitting the quizmaster captured in a cheeky grin.

'Whatever.' Joel continues to race through the answers like hound after hare.

While everyone is busy ticking off points and bonus points, I take a few more sneaky screenshots. For the future. We'll share the memories when everything's back to normal, whenever that is and whatever it is. Looking at the five faces, eyes down in phoney concentration, I suspect the old normality has long flown.

I then add up my total and am bizarrely chuffed when I get more than seventy-five per cent of the questions right. At least I don't have to compete with Joel for top spot, although the ease of his questions makes me think he hasn't put much thought into tonight's quiz. But it's hard not to be pleased at coming first. Alex looks suitably impressed and beams at me. Well, I assume it's at me as no one else is really interested in the random interloper.

There's a lack of the congratulatory whoops when I give out my score, a dearth of the usual sarcastic slogans of *who's a clever girl then, brainbox or smart arse*. The '*well-done*'s are muted, airy smiles floating through the screen.

Alex then speaks. He's been eerily quiet throughout, possibly in deference to being a newcomer. He genuinely doesn't seem to know anyone except me and no one else seems to have picked up that we're on familiar terms. All minds are elsewhere.

'Any answers to Barton's questions? Must be honest I've no

idea what the questions were but I was given instructions last week to ask.'

'Tell Barton, life's far too busy,' says Joel. 'I've had no time to look for answers, and actually they're all a bit personal.'

'Agreed. Hear, hear.'

'Same here. He's a nosey git.'

'Anyway, where the fuck is he?' Declan's tone cuts through the relieved assent of the quizzers but the razor-sharp edge to his voice acts like an electric shock, silencing the drunken agitated group. Then all at once his head and shoulders disappear from the hangout and he's gone.

Before I click *leave*, I make promises that next week's questions will be more challenging.

Joel tuts, raises his eyebrows and says, 'Whatever. Bye all.'

'Bye.' Tonight, the choir is out of sync.

'Bye. Thanks.' A half-hearted trill of her fingers and Annabel's profile disappears as well.

'Bye,' I mumble to myself as I scratch Fuzzy's ears and log out.

My furry friend eyes me, stretches out, and lets her claws massage my upper thighs, digging in and out. She's pleased to have me to herself again.

'Let's make next Friday the last one. What do you say?' The thrumming purr is my answer.

I turn off the computer, lift Fuzzy down and wander back to the sofa. It's ten thirty. I toy with watching the last episode of the twisted thriller, *You*, when my phone rings. It's a number I don't recognise.

'Hello?'

'Kristi. It's me. Listen, can we meet up? It's Declan by the way.'

'Sure. What's up?'

## 25

A SHOT IN THE DARK

**B**arton's feet pounded heavily as they slapped down the cobbled incline towards Prebends Bridge. His brain scrambled to stay apace and keep speed with his muscled calves and iron thighs. Heat, like sizzling red-hot coals, seared up his neck and face. Sweat oozed to douse the embers.

The black sky, leaden with moisture, grumbled in discomfort. As he raised a hand and felt the first skiff of the thunderstorm, he checked his watch. Five twenty. Pulling his hood up to shield his frozen ears from the bitter north wind, he slowed as he neared the river.

The Wear thundered along with a turbulent power beneath the centuries-old walkway. Durham cathedral, swathed in golden light, towered above dense walls of foliage and lit up the blackened sky; the building's majesty keeping guard over the swollen hungry water.

Breathing hard, he leant his arms along the wet slime of the wall and inhaled, dragging air through his wheezing lungs. He unzipped his jacket when his mobile beeped and read the new message.

Nearly there. See you soon.

～

He'd hoped the weather would make them cancel, turn back, but they'd been persistent.

As dawn broke, four texts and three calls had dragged him, thick headed and heavy limbed, out of bed.

'I hear you're in Durham. I'm close by. I can be there in an hour.'

Reluctantly Barton agreed to meet, share a drink but with a warning that he didn't feel so good.

'No problem. I'll not stop long. It'll be good to catch up.'

～

Barton honked into his handkerchief and jogged on with caution towards the towpath as the heavens finally burst, the sodden outpouring of fury drenching him in its wrath. One last spurt and he'd head back to the hotel. He'd easily make it by six.

As he rounded the bend, a spectral figure blocked his route. Where water lapped the banks, the path tapered sharply and there was no way past. He squinted through the thick glassy sheet of rain.

'A bit wet for jogging.' A muffled voice cut through the gloom; the speaker faceless in a dark mask which covered their nose and mouth.

'You could say that.'

He limbered on the spot, treading impatiently for them to step aside. Instead, they widened their stance, held forth a gloved palm and with the other hand raised a gun, nozzle directed at his head.

'I don't think you'll be going any further.'

The orchestral fanfare of thundering rain, bellowing wind and rumbling swirls of leaden liquid drowned out the scream, and swallowed up the single shot.

He stretched his arm towards the shooter, a futile plea, before his body convulsed and smashed to the ground. Black blood seeped from the entry wound and slithered towards the river, whose patient jaws gaped to guzzle up the slime.

## 26

'You saved my life, Kristi.' Declan peers into the bottom of his beer glass and swills the cloudy contents round.

'What are you talking about? I haven't seen you for, it must be at least two months.'

Declan has never driven to see me before, but he was insistent. He got back from Ireland late Sunday night and I've been his first point of contact. Strange, a bit freaky to be honest, but when he called on Friday after the quiz, he sounded desperate.

We're sitting in a country pub, all oak beams, low ceilings and dim lighting, about a mile from Hitchin centre.

'It's a long story.' He sighs, elbows propped on the rickety table, glass clenched.

'Go on. We've got all night. I'm listening.'

~

I've been furiously googling Declan Mooney since Friday night. Barton's questions seem suddenly important, providing a tenuous link to the Friday group members' weird behaviours. I don't know Declan that well, except as part of our regular quiz set. We met briefly at Annabel's wedding and again a couple of times when we all got together before lockdown. So, his call out of the blue was odd. Random.

*What secret society does Declan belong to and (bonus point) what does the induction ceremony entail?*

Declan Mooney, age forty-two, was born and bred in North Belfast, one of six. 'Runt of the litter. That's me,' he'd slurred through an alcoholic haze at Annabel's wedding. His twinkling blue eyes, shiny under thick black burgeoning eyebrows had glassed over in the telling.

'Brothers or sisters?' I'd asked.

'One dominating bitch of a big sister. Máiréad.'

'Why did you leave Northern Ireland? You went to Queens University, didn't you?'

'Couldn't wait to get away. Godforsaken hole.'

That was all the information I had to go on, as I snooped and pried on social media, scouring birth and death records and investment banking profiles. I guessed that his recent depression was down to the job redundancy at the bank.

'Let me get another drink and we'll talk. Same again?' Declan downs his glass, gets up, and goes back to the bar.

'Go on then,' I call after his retreating back. Once a drinker, always a drinker. Declan enjoys his drink, don't we all? But he's in denial. He drinks far too much, a weirdly functioning alcoholic. Annabel whispered, in the strictest of confidence, that his redundancy at the bank where he worked alongside Clifton was down to alcohol-related issues rather than pandemic cutbacks.

'I'm Irish. What do you expect?' Declan uses his Irish roots as flimsy justification when he knocks back whisky shots while the rest of us struggle to stay upright.

'Don't forget you're driving,' I say when he returns.

'The car's programmed to find its own way back.' He takes a sip and smiles. 'Don't worry. This'll be my last.' He automatically checks how much he's got left.

His hand trembles as he passes me my wine, and our fingers brush.

'You know when you phoned last week, when I was in Ireland? Well, I wasn't in a good place,' he begins.

Despite his loosened tongue, I read between the lines. He's depressed at being let go from the bank. He's fed up being single; this part was told with the pleading eyes of a puppy-dog, begging for a home. It's hard to take Declan seriously though. He's a Gemini, twin personalities, but I've long suspected he's hiding a third and possibly a fourth persona behind the blarney.

Clifton, smug and rapt in his own banking success and investing millions while the rest of the country is holed up under furlough and counting the pennies, is ignoring Declan's calls.

'I'm sorry. I didn't realise you felt so low. But how did I save your life?' I anchor my hand on top of his and will him to carry on.

'When you called, I was walking out into the ocean, heading for Scotland. You see, Kristi, I'd had enough.'

'Shit. You're joking me. Were you in the sea when I rang?' I pull my hand away, stretch out my neck and stare at him.

'I'd just started walking. Christ, the water was cold.' A faint humour pokes through his eyes.

'Go on.'

'A bloody dog bounded towards me and knocked me over and my phone slithered into the shallows.'

'A dog saved your life then. Not me.' I give a wry smile.

'The dog wouldn't have noticed me if I hadn't stopped to take your call. I'd have been long gone. Thanks, Kristi.'

'Christ, I'm sorry.' What more can I say?

## 27

My flat welcomes me back, Fuzzy scraping herself against my ankles, her tail rigidly skyward. Her hearty purr, a fanfare of joy, follows me through to the kitchen.

'Milk? Here you go then.' I dig out a few fishy treats and with a sideways glance she begins to guzzle.

I'm in shock, both at Declan's admission of attempted suicide, but also at how I seem to have become involved. But there's more. It's what he didn't say that's got me worried. I boot up my computer, pour myself a long cold glass of juice, and go back through my browsing history. I reread the article taken from the *Belfast Telegraph* twenty-four years ago in 1996. Declan would have been eighteen at the time.

### Kneecapping comes back to Belfast

*A dissident Republican group, known as the New Republican Army, have admitted to the kneecapping of six members of the same protestant family from North Belfast. One of the victims is in intensive care, fighting for his life. The police are questioning Sean Ferran, a former hard-line IRA leader of the early seventies as they*

*believe he may have played a part in the orchestration of the new*
*attacks. The police would ask members of the public to come forward*
*with any information by phoning the confidential number below.*

Sean Ferran lives in Bangor. The New Republican Army is believed to be still working undercover, rumbling patriotism a cover-up for threat and violence and it would appear that Declan's sister, Máiréad, is married to Sean's eldest son.

I close the computer down, my eyes bleary, with a sick feeling in my gut. Fuzzy has stopped purring and is watching me from the sofa through slit eyes. If I'm right, the answer to Barton's question is that Declan belongs to (or belonged to) the New Republican Army (NRA) and that the initiation ceremony involves kneecapping a member of an opposing idealistic faction. Although the NRA says theirs is a noble cause, a fight for freedom, I suspect this is purely alternative wording for terror with menaces; money being the driver. Mafia with a capital M.

Declan would have been eighteen in 1996. Old enough to know his own mind, but more likely brainwashed by those high up in the terror brotherhood. If he was kneecapping victims, this is what Barton most likely found out. If Declan's involvement with the terrorist organisation gets out now, his future career in banking is over. In fact, his future in any career is over. More importantly, it's not too late in the day for him to get sent to prison.

The father of the five other victims subsequently died.

# 28

It's hard sticking to dating rules, especially when you reach thirty. The urge to settle down creeps up like a persistent weed nudging through inviting cracks. The tick of the biological clock gets louder with each passing year.

I've scribbled reminders to myself of what I've learned through the disastrous experiences of my twenties and have outlined new rules for the upcoming decade. These are kept in a kitchen drawer, and after one too many glasses of wine, I dig out the scrap of paper and scan it with unfocused eyes and a mushy brain. It's a challenge at this point to keep myself in check, before I pick up the phone and babble down the line at the most attractive bachelor in my contacts list. Although it's been easier over lockdown summer to avoid the pitfalls; potential suitors haven't been forthcoming and rowdy party get-togethers are a distant memory.

When I confide in Annabel that I'd like to settle down, have a stab at domestic bliss, she offers sage advice.

'Act like the heroine in one of the old classics. Chaste, elusive and ladylike.' You have to admire her front. Great advice which she's totally ignored. Some good it's done her. She thinks because she's married the Jeff Bezos of the banking world, millions on tap, that she's now a font of dating knowledge for those who are still single.

Annabel's success, according to Annabel, at hooking Clifton had nothing to do with the fact that her father is on the board of directors at the bank where her husband works. She's adamant that her ladylike charms and enviable worth as a hostess snared the prize. Personally, I find it hard to view Clifton as anybody's prize as he's certainly not my type. Too short and yappy, with an unattractive arrogance. Also, Annabel avoids all mention of her early career as a model, especially the topless part.

Married men are head of my taboo list but there seems to be so much wrong with all the eligible single blokes in the over-thirties club. At least since March I haven't added to my catastrophes of drunken fumbles, accompanied by thumping hangovers and nightmarish regrets. Did I really sleep with a random guy in his car and then slope around sheepishly for a fortnight? Then of course, there's been the fiasco with Barton. In and out of bed, commitment promises from him like dangled carrots on elastic. These months of isolation have given me respite and time to reflect.

Now, of course, there's Alex. Yes, of course he's still married and to be avoided but what's wrong with a harmless bit of flirtation and fun. Especially as he's getting divorced. Deep down, I can see the rocks around the lighthouse, but am drawn towards the dimly flashing light in my rickety craft. The warning beacon is hazy in the fog.

The logic of staying in control is flimsy at best. I've ignored his calls, texts and messages for a week now and apart from the brief sighting on Friday night at the quiz, I've been holed up at home but weirdly willing him not to give up the chase. Declan's suicidal ramblings, neurotic coffee get-togethers with Annabel and Joel's eagerness to keep in touch have all conspired to make Alex more attractive.

Perhaps I need to give him a chance. Take my time and play the long game.

~

It's been this see-saw logic that helped me decide to meet up.

I check my watch again. It's 8.20. The small hotel on the roundabout, half a mile from the motorway exit on the outskirts of St Albans, seemed as good a meeting place as any for a quick catch up and when I responded to his text earlier in the day, Alex insisted he couldn't wait any longer. He was desperate to meet, which made me smile. Crumbs and all that, but yes, I'm lonely.

He's been playing golf near Bournemouth and wasn't sure how bad the traffic would be coming back, but there's been a dearth of texts keeping me up to speed. I keep checking my messages.

Sitting in the small hotel lobby, the male desk clerk smiles across. He's probably seen it all before. Pretty women get stood up all the time, especially by harassed married men. Perhaps the heroine from a Jane Austen novel would get up at this point, hoist her petticoats in the air and flounce off into the sunset, leaving her dark knight in despair a while longer.

At 8.45 Alex appears through the rotating door. He pushes it round with one hand and flattens his sticky-up hair with the other.

'God, I'm so sorry. The traffic was dreadful. Here, let me get you a drink. I could certainly do with one.'

'Don't worry. I'm fine. Yes, a drink would be good.'

'Have you been waiting long?' He takes my hand, pulls me out of the chair and leads me through into the bar.

'I've only got here,' I lie.

I wonder why I don't tell the truth, that he's unattractively late and I've been tapping my fingers for the last half an hour. But the fear of appearing too keen is instinctive. The game-playing helps me maintain a phoney control, a sense of mystery and cool indifference, but who am I kidding?

It's the same old ground as I soak up the sloppy behaviour.

## 29

'Any word from Barton?' We're an hour into our date when I ask the question. Alex's skin is aglow, all the fresh sea air has reddened his cheeks.

'No, nothing, which is strange. I've been at his flat over the weekend but he's not answering his phone. Anybody at work heard from him?'

'No. No one has a clue where he's got to. It's strange because he's usually so loud, in your face, when he's working on a scoop. Always desperate to prove he's the world's best journalist.'

But interest in Barton is brushed under the carpet as Alex changes subject without preamble. I take a copious slurp of wine, breathe deeply as his eyes drill through me. My stomach does a nervous flip.

'It's great to see you, Kristi.' He leans close and brushes my lips with his. He smells of golf course, bunker sand and fir trees. Perhaps I'm being overly romantic, but a bottle of wine in and he's taking on the allure of George Clooney. It's on my dating-rules list: avoid sugar-coated perceptions when under the influence. Alex is no George Clooney, but the next best thing in a drought. I smile, aiming for tip-tilted-lip sexy.

One thing I did learn in my terrible twenties, is never ask a man a question. Less asked, more gained. If he's expecting me to probe about his wife, the divorce, life in St Albans, he'll have a marathon wait. As if reading my mind, another tick in his suitability box, Alex feeds me unasked for information.

'My wife's staying with her mother, so I'm home alone for a few days.'

I don't want to talk serious issues, like failed marriages, mothers-in-law or divorces. I'm not there yet. Romance, fun and male attention make up my current agenda.

An hour later, we drink up and stroll out towards the car park. He unlocks his car, a shiny black BMW and stretches his hand into the back seat, pulling out a white rabbit which he hides behind his back. Well it might as well have been a white rabbit because of the surprise element.

'Oh,' I say, unsure at first of what he's handing me. A couple of seconds pass before I take the bunch of twelve red roses, believing him when he says he asked for a dozen, and warily grip the white cellophane wrapping. A determined thorn draws blood.

'Sorry. Here, let me kiss it better.' Alex licks the bleeding finger, sets the roses on the car bonnet and pulls me close. His body pushes hard into mine, our joint eagerness sparking an electric current.

Well, the Jane Austen heroine, all heaving bosoms and fluttering heartbeat would pull back at this stage and stare aghast at her beau. She'd be hearing wedding bells, eager to settle the matter of cow dowries and wedding feasts so she could finally lay rightfully alongside her prince charming in the four-poster bed.

But as our bodies gyrate in unison, I think I've already failed in following Annabel's advice. I'll not be settling dowries nor organising wedding feasts. One thing's certain though. I'm not sure how long I can resist jumping into bed with this guy.

## 30

G rayson, my newspaper editor, is standing in the foyer of the offices, his thick chiselled workout thighs straining to burst the seams of his shiny trousers. His suit today is surprisingly dark, the tacky sheen not so apparent.

'Kristi. Thanks for coming in at such short notice.' His hand is extended, which is oddly formal for a casual workers' meeting. The usual pat on the bottom, which should have sent me long ago screaming to join the #MeToo movement, doesn't materialise. Perhaps he's demonstrating a rare show of politically motivated social distancing, but something doesn't feel right. It's his uncharacteristic demeanour.

'Grayson. No problem.' His hand is clammy, and he proceeds to wipe the offending palm down his slippery thighs. I spray the sanitiser attached to a post at the bottom of the stairwell and rub the alcoholic gel through my fingers.

'Upstairs in meeting room two.' His eyes nod in the direction of the spiralling metal staircase. 'I'll be about ten minutes. I think everyone's here.'

I wander up to the first floor, edgy, unsure what the meeting's about. Redundancy screams through the glass-fronted offices with their empty desks. Think Wild West ghost town, a rotting shell of former glory, laid waste by drought and depopulation.

A lone cactus, shrivelled and spiky, sits forlorn on my own desk as I walk past.

～

Muted voices filter through the heavy black door of meeting room two. It sounds serious. I brace myself, take a deep breath and push the door open.

'Hi.'

My greeting is met with a muffled response.

The editorial and reporting staff of the LEHC (*London Echo and Home Counties*) newspaper are sitting sedately spaced around the lengthy expanse of the smoky glass-topped table. Tracy isn't perched on top as usual, having covered her shapely legs in grey linen trousers. I do away with the smile, set my bag down and pull out a chair.

'What's up? We can't all be getting sacked,' I ask.

'Haven't you heard?' Even Tracy's hair is acting weird, not scrunched up high and knotted off to the side but hanging lank.

'Heard what?' My heart races as I slide into my seat.

'Barton.' I'm not sure which member of our ten-man team has spoken.

'Hi, gang. Thanks for coming in.' Grayson suddenly appears gripping his Starbucks beverage, a bulging brown paper bag slung over his wrist. He's wearing the bland expression of an executioner about to throw down the axe.

The view of the Thames over Matthew Bolton's shoulder hasn't changed much since I was last at work, but the traffic streaming up and down the riverbanks is less frantic. Maybe it's purely a new perception. It seems a lifetime ago that I was in our offices at Canary Wharf. It crosses my mind that Grayson might be planning to move somewhere less expensive once he's cleared away the dross. This is most likely his intention, if the dour expressions round the table are anything to go by.

Grayson takes his seat at the head of the table, the headmaster staring down the assembly line of pupils.

'Barton.' He says the word twice. What's this all got to do with Barton? After a theatrical pause Grayson continues, 'I'm afraid he's been found dead.'

I scream as a window cleaner appears behind Matthew. He's dangling from a thin wire attached to a bosun's chair. The flimsy plank is rocking back and forth in rhythm with the squeegee which he swishes over the glass. Christ. Talk about timing. A broad smile beams through the hot glass.

'Morning,' he mouths. Those with their backs to the window turn their heads and stare. The cleaner, encased in a black harness, floats in the air like a hovering ghost.

Grayson's lips purse, the grave pronouncement having been swallowed up by the appearance of the *abseiler*. The guy, lips rounded in a whistle, his wide legs steady, finally dips out of view. A hard hat is the last thing to disappear.

We all look back at our boss, who sips through the slit in his drink's container.

'I was notified last night. Apparently, Barton's body was found along the towpath in Durham, by the River Wear. He was shot.'

It's as if we've collectively been given a terminal diagnosis. Silence hangs heavy in the air like the Ebola virus. I'm not sure whether to laugh or cry. Hysteria might cover the shock.

'Oh my God.' I seem to be the only one who doesn't know. 'When? Christ. That's dreadful.' I can feel the blood leave my face as a sickness creeps through my system. My stomach somersaults.

'The police think the murder happened sometime on Friday

evening. They've had a problem locating Barton's parents who are in Portugal and asked if I'd keep it quiet until they'd been contacted.'

'Shit, shit, shit.' Everyone looks at me, their mouths open as if watching a monkey at the zoo. I wonder which of them was told first and became the whisperer's echo for the rest of the staff. Tracy is the most likely as she's been Grayson's latest favourite acquisition.

*When's the funeral? Are there any leads? Why was he in Durham? Who would want to kill Barton?*

The questions flood out, the banks having burst under the weight of inquisitiveness, as we try to understand what's happened.

Grayson wanders round the table, offering little titbits of comfort to us one at a time. My ears follow his movement. A service is being held next week but the police aren't sure yet when the body will be released. No, there are no leads at present and he was in Durham researching a story on starting university during the pandemic. *Freshers' week by Zoom, you can't be serious?* This was the scribbled suggestion found on his desk.

'Who would want to kill Barton?' Tracy sobs.

I don't add anything to the summations.

But I have a list of at least five people who would have been more than happy to see the back of him.

# 31

Annabel and Clifton live in West Common, Harpenden, in a rambling mansion with electric gates and CCTV cameras working round the clock to capture images which are relayed to phones and random portable devices on the hour, every hour. Clifton jokes that Annabel has a miniscule camera sewn into her cleavage. Everything that belongs to him will be kept safe from thieving hands, including his wife.

'It's me,' I breathe into the entry pad on the gatepost. The concrete lions stare me down.

'Come in.' A muffled voice crackles back as the gates open, like heavy velvet curtains proud to unveil their theatre magic. I pull onto the gravelled driveway and park my Mini Clubman up behind a towering Range Rover. As I step out, the gates behind slide shut and lock me in.

Annabel hovers on the porch, holding a hankie to her nose and dabbing the tip. She flings her arms wide.

'Oh my God! Kristi.' The floodgates open and she flops her head on my shoulders. I suspect Clifton hasn't been overly sympathetic, leaning more towards welcome relief now that the alpha male is out of the way.

We stand, locked like long-lost cousins, until Annabel's distress gives way to a choking cough. 'Sorry. I can't stop crying. Come in.'

Annabel and Clifton Forrester's entrance hall is laid with a cream shiny-tiled flooring, and a grand sweeping staircase swirls upwards towards heaven. Think Tara, the plantation mansion of the deep South, in *Gone with the Wind*; although Clifton is more pasty-faced Ashley Wilkes than Rhett Butler.

'I've opened a bottle. Come through.'

I've never seen Annabel in bare feet before, but grief does funny things. I can see why she keeps them covered. Her big toes point east and west, each one trying to escape a pronounced bunion. Teenage years spent in crippling heels, but even now she's reluctant to forgo the painful glamour of the height advantage.

It's hard not to stare at her naggers' feet, as they lead the way to the *orangery* at the back of the house. The room got renamed, from conservatory to orangery, as Clifton's income grew, and ideas got grander.

I'm taken aback by the sight of a bottle of Moet nestled in a silver champagne bucket, wondering at the choice of drink as camomile tea would seem more appropriate in light of the shock. But the stopper's out, lying on its side.

'What happened? I can't believe it,' she says, quaffing the bubbles as she hands me a glass. She tops up her own, before emptying what's left of the bottle into my flute.

She lounges back on a cream leather sofa and indicates for me to make myself comfy on a smaller version opposite. I retell the story imparted by Grayson, embellishing the gunshot wound to the head. Annabel throws both of her hands over her face. 'Oh my God. Why? Who would do such a thing?' The tears trickle steadily, as if from a leaky roof.

~

Twenty years after meeting him, Barton was still in Annabel's head. Memories rummaged around, day and night, invading any chance of contentment. Lustful dreams intermingled with hellish nightmares. The faces of other women were a constant torment. But now the nightmares would be worse, sexual images replaced by deathly hallucinations.

Barton had been Annabel's first real love. They'd hooked up early on at university and were inseparable until Joel grassed up his best, probably only friend. Joel became Annabel's shoulder to cry on. But he was as much a bastard as Barton, milking his friend's duplicity for all it was worth. Barton never forgave Joel, and Annabel never got over Barton.

Clifton, out of nowhere, became her future, the high-flyer who offered the lifestyle expected of Harpenden residents. The wrong side of thirty, Annabel surrendered to her fate. Annabel's father had arranged the blind date with the bank's hottest employee, selling Clifton's suitability to his daughter by expounding on both his financial and cerebral assets. Annabel finally succumbed to a tepid relationship with London's answer to *John Rockefeller*. Problem was, he wasn't Barton, who was soon back sniffing around, more aroused than ever by the competition.

A click of Barton's fingers was all it took. Two weeks before her wedding, Barton had texted. *Are you sure about this? Are you doing the right thing? Why Clifton of all people ffs?*

Wedding preparations were at full tilt, guest arrangements, flowers, cars, and the honeymoon were being meticulously organised. Clifton got shovelled to the background, an incidental bystander at his future wife's wedding. A master of deception, Clifton pretended to be put out.

Annabel knew what a bastard Barton was, but it didn't matter. She couldn't get enough of him. Thoughts of him swam around in her head, ducking and diving through the murky currents, day and night. Nothing had changed; probably never would.

'Go on. A drink. Old times' sake?' Barton had grinned down the phone, his husky poisonous voice the sheen of silk. It was two weeks till her wedding. 'You'll be a married woman soon and then what's a guy to do? A drink. That's all. What's the harm?'

Of course, he was lying. Married or not made no difference to Barton. The harder he had to work, the keener and more determined he got. Once the walls were broken down, he moved on. A drink was never going to be enough.

'All right. Just for old times' sake. Where? The farther away the better. If Clifton finds out, he'll kill you.'

'Don't worry about Clifton. I can deal with him.'

They'd ended up in a five-star hotel on the outskirts of Cambridge in the honeymoon suite. It was perfect. Champagne in the bath, wild sex on silken sheets and breakfast in bed.

'What the fuck's that between your legs?' Barton's fingers had prised her thighs apart as they stretched out after lovemaking.

'Where?'

'That pointy black thing. Jesus, you've had a tattoo.'

'Oh, that's the Eiffel Tower. It's where Clifton got down on one knee.'

'You're joking. Who says romance is dead?'

'Don't ever mention it. It's an engagement secret. Clifton intends for me to belong to him for ever.'

As they hopped on the train back to Kings Cross, Annabel listened to Barton talk. Her own voice got swallowed up, along with any hope for the future.

She'd never get over Barton and had no idea how she was going to put up with Clifton.

## 32

'Barton's made a lot of enemies over the years,' I tell Annabel. 'He muckrakes for stories and scandal. He's like a detective when he's looking for dirt, digging sharply from all angles. You know that.' I take a deep breath before I carry on. 'What about our Friday quiz questions? I mean those were pretty loaded, don't you think?'

I narrow my eyes, the way Fuzzy does when she's half asleep but conscious that there might be the possibility of a treat if she concentrates really hard.

'To be honest, I haven't really checked them out. It was bad enough discovering that Clifton was engaged to Rihanna. I didn't bother after that.'

'What about your tattoo? How did Barton know?' I aim for the Achilles heel.

'Pardon?' Annabel looks out the window and I sense a change of subject, but it'll be hard considering the reason I'm here.

'The question about where your tattoo is?'

'If you don't mind, I'd rather not talk about it. It's old news, anyway.' Her cryptic answer isn't hard to solve. 'What about you? You'll miss having Barton at work?'

It's a rhetorical question. Annabel knows our history, having devoured my tales of misery linked to Barton's misogynism and she's now trying to draw out visible signs of distress from me to keep her own company.

'Of course. But I might as well let you know, I've met someone else,' I say.

'Who, for Christ's sakes? Why didn't you tell me?'

Annabel hops off the spotless sofa and scuttles off towards the wine cellar. It's up there with the orangery, in that it's mentioned whenever they have guests. Clifton disappears at every dinner party to toy with selections of Chateau this and Chateau that, and bores us all with vintages and bouquets before he pops the cork.

In less than three minutes she's back.

'Well, it's rather strange,' I begin, as the alcohol unfurls my tongue which has been tight like a rolled-up carpet. Annabel refills our glasses before bobbing across the room to collect the cork which has ricocheted off a wall and landed behind a potted lemon tree.

'Whoops.' She giggles. 'Sorry, carry on. What's rather strange?'

'You know Alex, who has joined our Friday quiz?'

'Yes,' she nods, her head bobbing eagerly. Her tears still drip but are getting wiped away by a heavy hand.

'I met him online. I played around during lockdown, delving in and out of dating sites.' Shit, it sounds embarrassing in the telling but Annabel's eyes, steely little magnets, stare at me determined to draw out more information. There's no going back and at least I'm taking her mind off Barton.

'When he turned up that first time on screen, I knew him as

Logan. He'd used a false alias online. You see, he's married. But getting a divorce.' My voice goes up a level at the justification.

'Oh, Kristi. It'll not end well.'

'Thing is,' I say, ignoring her prediction of doom, 'he knows, or should I say, knew Barton. He's been staying at his flat in London. That's where he's been the last couple of Fridays.' There's an awkward few seconds' silence before Annabel answers.

'Bit of a coincidence. Did Barton know you and Alex were dating?' She jiggles the edge of the flute against her teeth.

'I don't think so, although there's the possibility I let slip to Barton that I'd joined a dating site. It's called *Suave Singletons*.' I gulp the fizz, interested in her knee-jerk reaction. 'Barton might have told Alex to have a look, especially as he's separated. I wouldn't have put it past Barton to stir things up. He always thought he was so funny.'

Annabel's sympathetic smile is tinged with something. Pity? Glee? I can't be sure. But her flat silent response fills the room.

Our heads turn in unison as Clifton suddenly appears outside on the back patio and taps at the window.

'Can you let me in?' His *sourmug* bulldog face, with its flattened nose and thickset neck, squish up against the glass. The further in he leans, the more evident the wrinkles.

Annabel jumps up, puts her hand under a heavy metal doorstop and extracts a key.

'Hi. You're home early,' she says, unlocking the door and letting him in.

'I know. I've just heard about Barton. What the fuck happened?'

Clifton tears his tie off, shoves it in his trouser pocket and throws himself heavily into one of the designer rattan rocking chairs.

I look from husband to wife and back again and wonder why Annabel didn't tell him last night. I'm not sure how he found out, but he only heard this afternoon and has hurried home. I wonder what he'll have told his banking colleagues.

I watch as Annabel recounts the horror, fascinated by her steady tongue and calm ability to retell the macabre with a dry-eyed narration.

An hour later I'm driving back home through the country lanes. Rain lashes against the windscreen, but the wipers can't clear my vision.

Tears flow down my cheeks in a torrent of blinding sadness.

# WEEK 4

## 33

Annabel's email, which pinged through at nine this morning had the tone of an invitation to a funeral service, factual and grave.

Yet the Zoom link which arrived a couple of hours later, inviting participants to join the meet at eight seemed at odds with the situation. An invitation suggests partying, entertainment or at least another set of boring quiz questions to help pass a couple of dull hours.

Fuzzy is in her own bed, queen of the corner, emitting a noise like a muted road drill. My Prosecco glass is tucked away, out of sight behind the computer screen as I'm not sure if the alcohol will flow so freely tonight in light of the circumstances. But then again, I don't know what the rules are for virtual wakes.

Annabel invited us to meet as usual, to talk about Barton. God knows what she wants us to talk about, but she said that she didn't feel a quiz would be appropriate. I'm not sure the others would agree but as I knock back my first glass, I brace myself to click the link. It's ten minutes past eight as my finger hovers. Here goes.

Annabel, Rihanna and Joel are already present when I'm let in.

'Hi, Kristi. Glad you made it,' Annabel says. I told her yesterday I would but she's trying to control the tone of the gathering, like a teacher at the front of the class. It was her idea to bring us all together, share our respects, and she's coveting the role of heartfelt mourner. Her hair's not so bouffant as usual, but perhaps she didn't want to smother her halo. Yes, I'm being mean but she's so two-faced and naïve, thinking we can't read between the lines.

Yesterday when visiting Annabel, I made sure to sound surprised, play the childish game of 'let's pretend' when she eventually came clean about her dead lover. I was getting ready to leave, having turned down the invitation to share a strong coffee, when she confessed. The champagne had finally knocked the lid off the deceit and loosened her tongue.

'I might as well own up. I did sleep with Barton. That's how he knew about my tattoo.'

'When? I didn't know.' I'm not sure if I knew or not but it seemed the right thing to say. Clifton had disappeared again, eager to escape the tears and handwringing. I did wonder if a confessional might come but could have done without it before going home. The unwelcome images lingered until bedtime.

Barton's cheeky question about the tattoo and where it was located must have had everyone in our little group guessing. But having witnessed the wedding clinch between Annabel and Barton in the moonlit Sorrento garden, I've been one step ahead of the others. I can't help wondering what summations they've made on the first question about Annabel, without such clues.

~

Tonight, as I look at Rihanna and Joel, I know they're not remotely interested. Their faces with the blank smiles are like portraits on the cover of a not-so-glossy magazine.

'I assume Alex isn't joining us?' It's Joel's monotone.

As if on cue, a new screen pops up with Alex Allard's name across it.

'Hope it's okay for me to join. Kristi sent me the link.'

My blush stings, but no one notices or at least pretends not to.

'Of course. It's good to see you.' Annabel smiles, a less than subtle smirk presumably fired in my direction.

## 34

Alex phoned me on Wednesday, after my meeting with Grayson and the team. It had been less than twenty-four hours since we'd clinched in the hotel car park, but it seemed like a lifetime had passed.

We shared our shock, our frustrated passions temporarily swept aside. Alex had only heard the news, and he was on his way to Barton's flat to pick up some of his stuff which he'd left lying around. He hoped the police wouldn't be there and that he could pop in and out without detection.

This morning when I messaged him about Annabel's invitation to get together, he got back straight away, keen to join. He's probably lonely with his wife gone.

~

Tonight, the screen behind Alex is very different from the bland creamy walls of Barton's flat with its bright blue and yellow canvas showcased by a small gold strip light. Behind him now is the obligatory Zoom bookshelf filled with thick shiny coated textbooks and a row of black lever arch files. He'll be in his study, which he uses for working from home.

A photograph sits on a small shelf to the left of the screen, shoulder-height. I inch forward and peer at the monitor. It's of two people, in skiing outfits. Hard to say if they're both men, or a man and a woman. Most likely Alex and his wife, Elisa, in Chamonix where he told me they ski most years. He let this slip in an unguarded moment, but he's been careful not to talk about Elisa when we're together. He's guessed I'm not interested but more possibly he's erring on the side of caution, worried that too much information might make me turn tail.

His wife could be dead for all I know, or a figment of his imagination. As far as I've been told, she's still staying with her mother.

'Is Declan joining?' Joel asks.

'Yes. He's late again.' Annabel holds up her watch, the twin showpiece to Clifton's diamond studded Rolex. 'We're in no hurry tonight anyway.'

I'm not keen to hang around but there'll be no sneaky exiting early. Even Joel hasn't, as yet, mentioned a football game.

Rihanna is covered up tonight, her chest not so prominent and the fluffy pinks have been replaced by various shades of grey. Only Rihanna could find different hues of such a miserable colour. A small black collar circles her throat like a dark version of a vicar's dog collar. Her luxurious blonde hair is scraped back in a ponytail, fine wisps falling randomly across her face. Earrings are small diamond studs. Unlike Annabel, her lips are unpainted. Only her eyebrows, thickly and skilfully pencilled in, remind us all that it is in fact Rihanna on screen.

Declan's head finally pops up. He seems to have switched outfits with Rihanna because his pink, open-necked shirt (linen I think from the creases) lights up the gathering. He's ready for a night out on the town. His hair has been cut and if I didn't know

Declan, I'd have thought he'd been under a sunbed. Either he's been out walking or drinking early whiskies because his skin is ruddy, cheeks flushed but glowing.

'Hi, everyone. Sorry I'm late. Hope you haven't started without me.' His eyes twinkle and I edge towards the whisky assumption. He's certainly not been crying.

'No, you're fine. There's no quiz tonight, Declan. We're only here to talk.' Annabel sounds like a therapist, and we are the group of mentally challenged patients whom she'll encourage to open up.

The mood is hard to describe. There are definitely two sides to the conversational coin. On one hand there is sombre respect, but there's also the less than subtly masked sense of relief in the air. Declan is back to the Irish jokes, straight away picking up on Rihanna's outfit.

'Jesus, Rihanna. Have you joined the Carmelite nuns? What the fuck are you wearing?'

Joel doesn't say much, but twenty minutes in, he asks if the police have any suspects. It's a strange introduction to the conversation.

'Not yet, I don't think. It looks pretty random but who knows.' Annabel's voice quavers.

'Have they spoken to anyone here?' Dog with a bone, that's Joel. His beer has been replaced by a mug of something hot. If his thick baggy eyes are anything to go on, I suspect coffee.

'Not yet, but they've asked us all at the newspaper offices to come in on Monday morning first thing to give statements,' I say.

'Oh.' Joel lifts his mug with both hands and makes a large circle with his lips before clamping them onto the rim.

'Let us know how that goes, Kristi.' Alex smiles. He's toying with the crowd as we've already arranged to meet up for a romantic meal tomorrow night. No one knows our connection, except Annabel, and Alex is enjoying the charade. No doubt the evening's host will alert me later of her suspicions that he might be a player. She'll want to warn me off, especially from someone so obviously successful and handsome.

'Yes, do, Kristi. Keep us posted,' commands Declan.

'Likewise,' the others chorus, like choir members with husky throats and an amateur conductor.

'The memorial service is next Friday,' Annabel announces when conversation dries to a trickle. Declan's continued attempts at levity are falling flat, forced responses producing the tinny canned laughter used to bolster a comedy show flop.

'Have they released the body?' Joel, mind of a detective.

'I'm not certain but the family's holding a memorial service anyway. I'll send you the details. And I was thinking, why don't we all meet for a few drinks and a catch up after the service? I think our quiz evenings might have reached the end of the road.'

'Good idea,' I say.

'Yes, why not.'

'I'm game.'

'Okay.' It's the first thing Rihanna's said, other than hello.

'Can I come?' Alex is smiling, all teeth and crinkly eyes. Jeez, he is handsome.

'Don't see why not. All right with everyone?' Annabel asks.

It's past midnight and I'm lying alongside my furry bed companion, staring up at the ceiling, thoughts and questions swirling round my brain. I've cracked the window to let in some air, and the screech of night riders, tearing down the road outside, intermittently break the silence.

Why was Barton in Durham? Was it connected to the freshers' week story? Who wanted him dead or was it a random, perhaps a drug-fuelled, attack? But a gunshot doesn't seem random. A knife perhaps, but a gun suggests some amount of forward planning. The likelihood of pre-meditated murder takes hold.

As I drift in and out of sleep, I keep coming back to the six questions that Barton sent to our Zoom group. The questions were loaded, each one aimed at particular Achilles' heels. I'm not a fan of coincidence. The questions came a week or so before he was murdered. There's a nagging thought that the answers might bring up more dirt than was initially apparent.

What if one of our group had some really bad secret in their past that Barton knew about and that person was desperate for it not to get out. Could one of us really have been capable of murder to keep Barton quiet?

Then there's always the possibility of blackmail. Perhaps Barton had latched on to someone's secret and had begun to turn the screw.

## 35

Clifton's hand was hot, sweaty, as it clamped over Rihanna's. She knew they only had a couple of hours together, but she was getting used to small favours. Lockdown had made her even more grateful, desperate for snatched moments to lift her mood.

Sundays had always been a dark time. Mondays, as a child, back to school still haunted her and, as an adult, it was work. During lockdown, every day felt like a wet Sunday afternoon, with nothing to look forward to. Except, of course, Clifton. Brief clandestine meetings were better than nothing; kept her sane.

'When do you go back to work? I can always help out if you're struggling,' Clifton said.

'Next weekend. I've been putting it off. The gym's open again but the Pilates classes are smaller than usual. People aren't rushing back.'

A light persistent drizzle had begun to fall, drops of damp depression wetting her hair. Clifton threw up his hoodie and pulled her in close.

'Come here. Don't worry. Please be patient a little while

longer. If that bastard, Barton, hadn't shit-stirred with his bloody questions, Annabel would never have found out about us and I could have picked the best time to leave. Now she's like a dog with a bone, going over and over the same old ground. She'd sting me for everything if I left now.'

The squelching mud underfoot made gloopy sucking sounds. Rihanna looked down at her new trainers, the pink canvas dotted with filthy brown splodges. It's how she felt, smeared with dirt. Problem was, she couldn't walk away. Didn't know how.

'She'd have found out sometime. You can't really blame Barton,' she said.

Clifton's pace quickened as the increasingly heavy pellets cascaded down on top of them. He was like an impatient dog, panting hard as he pulled her along.

'Listen, I'll drop you back. Are you around Tuesday for drinks? I can get off work early and meet you at the usual place.'

'Yes, I should be around.' Rihanna's stomach suddenly knotted, a sharp pain shooting through her side. 'Shit.'

'Are you okay?'

Rihanna clutched her stomach, bent over and fell against Clifton's chest.

'Yes, I'm fine. It'll pass.'

It was only another five minutes up the hill and Clifton slowed his pace, checking every few seconds if she was all right. He'd left his car in the pub car park when they'd decided to go for a walk, but they'd gone farther than planned. When his car came into sight, Clifton zapped it open, and Rihanna fell heavily into the passenger seat.

As he started up the engine, he turned the radio on low.

'I'll put the heated seats on, warm you up. Has the pain gone?'

Rihanna fumbled with numb wet hands to pull the seat belt firmly round her. She didn't know how to tell Clifton. It was only eight weeks, but the baby was already fluttering inside her.

'Yes. Much better, thanks.'

## 36

The email has been sitting in my spam folder. Barton sent it from a personal Hotmail account which my computer didn't recognise. My stomach clenches, the coffee gurgling like bubbles in a whirlpool. I set down the dry toast, flicking the crumbs onto the floor. Fuzzy loiters, sniffs the debris and moseys off.

The Sunday morning hangover isn't as bad as anticipated as I've learnt not to overdo things on 'dates with potential'. Alex has been slotted into that category but until I know him better, there's a long way to go. I need to be cautious, tiptoe carefully over the loaded minefield. Fingers burnt and all that. At my age there aren't as many chances left to make mistakes, learn lessons and move on but it's tough accepting that I should be experienced enough to make something with potential work out. It's scary.

The email which I'm staring at was sent on Wednesday 16th September, two days before Barton was murdered. Shit. Shit. Shit. My hands tremble as I fiddle with the mouse. The subject line contains the one word: ANSWERS.

To: krisdex1234@hotmail.com
From: bjhinton7890@hotmail.com


Hi Kristi
   Hope you're well. Sorry I've not been around, just needed time out.
   Anyway, I'm up in Durham, digging around for an angle on the return of students to Uni and freshers' week. It's bloody cold up here. I'd forgotten the shitty north wind, as sharp and cutting as a serrated knife. I'm going to stay a while longer and speak to students, if I can find any. They're as rare as priests in a nun's vagina. Hopefully I'll not have to track them down online and Facetime for their opinions on the new normal for student life. Poor buggers. What's the fun in a virtual freshers' week? Maybe they'll all get drunk and share topless photos with new socially distanced mates.
   How are you getting on with the questions I sent through?? It was only meant to be a bit of fun. During lockdown I poked around on the internet to see what sort of dirt you could get on people… eye watering, to be honest. Out of our Friday troupe, I think you're the only one not hiding a dirty little whopper. Well not yet anyway!
   I've toyed with a story angle, although will come clean that there's no film

commission. Just messing on that one. I thought I could change the names, keep the characters and backstories and write that novel that I've always been threatening.

Okay. So, I'm a shit-stirrer… but it's what I do for a living. I've got plenty of enemies but that's part of the job. Anyway, since I sent out the questions to our Friday group, I've started receiving menacing threats on my phone. They were pretty tame at first but now they're coming through every day, sometimes several times a day, and are getting increasingly sinister. **'I'll slit your throat, you bastard. Believe me. I'm on my way'** was the latest missive. I've no idea who's sending them, but I've obviously hit a very sensitive nerve.

When I get back, I'll show you. I think best I drop the storyline as it's not worth the aggro and anyway, wouldn't want to lose the few friends I've got left.

But… thought you might be interested (for your eyes only) in the answers to the questions. Maybe best you delete them after, but they make for fascinating reading. I've attached each answer as a separate document.

BTW, what's your new column called? I hear from Grayson you've come up with something like **Lies and Lockdown**. Ha ha. Apt!!

Should see you sometime next week. Oh, nearly forgot. How's things going with Alex? Sorry I couldn't help pointing him in your direction. He's quite a catch. If you get a chance, ask him about his villa in Marbella. It's very cool. I'd steer clear of his wife though.

Best

Barton (big kiss)

## 37

Q uestion 1: *Who was Joel's first ever serious girlfriend and (bonus point) how long after their first date did they sleep together? (nearest answer gets the point)*

Joel was like a scrawny mongrel on heat when he met Olivia, first day of freshers' week. He was my neighbour on the hexagonal landing of Trevelyan College at Durham University. The walls were so thin, we might as well have been sharing. Olivia was in the room next to Joel, in a similarly bijou cubicle. We had all opted for single occupancy in the first term which might have played into Joel's hands in the early days.

Joel met Olivia on 4$^{th}$ October 2006 and slept with her the next day. Full marks for speed, I'll give him that! Joel's never been one to hang around. Anyway, it lasted all of three weeks, when Olivia finally ventured out into the big wide cosmopolitan student world and mixed with more dynamic, good-looking and like-minded students. Ahem. Yours truly. Not being boastful, but I managed to get her into bed on 5th November, if I remember correctly, at the end of a Halloween bash at Durham Castle. There were certainly fireworks that night.

So, on the face of it, Olivia was Joel's first ever girlfriend and they slept together one day after meeting… perhaps this could be construed as their first date.

But after some mammoth lockdown digging, propelled through chronic boredom to trawl photos and snippets of postings from his old classmates, 2005/06, some very interesting facts came to light. Also, I've never really forgiven Joel for interfering and buggering up my own love life back then. More on that later.

Apparently, Joel dated a girl for six months in his last year at school. He hooked up with her at the Christmas party, 18th December 2005. Thing is, he never owned up to anything serious. He laughed it off as a drunken fumble behind the bike sheds and told his friends he had no intention of seeing her again. That was his story and he stuck to it. He's a sneaky little weasel.

But he lied. He carried on seeing her on the quiet, taking her to the pictures and farther afield to country pubs in his bashed-up Ford Fiesta, drinking and driving with abandon. He broke the law. He got breathalysed more than once and eventually got a three-year ban.

You see, he broke the law in more ways than one. His girlfriend that year was called Josie. A pretty little brunette, long skinny legs and false eyelashes. Recent selfies still can't camouflage the fulsome cleavage. She's now married to a bricklayer and lives on the Archway Road in North London. Yes, Josie was his first serious girlfriend (not Olivia) and Joel slept with her on New Year's Eve. His parents had gone to France, Le Touquet to be precise, to see in the New Year and they agreed that Joel was responsible enough to invite a couple of friends round. He didn't. He stuck to one, Josie. And that's the answer to the second part of the question. It was precisely thirteen days after their first date, and meeting, that he stole her virginity. (He probably lost his own that evening too.)

Right, now you want to know what's so secretive about this less than colossal piece of information. You see, Josie had just turned fifteen. Joel broke the law twice. As a drunk driver he escaped with a ban and a £300 fine but with Josie, he would have been looking at a stretch inside. Lucky for him, she never let on.

Now, aren't I the clever sleuth? Just call me Sherlock.

The thing that bothers me, is that now Joel

is teaching geography to fourteen and fifteen-year-olds at St Martin's School, does he still have a penchant for young girls?

Yes, I'm a shitty nosey bastard, but you see my point, don't you?

## 38

Q uestion 2:What's Annabel's tattoo of, and where exactly (for a bonus point) is it located?

Annabel's always been like a bitch on heat. Let's face it. I've known her since university days, and she's put it about more times than a randy rabbit. Clifton was a catch, certainly in terms of wealth and status, but also in that he seems able to turn a blind eye to her penchant for hunky toy boys. Maybe you're thinking I'm no toy boy, but I'm still in the hunky category. You've got to agree.

Annabel and I hooked up first term at uni. She was quite the firecracker in those days and even taught me a few early lessons in fumbling. But there were so many pretty girls around at the time, I found it hard to remain completely faithful. This is where that little shit Joel comes in. He told Annabel what I got up to and spoiled our party. She didn't forgive me, for quite a long time, and when she did come running back, I'd sort of lost interest.

Anyway, Annabel and I have kept in touch and shortly before her wedding (okay, I couldn't resist) I called her and we had, wow, a night to remember. Took me back to why I first fell for her. Champagne in bed, sex in the bath… you know, usual stuff.

Well, of course, I discovered her pretty little tattoo. The point of the Eiffel Tower is so far up her crotch, it's almost inside. Clifton gave it to her as an engagement present, always meant to be for his eyes only. Prick. Who was he kidding? They're a match made in hell and he'll never keep her satisfied.

I suspect you might have solved the second part of the Rihanna riddle; you're one nosey bitch, Dexter, but nearly as good a detective as yours truly. You can see that it's not just Annabel who plays dangerous games. Clifton, engaged to Rihanna years ago, can't let her go either. He's still stringing her along, pretending that one day he'll leave his wife. I suspect his interest in Annabel was more down to the fact that her father is head of the bank where Clifton works, rather than fascination with her physical and mental attributes. He's now one loaded sycophantic fat cat.

I know it was pretty shitty to hook up with Annabel before the wedding but she's quite the nymphomaniac, and what's a man to do? Oblige, of course.

I suspect I'm the only other person in our little Friday group who knows the answer to the Annabel question, and of course you do now too. If Annabel ever pisses you off, you can mention the Eiffel Tower. She's certainly pissed off enough people in the past and I've learnt it's always good to have these little titbits of informative shit up one's sleeve.

## 39

Q  uestion 3:What dating site does Kristi use and what's the
name of her current mystery single lover? (bonus point)

Not much dirt on you, that's for sure, Miss
Moneypenny. Pure as the driven snow. Except
dating married men isn't the wisest move,
certainly not in your thirties.

No doubt Alex has told you he's getting
divorced. I'd check this out. His wife's a
sexy little pocket rocket, all of five foot
three, but pretty loyal. For my part, Annabel
was a much easier trophy and to be honest,
I've failed miserably where Elisa is
concerned. But then, Alex is much more of a
man than Clifton. Perhaps you've already found
that out? Perhaps not. You're smart enough to
play it carefully though. Good luck is all I'd
say. Alex is a bit of a dark horse, a bit more

to him than is first apparent. I've known him since school days, and he hasn't changed much.

We were fourteen when he stole my bike. Told me he'd seen a young lad picking the padlock and riding off into the sunset. He's always underestimated me. I was suspicious and watched him ride it a couple of times before dumping it down by the river. I never told him I'd seen. Remember, it's always good to have one over on people and Alex is no exception.

As I hinted in the email, don't forget to ask him about his villa in Marbella. Yes, Marbella. He might tell you it's a two-bed apartment in the Costa Blanca, but he'd be lying. And remember to ask yourself why.

Listen, I'm always around for a bit of fun. Perhaps you fancy a weekend away sometime again soon? Like old times. I might be getting ready to settle down you know, and you'll definitely be my first port of call.

B X

## 40

Q uestion 4:What was the name of Rihanna's first pet and (bonus point) first fiancé? (although I don't think there's been more than one! Ha ha!)

I think you'll all have worked out the answer to the second part of the question by now. Thing is, Annabel genuinely didn't know. Clifton likes newer models, always scouting round for the latest car with the shiniest bonnet and the girl with the biggest bumper. But he also can't let go of possessions. Rihanna was once his and she's perfect for a bit on the side; **lights on but nobody's in** is his naïve simplistic view of Rihanna but he should pay her more attention, because she's not as fluffy as she appears. I've still no idea why she turned me down… maybe one day.

But, like Annabel, when it came to settling

down, Clifton needed the full package. Annabel would be the well-groomed wife from a suitable background, not to mention a father-in-law with a few million in the bank. Clifton needs money and possessions to make him look taller, disguise the fact that he wears built-up shoes.

Rihanna was only in her teens when she got engaged to Clifton. Eighteen, I think it was, and he was twenty-eight. Rihanna has broken a few hearts in her time, but Clifton was among the first. However, when she wanted to settle down, get a commitment, he scarpered faster than a rabid rat. He asked her to wait for him. What a shit! I mean she was such a pretty little thing, still is and he's such an arse. Why the hell would she wait for him?

I don't think Annabel has twigged that they're still seeing each other. I mean, she can't moan considering that she begged me for sex a couple of weeks before her wedding. I doubt Clifton would be so understanding. They'll spend their married life tiptoeing round each other, playing the dutiful and long-suffering spouses. Although I don't think I want to be around when Annabel discovers the perky Rihanna is still seeing her husband. Do you?

On the question of what Rihanna's first pet was… the best way to find out would be to ask Clifton. As to what happened to the pet… well, suffice to say, Clifton's a sadistic little shit. Rihanna shouldn't have tried to play him at his own game by dating other guys when he told her he wasn't ready to settle down. She's much more of a fighter than she appears. Yet, I'm surprised she's forgiven him for what he did to the cat.

# 41

Q uestion 5:*What secret society does Declan belong to and (bonus point) what does the induction ceremony entail?*

I'm not a fan of Declan Mooney's. Far too much slimy Irish charm and blarney. He's not to be trusted and watch out because he's got his eye firmly fixed on you, Kristi.

His secret makes him a dangerous commodity. Being Irish might give you a clue as to what society or splinter group he belongs to. He joined up when he was only fifteen. Well, maybe 'joined up' is a bit simplistic and wide off the mark. His family initiated him into the brotherhood, brainwashed him, and he didn't really have a choice. I suspect he still blames everyone up the Falls Road in Belfast for his involvement in the republican cause. Either way, Declan became a fully-fledged member of the New Republican Army (NRA) before he finished school.

He was too young to break away, no money and plenty of excuses to tag along and partake in the terror war against the protestants over on the Shankill Road. He thinks no one on the mainland knows about his past. Other than myself, I suspect this could be true, because is anyone really interested? It all happened so long ago. Declan will be though. He'll be petrified that anyone might find out what he got up to, especially now that he's been made redundant from the bank. The chance of another job is slim, especially with his current penchant for one too many whiskies at lunchtime. I'm not sure that even a glowing reference from Clifton will help him get another decent job in the banking world. Clifton has been trying to distance himself since even before his wedding to Annabel. I'm not sure if Clifton knows about Declan's connections, but perhaps he should be wary of the Irish dissident. Declan is no saint.

You might have guessed at the induction ceremony. It took me a while to come up with the second part of the Declan conundrum but I'm good at scouring through archive newspaper clippings. Lockdown has given me plenty of time to probe, and lo and behold I came across a very interesting story. Kneecapping was a favourite pastime during the early seventies, but it's carried on as the MO, modus operandi, of the New Republican Army whose activity is still simmering in the shadows today. Sean Ferran, the head of the NRA, has for decades been recruiting young guys eager to join the cause.

In 1995 a whole family of protestants who wouldn't pay up (think Mafia, drug-running scenarios) were kneecapped. The father ended up in intensive care and died a few days later. Declan was never caught but was handsomely rewarded by compatriots for his part in events.

Problem now for Declan is that Sean won't let him go. Declan's tried hard enough to leave the past behind, but every time Sean needs one more job doing, he clicks his fingers. You see, Declan can't escape his past. He's actually wanted for murder, but the file was archived a long time ago, and the Troubles in Belfast have been hidden under the phoney carpet of the Good Friday Agreement of 1998. No one wants to go back and relive the horrors. But, hey ho. Poor Declan. He still doesn't know which way to turn.

Don't feel too sorry for him though. He's guilty as charged. If he owned up, he might be able to get sober and gain protection in return for releasing names, dates and details. Perhaps a new life in Brazil wouldn't be so bad for him now. He's not got much else to look forward to.

~

A lot of info. I'm good, aren't I?

You're the only person I've shared all this with. I've been so bored during the last few months that I had to find something useful to spend my time on. Well, maybe it's not that useful but it's been fun.

At first, I thought it would all make a good story, even a brilliant film, but in light of recent threats, I'm putting it on the back burner. Perhaps some things are best kept hidden.

Anyway, I'm looking forward to hearing all about your new column. *Lies and Lockdown*, I think Grayson said. Sounds a great title. What do you have in mind?

Cheers and see you soon.

B X

PS Maybe grab a bite and a few drinks? You'll always be my favourite girl.

## 42

The glass doors are all thrown wide, inviting us to wander freely and share our discomfort. Starbucks coffee mugs are lined up on the long table by the window of the large meeting room.

'Help yourself,' Matthew Bolton says, a bony finger pointing at the line of cappuccinos and Americanos in cardboard containers, arranged like terracotta warriors in neat little lines.

'Thanks,' I say when he indicates the one with my name on.

It's long been the newspaper's custom to start the workday off with a shared coffee. But having foregone breakfast, it's a risk. Alongside the sterile refreshments, is a bottle of sanitiser and a fresh packet of masks with no sign of the welcoming croissants.

'Mask?' Matthew walks round the circle of sombre staff and dangles the pale blue accessories which look like bikini triangles. Perhaps I could have three. Two for my compact breasts and one for the fig-leaf area.

'Thanks,' I repeat, taking one and stuffing it in my pocket. I'm not sure when we're supposed to wear the masks as everyone is sipping greedily through the miniscule holes of plastic coffee lids. Tracy has put the elastic round her ears and the useful part is under her chin. At least she's showing willing.

'Hi, guys. Thanks for coming in.' As he enters, Grayson's voice booms off the glass windows and doors, the echo reverberating round the room. Alongside him are two casually dressed men in dark suits. *Covid* cops probably, starched and laundered uniforms archived at the back of wardrobes.

'Have a seat everyone. This is DCI Trottman and PC Weatherton. As I told you, they want to speak to you in a group and then take individual statements from each of you, regarding Barton Hinton's murder.' Grayson speaks with authority as if he's heading up an international summit on climate change or melting polar ice caps.

With muted 'of courses' and 'no problems' the editorial staff of the *London Echo* shuffle round the table. Grayson, sitting at the head, flings back his chair and narrowly avoids banging his crown on an overhead projector. The policemen stand like sentries, one on either side.

The coffee spikes my nerve endings, sharp little twinges pricking with every sip. It'll take more than one to unravel my gnarled cogs.

After I'd copied Barton's email and question and answer documents onto a couple of memory sticks, stashed away like blood-splattered instruments of a sordid crime, I deleted all the loaded material and associated communications from my hard drive.

I have in my possession enough reason for any one of our Friday Zoom group to have wanted Barton dead. Not to mention that there is enough dirt on at least Declan and Joel to have them put away for a very long time, even if they haven't been the ones to have had Barton shot through the temple.

But currently, I'm also a criminal knowingly impeding an enquiry by withholding vital information. Problem is, I have absolutely no one to talk it through with. Perhaps I should tell Alex, but perhaps not as I don't know him that well.

'Good morning. I'm Detective Trottman and this is my colleague PC Weatherton. We're here to run through events surrounding the heinous murder of your colleague, Barton Hinton.'

DCI Trottman's voice drones like the hum from a hornet's nest. His delivery lacks tonal peaks and troughs, and his lacklustre droll is taking the edge off our collective curiosity.

Matthew fiddles with his mask, teasing it up and down. Not sure it'll help his asthma and Tracy is looking down at the glass-topped table, her head nodding every so often in acknowledgement that someone is speaking. Grayson leans back, legs splayed out, relishing his managerial role in the tragedian performance. The other six members of staff, a couple of secretaries and four junior editorial assistants are like cardboard cut-outs. Young, eager to please and even more eager to hold on to precarious jobs; they collectively stare, unblinking at the dull detective.

## 43

It doesn't take long for the individual interviews to come around, the police not wasting time on random questions that come their way. They're not at liberty to answer even the most pertinent concerns at this early stage in the investigation.

I'm third in line for interrogation and I sit on the edge of my chair, eyes glued to the dark blue carpet tiles. My legs jiggle up and down, feet close together. It's like the dentist's waiting room minus the threatening tone of a sadistic drill warning of the pain to come.

I plan to stick to my original story that I haven't heard from Barton since Friday 4th September, our Friday quiz night, when he was question master. I won't mention the bonus round and suspect that once the police talk to the other members of our group, that none of them will mention them either. I mean which of us would?

Annabel or Clifton could certainly have been angry enough to want harm to come to Barton. Joel certainly won't want his past dragged up. Rihanna knows when to keep her mouth shut, I'm almost certain. She's got as much stuffing between her ears as a Steiff Teddy Bear but she's not as soft and cuddly as she makes out. Barton's observations have backed up my own summations. Declan, for certain, isn't going to own up.

I suggested earlier to Alex over the phone, on my way in to work, that he shouldn't mention the questions either.

'No worries. They weren't anything to do with me anyway.'

Alex is going tomorrow to the police station to make a formal statement.

'Kristi Dexter? If you'd like to follow me.' PC Weatherton's voice interrupts my thoughts. His accompanying smile tries to assure me that the procedure will be painless.

'Sure. Coming.' My voice is jittery, a criminal edge to the diction, but my eyes prepare for full unwavering contact.

The small meeting room, with its hard black door rather than showy glass panels, is located at the end of the corridor next to the men's toilets. A loud blast of air rumbles out across our path.

'Come in.'

I follow Weatherton through into what has been set up like a police interrogation room on some made-for-TV crime drama.

'Miss Dexter. Please, have a seat.' I resist the urge to sit alongside the detective but instead proffer a winsome smile as I drag back the blue-upholstered seat on the opposite side of the table. This is the room where you know you're in trouble when Grayson suggests it as a meeting venue.

'Okay. Perhaps you'd tell me how well you knew Barton Hinton?'

It's like an exam, easy questions first. I'm good at multiple choice, spotting when a tricky question is slotted in among the more obvious. Today I'm aiming for at least ninety per cent.

It's hard telling lies, especially in a murder case, as we all know the consequences. Cop shows home in on criminals who make shifty gestures, arrogant asides, assuming they're smarter than the whole of Scotland Yard. Problem is, I'm not confident of my ability to pull the wool. A dry irritating cough isn't helping me.

'Can you think of anyone who would have wanted to harm Mr Hinton?' Weatherton's lips vibrate like a violinist's vibrato when he talks.

'No. I've no idea.' I open my eyes too wide. Jeez, I need to lower the pitch of my voice.

'No one at work? Friends?'

'Not that I know of.'

'Did you know the deceased well? I have here on record somewhere,' he shuffles papers around, 'that you dated Mr Hinton for a while.'

'We went out a couple of times, that was all. Obviously, I work with him but haven't been on a date as such, since a friend's wedding last year.'

'Would that be Mr and Mrs Forrester's wedding. Italy, I think it was?' He checks his notes.

'That's right.'

The detective scratches his head, a thoughtful gesture rather than to alleviate an itch. The few seconds that pass feel like an eternity.

'Right. I think that's all for now, but we may need to ask you some more questions at a later date.' His eyes bore through me, attempting to gauge my response. Will I answer too quickly? Do my eyes have a direct honest approach? Will my intonation feed him doubts?

'Can I ask, do you have any suspects?'

'Unfortunately, I'm not at liberty to say at this stage, Miss Dexter, but we are currently looking into several lines of enquiry as well as possible motives. But as yet no one has been charged.'

My legs wobble like unset jelly, my head light and fluffy as I stand up and push back my chair. I use the flat of my hand on the table to steady myself.

'Thanks,' I say, unable to read from the detective's expression if I passed the test.

As I head for the exit, I feel the detective's black pellet eyes follow me from the room.

## 44

We're in the White Lion pub in St Albans. Alex no longer has the luxury of Barton's flat to escape the problems at home, but as his wife, Elisa, is still with her mother he's enjoying the quiet familiarity of his own place.

'You should have come to me,' he says. 'I'm good in the kitchen and could have rustled up a meal with a couple of romantic candles.' His lips curl at the corners.

'Probably best not. It wouldn't feel right. Perhaps, when your divorce comes through, I'll risk a visit.'

It's still early, only 6pm and the evening trade is sluggish. A bar girl is wiping a soggy cloth up and down the heavy counter.

'It used to be heaving in here after work. Certainly not like the old days.' Alex licks his full lips after each mouthful of lager.

'What? You mean like in medieval times?' Keep it light, wispy. I've got a few questions to ask but intend to slip them in randomly before he's aware of an agenda.

'Ha ha. Very funny. It seems ages since things were more normal,' he says.

There are only two other couples in the pub, sitting far apart from each other. I think of lepers, riddled with scabs and disease but perhaps these pairs are married, glad of the space.

'You can say that again.' I smile over the top of my glass.

'It's dreadful about Barton. I can't get my head round it.' Alex's smile droops as he speaks.

'We had the police at work, getting us all to make formal statements. No one seems to know anything. And, by the way, I didn't mention Barton's probing questions that he set us when he was quizmaster. Saw no point,' I say.

I still wonder if Alex knows what the questions were. I'm not sure. He mentioned that he didn't know, but wasn't he curious? I remember him telling us all, the following week, that Barton had asked him to see what we had come up with as answers. 'Don't shoot the messenger' crosses my mind. It seems unlikely that Barton would have told him. But then, I don't know how close they were. Alex's free use of Barton's bachelor pad throws up doubts.

'I didn't say anything either,' Alex continues, sitting up more rigidly. 'I've no idea what the questions were and anyway, after you called, I saw no reason to bring up the subject. I didn't have much to tell the police as I hadn't heard from Barton since that first quiz night. He told me he was travelling around, sniffing out scoops and headlines.'

Alex slips along the bench, nudging his shoulder against mine and gives me a light kiss on the cheek.

'Hm. You smell good,' he says. It's a subtle change of subject. I'm not sure if Alex is steering the conversation away from the snakes breaking loose from their pit, but I certainly am. The wine is making me edgy but boosting my confidence and determination.

'Have you had a holiday this year? I could really do with a break,' I begin, threading the needle with a tenuous thread.

'No. I was planning a trip to Spain until everything went pear-shaped. What about you? Any plans?'

'Spain would be nice. Have you been before?' I ask.

Alex's shoulder sidles back and he leans forward, resting his elbows on the thick wooden table. 'Yes, I've been a couple of times.'

'Whereabouts? Any recommendations?'

Barton's email is ringing in my ears, pushing me to ask about a villa in Spain. Marbella. My dead colleague's ghost is nagging.

'Murcia a couple of times. La Manga Club to play golf. Spain is heaven for golfers.'

'I quite fancy a trip to Marbella. Find myself a millionaire toy boy.' I laugh, the tinny sound bouncing off the papered walls. A couple of seconds pass while Alex checks his phone screen.

'A top-up?' His question is an answer. My stomach knots when he ignores my words, his silent response telling its own story. If Alex and I stand any chance of a future together, I need to smash apart the lies and fill in the omissions.

'Yes please. Another white wine would be lovely.'

Around midnight, I crawl into bed, Fuzzy having already sneaked under the duvet. It's going to be a restless night. Alex is keen for us to consummate our relationship, but my head is going to rule my heart; it's the only way forward. There'll be no sex until I can trust him. I'm determined that I'll not be the one crying into my pillow when he decides his wife isn't so bad after all.

Unless he comes clean and opens up, Alex is going to have a long wait.

## 45

Grayson likes the idea for my new column, *Lies and Lockdown*, but he's menacing with his sharp pointed tongue telling me to come up with something really gritty. Readers are fed up with dull, depressing headlines about lack of PPE, death statistics and governmental failures. He's not a hundred per cent sold on the word *Lies*, but he's prepared to see what angle I use.

'Let's get back to some good old dirty gossip. The depressive life angle for thirty-something singletons, has become bloody repetitive. Somebody somewhere must have been having a good time, surely. Perhaps breaking curfew and sneaking out for a bunk up with the neighbour's wife in the garden shed or driving a few hundred miles to reconnect with an old flame without a mask. Use your imagination. Come on, Kristi. Something meaty.'

He's a dirty old git, Grayson, but he's right. I need to come up with escapism stories showing that some people have made use of lockdown to enjoy themselves, rather than spent the time plotting how to end it all... a bottle of paracetamol or a razor blade?

~

Fuzzy has been out all night, so I can't concentrate. She's done it before but, as I glance at the kitchen clock, I realise she's usually back by nine, latest, guiltily depositing a mouse or baby bird on the floor and sloping off to her bed. It's now ten o'clock.

I pull on a sweatshirt and dig out my trainers from the hall cupboard, slapping the soles together to loosen the dried mud. Fuzzy can't have gone far. The wind is still swirling in violent gusts with eerie lulls in between. She's probably found a warm sheltered spot and I'm hoping it's not with her favourite neighbour, Mrs Crabtree, the lady who feeds my cat indigestible dried chicken pieces and lets her doze in the airing cupboard.

Through the window I notice a branch has snapped off from the sprawling chestnut tree in the middle of our communal green. The old man from a couple of doors down has dragged it off to one side and is now attacking it with a giant saw.

As I lock the front door behind me, I check the cat flap hasn't stuck, prodding it backwards and forwards. I pull my hood up, cocooning my ears from the cold tornado-like onslaught and start jogging lightly round the estate.

Even though there's no sign of Fuzzy, I carry on to the park, my feet pummelling the pavements, the blood coursing through my veins. I need to keep going. I know I'll come up with inspiration for the column, I've got over a week, but in the meantime I've no idea how to deal with all the shit Barton's death has left behind.

I stop by a bench, stretch out my tortured calf muscles by lengthening my leg along the seat, when my mobile suddenly vibrates. I unzip the pouch strapped round my waist, lift out my phone and check the screen. It's Declan. When I don't pick up, a message appears straight away.

Hi. I'm in your area. Are you working from home? I could pop by for a quick coffee.

D x

I cling on to the back of the bench as a hurricane-force wind tunnels along the footpath. My hood flies back and sends my hair swirling round my face.

Ok. I'll be back home in half an hour. Just a quick one though. I'm supposed to be working!

On the walk back, I peer into gardens, up trees and under cars but still no sign of Fuzzy. A sickness grips as I gather speed. My elderly neighbour has built a sizeable pile of log cuttings from the fallen branches and smiles as I pass. Outside the entrance to my house, a white van is parked askew on the pavement. *Haldeans Fruit and Veg* is painted along the side, with brightly coloured fruits plastered above and below the wording.

As I come alongside, a man gets out holding aloft a small box of produce, a bunch of bananas balanced precariously on top. A sterile starched white cap sits on his head like a cloche, and pristine white overalls cover him to below the knees. I squint into the sun. Who the heck is sending me fruit? Perhaps it's for the old boy cutting the branches.

'Don't you recognise me?'

'Declan?' The lilting Irish brogue is distinct. 'What are you doing?'

'A little present to say thanks.'

'No, I mean the van, the outfit.'

'A man has to earn a living. It was either this or chucking packages on doorsteps for Amazon. I was delivering to a store in the area and thought I'd pop by.'

'Come in. It's good to see you.'

Declan follows me in and sets the box of fresh fruit and veg on the kitchen top. He takes his hat off revealing hair that looks like a sculptor's block of unmoulded clay and shakes his head, using the tips of his fingers to loosen the clump of matted strands.

'I'm worried about Fuzzy,' I say. I click the kettle on and turn to face him.

'Why, what's up?'

'She's been out all night. I'm worried because she's been restless the last few days and not eating properly.'

'Hmm. You're certain she's not in the house somewhere?'

'No. I've checked.'

Declan ignores me and wanders through into the lounge and pokes around, his head dipping under the sofa and chairs.

'I'd have heard her if she was inside. She hangs around my ankles.'

Declan straightens up again and scans the room for hiding places before he asks if he can use the bathroom.

'It's been a long drive up from Finchley.' He un-pops his white coat, drapes it over a stool and disappears upstairs. Two minutes later he's back down.

'You need to come up,' he says, a nervous grin on his face.

'What is it?'

In the few seconds it takes to climb the single flight of stairs, I consider a wasp's nest, mice droppings and perhaps a broken bathroom window, smashed for the umpteenth time by a rogue cricket ball.

Declan leads me into the bedroom and for one awful moment, the possibility that he might be making a play for me crosses my mind. He stands on my bed, steadying himself on the wardrobe which sits tight up against the frame.

'I think this might be your missing housemate,' he whispers.

A large white ball of fluff is camouflaged on top of my winter duvet. A soft wet tongue is furiously licking her belly. A violent hiss is directed towards Declan and he wobbles.

'Oh my God. Fuzzy. What's she doing?'

'I think she's bringing you a few more little housemates.'

'What do you mean?'

'Can't you work it out?' Declan clambers down and helps me up.

'You're joking me. She's pregnant?'

'I think she's not only pregnant, but in labour.'

Suddenly Fuzzy lets out a deafening yowl and her body starts to vibrate.

'Shit. We need to get her to the vets.'

'Too late. I think the first kitten is on its way.'

It's four o'clock in the afternoon and Declan makes a fourth round of coffees. Four slivers of fur nuzzle up to a proud, exhausted mother in a cardboard box which he dug out from the back of his van. Four is my new lucky number.

'That wasn't so hard now, was it?' The twinkle is back in the Irish eyes. Declan grips a hot mug, greedily guzzling the emergency chocolate biscuits.

'What can I say? I couldn't have done it without you. You've been marvellous.'

'You'd have found a way. It's nature after all, the most natural thing in the world. Listen, I need to get going. The flat tyre story won't placate my boss much longer.'

Declan stands up, stretches his arms out to the side.

'Thank you. You've been a life saver.' Without thinking I lunge forward and throw myself at him. Strong arms pull me in as I tuck my head under his chin. His body heat covers me like an electric blanket and his fingers run gently through my hair, up the back of my neck and coil the straggling ends behind my ears.

'You smell good,' he says.

For the first time all day, I'm lost for words as tears dribble down my cheeks.

# WEEK 5

## 46

Off screen, there's nowhere to hide.

Real life has exposed, like a rocky outcrop, our quiz group in full raggedy-edged 3D definition. Width, length and depth portray the reality of our appearances and personalities. The relaxation supplied by slippers, bare feet and full bottles of strong wine has been replaced by edginess. It's as if we're seeing each other for the first time; like a random group of commuters who pass each other every day but are now sitting round a table, close-up and uncomfortable.

Annabel is in the middle of the rectangular table, facing Alex whose chair is disturbingly close to my own. Declan's twinkling eyes have lost the sparkle that glistened as his bloodied slithery fingers gently slid the third kitten, encased in a wet glistening sac, into the world. His eyes are moving rapidly in all directions, as if he's in a disturbed state of sleep.

Declan is opposite me, his legs tightly tucked away, feet neatly crossed at the ankles. His hair is lightly gelled, spiked up at the front with the strands criss-crossing. Joel meanwhile is staring into the bottom of his beer glass with a glance every so often at Rihanna's breasts.

'This is the first time we've got together since the New Year.' The compulsion to take control makes Annabel speak first. 'Cheers, everyone. Good to see you.'

'*Cheers.*' '*Yes, good to be out.*' '*Long time indeed.*'

∾

Barton's family opted for a closed remembrance service, his body not having been released, pending further investigation. Our small group's good intentions to turn up and share silent prayers have been scuppered.

Annabel emailed us individually to see if we fancied meeting up anyway. When she texted to see if I wanted Alex included, she'd already asked him. I joked with Alex that she might have a soft spot for him now that Barton was gone but Alex laughed and assured me, she definitely wasn't his type.

Yet Alex feels more like a plus one, an imposter hovering round the edges of our established Friday night brigade. Although Alex and I have had a few dates, the group can only surmise at what's going on between us and now certainly isn't the time to fill them in.

The tapas bar is located at the back of Kings Cross, Rihanna's suggestion. The queues usually snake all the way down the street apparently, it's that popular. But tonight, the line of customers is small, neatly spaced and anticipatory weekend chatter has given way to quieter respectful tones. We may as well have been queuing for a funeral service.

Declan winks at me, before raising his eyes heavenwards, as conversation takes off. Barton, as usual, has claimed centre stage. *Who would have wanted to kill him? Why Durham? A hitman versus a personal face-off?*

Declan has the expression of a hangdog puppy, eager for a new home, with his heavy droopy eyes. Weird I know, but sitting between Alex and across from Declan makes me feel as if I'm two-timing. Declan has thrown a spanner in the works with his soft and gentle treatment of Fuzzy. Alex hasn't picked up on Declan's and my drama as I haven't recounted the full Fuzzy saga, but he won't perceive Declan as a threat; Alex's confident manner, with its thick black edging of arrogance are a large part of the attraction. As his hand rests lightly on my thigh, it's hard not to compare the two guys. Alex is definitely Alsatian; heavy set and thick furred with bared teeth, whereas Declan is springer spaniel; bouncy and excitable.

Conversation flows like a river over leaden boulders, this way and that, smooth passage interrupted by incoming tributaries that disrupt the course of the mainstream. Joel's sudden interjection feels like arrival at a thundering waterfall.

'You know the questions Barton sent us? They were pretty loaded. Has anyone mentioned them to the police?' Joel sits up straighter, directing his gaze towards each of us in turn. His expression is deadpan. It could be accusatory or questioning.

'I didn't see the point,' says Declan.

'Same here.' Rihanna's nervy voice pipes up.

'Bastard. I'm certainly not going to say anything. He was a real shit-stirrer,' Annabel says, her voice slicing through the restaurant buzz. Her reverential tone has been buried under the venom. She turns pointedly towards the squeaky mouse on the end and stares her down.

I'm impressed that Rihanna turned up at all now that Annabel knows about Rihanna's past engagement to Clifton. But the ladies, in respect to Barton, haven't drawn blood although I reckon tonight will be their last outing together.

'Shall we all forget about the questions then?' Joel leans forward, his skinny ribs stabbing through a yellow T-shirt.

'Suits me,' says Declan.

'What were these questions?' Alex's voice, deep like a bass

drum, drowns out the percussion. He's moved his hand from my thigh, brought it up and settled it on the table. His hands are smooth and strong with sharply defined veins weaving through the backs like well-established tree roots. The cuffs of his long-sleeved work shirt are smartly buttoned, but his bulging biceps and triceps draw the eye.

'Just some stupid questions Barton sent us all. Before you joined quiz night.' Joel lounges back again, his casual body language trivialising the subject matter.

'Yes. He asked me, when I came along that first week, to see if you'd all come up with the answers. I was curious.' Alex's full lips attach to the glass as he sinks his drink. 'Shall I get another round in? Same again?'

The room suddenly feels very hot. I peel off my lightweight sweater, tying it loosely round my neck. Alex motions for a waitress and while his attention has turned, Declan subtly steers the agitation away from Barton's conundrums and recounts the full Fuzzy saga.

'You didn't tell me?' Alex's hand is back, rubbing teasingly up and down my legs.

'Sorry?'

'About Declan being vet of the year. A regular James Herriot.' Alex smiles from me to Declan.

'It was lucky I was in the area.' Declan's smile is every bit as bright.

Six months of isolation, and all of a sudden, I'm stuck between two warring guys.

## 47

Quiz nights are now officially cancelled until further notice. It'll take more than a second spike to bring the six of us together again. We were all quick to pull our jackets back on and say our goodbyes. Joel and Declan overdid the elbow touching, everyone relieved that the phoney air-kissing has been consigned to history. The group scattered like a plague of ants sprayed by poisonous powder.

Alex walked me back to Kings Cross, managing to lose the others before the platforms, by pulling me into a pub en route for a nightcap. A goodnight kiss wasn't as potent as the one in the hotel car park. In a previous existence, I would have linked Alex's lack of passion with my own insecurities, but tonight my mind is all over the place. Relationship issues are the least of my worries.

Once I'm on the train rumbling out of the station terminal back to Hitchin, I close my eyes against the heavy motion. My thoughts are skewed. Our group have all agreed not to mention the questions, but this means we are all complicit in covering up evidence. While the others don't know the full extent of the shit

Barton unearthed, I do. Am I more culpable than the others if I don't speak out?

As the carriage rattles on, lights flicker on and off and the silent masked travellers, like aliens from a distant planet, make spartan conversation. I start to question what really might be going on. Barton is dead. As well as some random member of the public whom he most likely screwed in the media, our Friday night group members all had good reasons for wanting him out of the way.

While I should bury my doubts and leave the investigation to the police, it's not that easy. I'm like Miss Marple who is friends with several suspects in a very sordid murder case. Yet these friends are too keen to shovel some loaded clues under the carpet. It crosses my mind, as I stare out at the deserted platform of Finsbury Park, that perhaps two or more members of our group might have worked together to dispose of Barton.

Names, possibilities, motives, opportunity... what am I missing? My thoughts weave in and out the crime tapestry. *Perhaps it was him? Perhaps her? Or maybe?* My eyes are heavy, eager to draw the lids closed for the night.

*Hitchin. Mind the doors please.*

'Shit.' I grab my bag, jolted upright from a nightmarish slumber as the announcement breaks the silence. I scramble for the doors and manage to escape a second before they clamp shut.

## 48

Rihanna's face is blotchy, like a piece of blotting paper that has soaked up rogue ink spills. Facetiming isn't helping to disguise her mood, which is as raggedy as her appearance. My mind is half on the random call, answered a bit too rashly, and the other half on my column notes scribbled on a pad in front of me. I tap my pen against my teeth.

'Rihanna.' My surprised tone mingles with exasperation at the interruption. But something in her gloomy expression makes me put the pen down. 'All okay?'

'Not really. Do you mind if I pop round? It's hard to talk properly on the phone.'

I ask myself, why me? I've only met Rihanna a handful of times in the flesh, so to speak; once at the wedding in Sorrento, Friday night just past and a couple of times during the year when we all met up for drinks and mild flirtation. Problem is, I don't really know her and she's not the sort of person I'd normally choose to hang around with.

Firstly, she's far too pretty and a few years younger than me; plus, she's also single. Rule number one for dating in your thirties, avoid socialising in twos, especially with a pretty airhead like Rihanna. Despite the flawless complexion, sculpted lips and all-over spray tan, she sports a natural vulnerability that attracts men, like bees to honey pots. Lockdown, with the challenges of isolation and frequent bouts of the blues, still hasn't increased my desire to befriend her. I'm at that stage in life where I need to hunt alone, rich harvests thin on the ground.

Rihanna's much too self-conscious to confide over a screen and Fuzzy's kittens have provided her an excuse to drop by. She only lives a couple of miles away in Tadmoor Village, an isolated hamlet which bolds and underlines the 'I' in isolation. The village High Street *is* the village. Rihanna's cottage is stuck between the post office and The Nag's Head pub. A two-room doctor's surgery is the only other building of note, a recently erected one-storey brick cube at the end of the street, which either welcomes you to the village or bids you farewell, depending on which way you're headed.

Half an hour later, Rihanna is standing at my front door, having given me just enough time to brush my hair and get out of my PJs. She looks even worse in person than on screen.

'Come in. Coffee's on.'

'Thanks, Kristi. I hope you don't mind but I've got no one else to talk to.'

Rihanna follows, like a simmering hand grenade, into the hall and gently pushes the door behind her.

'What have you been up to? During lockdown. It's been a long old haul,' I say, desperate for another strong coffee to prepare for what's about to come. Rihanna hovers as I froth the milk.

'I jog every day. Up hills and down the other side. Sometimes I cycle. Exercise is the only thing that keeps me sane.'

The box with Fuzzy and the kittens is moving from side to side, the furry little fiends battling to the death for their mother's milk. 'Oh my God. They're just so cute.' Rihanna coos and stares down at the fluffy balls.

'Milk? Sugar?'

'I'll stick to tea, if you don't mind. Do you have mint tea by any chance?'

I root around the cupboards for rogue herbal tea bags stuck to tatty cardboard boxes. I sniff the dried-out raspberry and echinacea sachets and Rihanna's sickly face lights up. Rapture is a bit of an extreme description, but it's the first time she's smiled since she arrived.

'Yes please. Perfect,' she says, while I stick the kettle on and get myself a second coffee from the cafetière I'd prepared for her arrival. I mean who doesn't need a heavy lift on a Sunday morning? The caffeine fix is like a crane hoisting aloft a smashed-up motor. My solo Saturday night binge session involved not only a full series of a Swedish-noir crime series, but a bottle and a half of white wine.

We carry our drinks through to the living room.

'What's up?' I ask as I settle on the sofa, feet curled under my jogging bottoms, with Rihanna sitting erect on a chair opposite. 'You look tired.' An understatement, but where else to start?

'Not really. Everything's a mess.' Rihanna might look flaky, but she's not a crier.

'Go on. I'm listening.' Christ.

'It's Clifton and me. I don't know what's going on. Ever since Barton sent through those stupid questions and Annabel found out that I'd been engaged to Clifton...' she pauses here. 'You did know, didn't you? That we'd been engaged, I mean.'

'Yes. I found out the answer to that question.' I grit my teeth, embarrassed that I bothered with the questions at all but also uneasy facing her now that I know the answer.

'Ever since Annabel found out, she's been making Clifton's life hell and he's worried that she'll find out we're still seeing each other.' Silence. Shit. Why is she telling me this and should I care? But like it or not, I'm being sucked deeper into the whole mess.

'You're still seeing him? Do you think that's wise? He's married, Rihanna. It'll not end well.' My pronouncement hits a nerve. Who am I kidding? Alex is still married. Getting a divorce might make the timescale different, but does that matter? Perhaps Clifton has spun Rihanna the same line.

'I'm pregnant,' she says. The bombshell. Another one for my field of landmines. 'Clifton was furious, murderous in fact, when Barton stirred the past up. When Annabel found out, after the quiz night, that Clifton and I had been engaged, Clifton set off to confront Barton. I've never seen anyone so mad. He called round with me first, ranting like a mad man. His face was puce.' Rihanna's upholstered lips quiver and I hand her a tissue.

'Here.' I'm not sure what else to say, but I don't have to. Rihanna fills in the spaces.

'You see, Kristi. I'm worried Clifton might have been the one who had Barton killed.'

# 49

Lockdown's quiz night has tied our random group of individuals together, like a poorly packaged Christmas present wrapped in flimsy paper. But apart from Alex and Declan, I want to walk away from the rest. The fallout between Annabel, Clifton and Rihanna has nothing to do with me and it's the last thing I need right now.

Joel's irritating invitations to meet up only started after Barton's shit-stirring and I'm not sure why he keeps texting. He knows I'm seeing Alex and that Declan is also sniffing around. It's as if Joel thinks I know something more about Barton than I'm letting on.

Rihanna cried for the next twenty minutes after her loaded outburst before she finally shuffled out the front door. After announcing her suspicion that Clifton might have had Barton murdered, she clammed up. Perhaps in deference to her current situation with Clifton, the father to their impending baby, she felt she had gone far enough. Maybe too far.

I certainly didn't want to hear any more, and my gentle suggestion that perhaps she go to the police with her suspicions, was ignored.

After Rihanna left, I forced myself back onto the computer and loading the memory stick, I reread Barton's last email with the attached documents.

My mind swirled with questions. Was Barton warning me that he felt under threat by one of our group? Why did he want me to know all the shit about everyone? What am I missing and again I wonder, why am I centre stage?

Rihanna's visit has left me queasily uneasy. She really seems to think Clifton capable of murder. If he was capable of murder, what about the others? Declan had reason and so had Joel to keep their secrets hidden. But it all seems too far-fetched.

I gently slide my hand down beside Fuzzy and her babies. I stroke Fuzzy's head, but she lets out a faint hiss. I manage to stroke the four miniscule heads, a personal baptising ceremony, before Fuzzy agitates and bares her claws. Instead, I lean over the tiny bundles and inhale the sweet scent of innocence. Declan has already bagged the smallest, the runt of the litter. *Periwinkle* he's named it, not sure yet if it's a boy or a girl, but the four white ankle socks on the little jet-black mass had him swooning.

Alex, on the other hand, laughed when I suggested he might adopt one, as he doesn't do animals. Apart from in his dreams when an Irish wolfhound keeps him company on jogs around the park. He said he's not into hairs, mess and burdensome commitment and he hasn't got the time. The bit about 'not into commitment' struck an off-key chord.

By eight in the evening, I'm exhausted from housework and mundane weekend chores, but more so from all the anxiety. I head upstairs early, hoping a good night's sleep will clear my head for work tomorrow. It's still early but I'm exhausted. I slink down into a hot bath, read a few chapters of a random chick-lit novel but my eyes keep closing.

When I finally clamber into bed and turn the lights out, Barton's voice spins round in my head. 'Check out Alex's villa in Marbella. You'll not believe it.' What villa? Why has Alex not mentioned it? And when will his wife be back?

Nothing stacks up. I'm definitely missing something but no idea what.

## 50

The car zigzags through the country lanes on the back roads to St Albans, sheering left and right as it skids off debris which has detached from overhanging branches. A large van suddenly skews around the corner and heads towards me like a bull at a red flag. I bash my fist on the horn, warning the driver who narrowly misses my wing mirror.

My nerves are tight, jangling like chimes in the wind and my mind won't slow down. It's as if I'm in a vehicle careering at hazardous speed down the outside lane of a motorway, the braking cable adrift.

Since Rihanna's visit on Sunday, I haven't been able to concentrate on anything. Yesterday I ploughed through some mind-numbing editorials for work, but today I've had to get out of the house, or I'll go crazy sitting in front of the computer screen.

There's a fine line between curiosity and paranoia. I tell myself I'm curious but the somersaults in my gut say otherwise.

I've got that awful instinctual feeling that things aren't going in the right direction with Alex and that we've reached a brick wall. The word 'commitment' hasn't been mentioned, but then perhaps I'm being naïve to expect any promises from a man whose wife hasn't really moved out. 'Staying with her mother' isn't the same as 'filing for a divorce'. Also, my mantra is: 'If you don't understand something, don't trust it.' Alex is hiding something, and I'm determined to find out what.

I check the Google map on the dashboard and enlarge the display. Alex lives on the south side of St Albans, about a mile from the M25 junction. 'It's perfect commuter belt,' he bragged. 'Twenty minutes to Kings Cross and less than five minutes to the motorway.' The location of his house, with its speedy links to elsewhere, ticked his boxes. The pull of nature, rambling trails and peaceful countryside, a few miles further north, hadn't appealed. 'I can pop to country pubs at the weekend. Weekdays, it's all about making money and keeping up.' Chalk and cheese from Rihanna.

I manoeuvre across the main thoroughfare into the slip road which leads to a white-painted housing estate, 1970s with wooden facias, wooden fences and wooden residents. The road curves round and properties become grander, fancy worded plaques replacing rusting numbers on individual properties.

I slow to a crawl, nervy but alert in case Alex's plans have changed. My suggestion last night when he called, to meet for lunch, has been pencilled in for Friday; he couldn't do today as he's due up in London with clients.

'I'm sorry. I'd have loved to meet tomorrow but hope Friday works. I'm missing you.'

His husky voice schmoozes down the phone, like foreplay,

teasing with promise. Alex's patience and apparent acceptance to keep things platonic for a while longer are earning him brownie points, helping to bolster my slim belief that we might have a chance at something serious.

Alex lives at number fifty-four. I count along, desperately looking out for random numbers in place of name signs to let me know if I'm getting close. Trees, ancient, gnarled specimens whose trunks are encased by huge uneven paving slabs, line the street. The detached houses possess a medley of design; varying shapes, sizes and random extensions stamp individuality on the properties. A bungalow nestles alongside a gated mansion, and suddenly three identical timber-framed Swedish-style homes appear to break up the raggedy pattern.

A little further on I pull up outside a house with a gold-plated number 54 attached to a gatepost. The house reminds me of a child's drawing. A regular square facade, four rectangular windows and a large white front door bang centre. The area to the front of the house is paved in criss-cross blockwork, and two large terracotta pots planted with enormous fir trees sit either side of the porch. Elisa probably strings fairy lights round them at Christmas time. I shiver.

There are no cars at the front, but the drive sweeps round the right-hand side of the house where the rear bumper of a blue car juts out. My eyes scan the house for clues, but of what I'm not sure.

The window frames look as if they've been recently painted, the blinding white gloss shining in the sunlight. I squint towards the upstairs window which is ajar. Actually, more than ajar; it's pushed out a significant distance. My heart pumps, as I desperately try to restart the car, turning the key with sweaty fingers. The car hiccups as I let the clutch out too quickly before I manage to reverse back a few yards away from the entrance.

If Alex is in London, then who is in the house? Perhaps it's a cleaner but rather than risk being spotted, I stay where I am, slink low in the driver's seat and wait, deciding to give it no more than half an hour.

Twenty-five minutes later the blue car drives out. I duck down behind the dashboard, banging my leg against the steering column when I recognise the driver. The large blue Range Rover glides left away from the property, in the opposite direction from where I'm parked. I straighten up once the car has turned left again, back towards the London Road and out of sight.

Why the hell has Annabel been at Alex's house? How does she know him? She's never mentioned ever having met him until the quiz night and seemed as surprised as everyone else that a stranger had taken Barton's place. In recent conversations, when she admonished me for dating married men, she's never once said she knew Alex other than as a random interloper to the Friday hangouts.

My mobile breaks the silence and makes me jump. Shit. It's Alex. I stare at the screen for a couple of seconds before I turn my phone off and speed away.

# 51

Nine o'clock sharp and Grayson Zooms into view.

'Kristi. How the hell are you?'

'Fine thank you, boss.'

As he never calls about anything other than work, I jump in and avoid the need for pleasantries. 'Don't worry. I'm working hard on my column,' I say.

Grayson isn't so daunting on screen, the toxicity of his halitosis a welcome subtraction from the new-normal interaction. His blue slim-fit shirt has a couple of buttons missing near the collar allowing his hairy chest and throat to create a thick invasive forest effect. His balding pate hasn't been so lucky though in foliage maintenance. A Bobby Charlton style comb-over is less than subtle but a thickset throat hints that he's been making regular use of his home gym.

Natalie, secretary-cum-girlfriend, moved in with her boss early March but is planning to move out again, according to office gossip. Cooking, cleaning and ironing weren't part of the original deal, but Grayson has no idea. He's like a pig in the proverbial.

'Wanted to run a few things past you.' Grayson leans back,

settling his legs along a chair pulled up alongside. I catch a glimpse of shiny tracksuit pants, barely able to contain the smirk when I realise he's forgotten that his bottom layer doesn't match the Savile Row shirt.

'No problem. Fire away.'

The fact that I'm only fifty per cent through the first draft for week one of my new column would once have had me in fear for my job, but everything about my career at the *London Echo* has changed in the last couple of weeks.

Concentration, for one, has been squashed like a weakly buzzing fly on death row. A few months ago, I was flying high, Grayson's great prodigal hope for headlines, kicking hard at Barton's heels for recognition and promotion. As I stare at the face on screen, Grayson doesn't seem so chipper either. His macho bark, famous for its hollow timbre has mellowed to an irritating yap. I'm not sure which is worse.

Barton's death has led me to what I can only describe as PTSD (post-traumatic stress disorder). Lack of sleep compounded by recurrent nightmares of prison cells, solitary confinement and a bread and water diet has left me in a state of conscious anxiety. I feel like a criminal on the run, my only crime being in the wrong place at the wrong time. It's not Barton's death as such that's causing me the most trauma, rather the unlawful role into which I've been cast. The email answers to Barton's loaded questions, which I've kept secret, mark me out.

'You all right, Kristi? You look a bit peaky.' Grayson's thin lips stretch back like strained fabric to reveal a full line-up of perfectly bleached white teeth. The yellowing has gone. Natalie, once a dental nurse, has no doubt helped him achieve the perfect smile.

'I'm fine. Just a bit of a late night.' I lift my coffee mug and cover my response with the receptacle.

'Well, a couple of things,' he continues. 'There's this latest idea going around that with more people working from home, there's also the possibility of more people working slightly further afield.' Grayson clears his throat, a musty foghorn warning.

He pulls out a cigarette from a packet in front of him and clicks a silver lighter. 'It's heaven not having to scuttle down into the street for a fag.' He takes a deep draw on the death stick, closes his eyes and emits a heavy vaporous mist which temporarily clouds the screen. 'You see, Kristi, my plan is to move out to Spain, run the newspaper from there. It can all be done online. My neighbour has recently moved to Barbados where they're offering cheap visas to encourage people to emigrate and work from the paradise of a sandy beach. What do you think?'

I think it's a completely mad idea. 'Yeh, sounds like a plan.'

'Anyway, I can pop back and forth to keep an eye on you all.' His laugh sounds like he's being suffocated by a chloroformed handkerchief. 'And, Kristi, I'd like you to be in charge on the ground, so to speak. You'd report directly to me and keep me in the loop. What do you say?'

Barton had been itching for months for promotion. His death has given me an opportunity that I'd probably have had to wait years for. I'm not a gusher by nature, but it's hard to keep a lid on my enthusiasm.

'I don't know what to say.'

'*Yes*, will do.'

'Definitely. I'd be delighted. Any idea of when you'll be moving?'

'As soon as possible, although the police don't want any of us going anywhere until they're a bit further down the line in finding Barton's killer.' Another choking laugh turns Grayson's face red. 'Actually, now you've got Barton's earmarked promotion, you could be added to the list of suspects. The pay rise is that good!'

Grayson reels his legs back in and stubs out the cigarette butt on a coaster. Burn marks pit the zigzag pattern. 'One more thing, before I let you go and get on with your column.'

I feel as if I'm in a surgery when the doctor tells me my blood pressure is good, my vitals healthy, no problem with my heart, liver or kidney, but... The pause hangs for a second too long.

'The police popped round yesterday asking about a list of questions Barton had drawn up. I think they had something to do with you guys who do a Friday night quiz. Do you know anything about this?'

# 52

The silence and loneliness of lockdown has often felt like being cast adrift on a desert island. Think Robinson Crusoe. Recently the grip of a mobile phone has held little comfort. Voices of friends, work colleagues and clients have the distant tone of an African drumroll. Emergency assistance is carefully considered for elderly infirm neighbours, but the young successful businesspeople are assumed to be of sound mind and health, well able to look after themselves. *'You'll survive. It'll not last for ever.'* *'Have an extra glass of wine.'* *'Call me anytime.'* Scraps of encouragement feel as tuneless as the ardent melodies performed by the fiddlers on the *Titanic* as it went down.

Being thirty and single has definite advantages, but when you're left for dead on a lone stretch of beach, it's definitely not quite so attractive. Isolation has etched its mark and I realise I no longer want to be alone.

Rihanna has convinced me of the mental health benefits of jogging. She's desperate for a friend and is reeling me in, like an angler with a long rod and sharp hook, by sending through all manner of articles related to health matters. As well as teaching

Pilates, Rihanna gives nutritional and lifestyle advice to all and sundry. She knows I'm struggling, loneliness at the core, but little does she know the extent of my worries.

∼

The traffic is back, snarling early up Hitchin Hill, as I pound the pavements towards the town centre. Chirpy birdsong has been replaced once again by grating horns and grim-set faces. Perhaps Grayson is right to move away, take the chance for an easier lifestyle while the world isn't so uptight on judging.

I slow down and walk the last hundred yards to the coffee shop in the market square. I peer through the steamed-up windows before I go in. It's quiet inside but the robust aroma of freshly ground coffee provides a familiar comforting welcome.

'Good morning. It's been a while. Usual?' Robbie, the young chirpy proprietor kitted out in black overalls and a black and white chequered cap, twiddles with the knobs on the coffee machine.

'Yes please.'

My once-regular weekend seat in the corner is lit by an industrial hanging light, its black metal shade floating above the reclaimed wooden tabletop. I slip my pen and notebook out from my running pouch and nestle into the cushioned bench. I've got half an hour to kill before she gets here.

I scribble wild notes, question marking additions as I go. I underline in thick black pen knotted thoughts that I have to get down on paper.

- Annabel. Why was she at Alex's house? What's the connection?
- Clifton. Could he really be capable of murder?

- Declan. His background suggests he's already killed in the past.
- Rihanna. Am I missing something? Her future might be turned upside down after Barton leaked her past history with Clifton.
- Joel. A silent assassin with a seedy past to protect.
- Work colleagues or others with a vengeance. Need to dig through old reports and newspaper clippings.
- Me. Should I come clean to the police about what I know? It might put Declan and Joel in prison for past offences, as well as highlight a reason why Clifton could have had it in for Barton. Also, after the time that's passed, I might become a suspect. Withholding vital information could lead to me being charged with perverting the course of justice.
- Who would have access to a handgun? I've googled gun crime in the UK and handguns can be sourced by various means: shady contacts, theft of legally registered firearms or smuggled in from Europe or the States. The possibilities are endless, for someone desperate enough. Everything can be bought for the right price.

It's all too much. My head swirls with the various computations but something draws me back to the questions Barton threw at us. Why? What had he to gain? It all seems too coincidental that he got murdered once the answers came to light and I'm not big on coincidences.

Suddenly a loud voice above my bent head makes me jump.

'Quaint little place. A bitch to find though. How are you?' Annabel's eyes land on my scrawled notes as she unwinds a floaty silken scarf from her pale neck.

I jerk backwards. 'Shit, you scared me. I was lost in thought.'

I snap shut the notebook and zip it away again. 'What'll you have? The coffee's strong but works a treat.'

'A cappuccino would be nice. Maybe share a pastry?' Annabel slips into the hard wooden chair as a young waitress approaches. 'Jeez, it's so nice to get away from the house. Did you jog down?'

'Yep. Rihanna's influence.' I blush when I mention Rihanna, momentarily forgetting it's a name best avoided.

'I need to get back to the gym. Lose a few lockdown pounds.' Annabel lets go the mention of Rihanna, patting her stomach instead.

Perhaps it's my suspicious mind, but Annabel buzzes from subject to subject, like an agitated wasp. Eye contact is fleeting, her voice singsong.

'Clifton and I are going away for a few days. It's been a long old stretch at home. We've booked a week in Spain and I can't wait,' she says.

'Sounds lovely. I wish I was going somewhere hot.' Then something clicks, a rusty lock creaks open. 'Spain. Whereabouts?'

'South coast. Found a lovely villa, private pool, landscaped gardens.'

'Marbella, by any chance?'

'Marbella. How did you guess?'

'Millionaires' paradise. Sort of guessed it would be Clifton's choice.' Keep it light, a long noose, plenty to hang herself with.

Forty minutes later the silken scarf is rewound, feather-light air-kisses proffered from a distance before Annabel wafts out as seamlessly as she appeared.

I leave the café shortly after, and set off for home, back up the steep hill. The acceleration of thoughts helps fuel my aching body and halfway up the hill, my jaw finally unclenches, and blood pumps more freely as I race for home.

A sudden stitch threads its way into my side, the needle point piercing. Outside my front door, I bend over, my hair flopping like a curtain across my eyes. As I straighten up again, I notice a large package on the porch.

My eyes swivel round the street which is deserted apart from a couple of kids dicing with death on skateboards, before I open the front door. I lift the parcel inside, swaying it to see if the contents slide about. I hunt around for the sharp paring knife in the kitchen drawer and slit open the sealed edge.

An envelope with Kristi scrawled in childish handwriting, is stuck to the bulky item which I tear open.

*This isn't really for you. Rather a present for Fuzzy and the brood.*
*Need to take care of my new baby. Declan x*

A series of team meetings followed by mind-numbing editorial work, and the afternoon soon passes.

When I finally log off for the day, I become aware of Fuzzy purring loudly, the first time I've heard such a rhythmical trumpet in days. The four globes of fluff, arranged in a line like furry tennis balls in a can, are asleep. The new luxurious cat bed with its soft raised sides and padded mattress is a great success.

As I pour a long cold glass of wine, noticing it's only five o'clock, my delight at Declan's present has only added to my list of quandaries. He's a good kind guy, slowly knocking at my heart with all manner of thoughtful gestures.

How the hell can I tell the police about the questions without landing Declan in a cell for kneecapping a family and killing the father more than two decades ago?

As I glug from my glass, I wonder at Declan's sudden keenness to buy into my life. He hints it's not sudden, he's always fancied me and after I saved him from walking into the Irish Sea to certain death, he felt it was a sign that he had to follow through.

But why am I so suspicious?

# WEEK 6

## 53

Alex's hand links through mine, his fingers coiled like baby snakes, as we stroll through Covent Garden.

'What's up?' he asks. 'You're not your usual bubbly self. Is it work?'

'Nothing. I'm fine. In fact,' I pause, pull my feet together, 'Grayson has offered me a promotion.'

Alex swivels round, a theatrical pirouette, and brings his face up close to mine.

'That's brilliant news! Why didn't you tell me?'

'Not much to tell really. I think Barton was originally in line for the promotion.'

Without so much as a hesitant moment of reverential silence, Alex picks me up and swings me round. His enthusiasm is bizarrely over the top.

'Let's celebrate. I've only got an hour now for lunch but perhaps a proper celebration tomorrow night?'

*If he asks you out on a Saturday night, then he means business. Otherwise, forget it.* Annabel's been negative about Alex since I told her we were dating. She's supposing, because he's married, that he's lying. Lying about getting a divorce. Lying that his wife doesn't understand him. Lying that she's staying at her mother's. It makes me assume Clifton is a habitual liar.

But now I know that Annabel is on familiar terms with Alex, or perhaps with his wife, Elisa, I suspect her warnings have been loaded with more than friendly misgivings.

~

'What about here?' Alex stops outside an Italian trattoria and scans the menu by the door.

'Yes. Looks nice.'

My plan, since spotting Annabel at Alex's house on Tuesday, is to be patient, steer the conversation carefully like a barge through narrow locks.

The mix of rosemary and garlic tickles our nostrils as we enter, and the sight of dim candlelit tables threatens to weaken my resolve of sticking to planned conversational topics. Yet I know I mustn't let my guard down until I've got some answers.

Customers are separated by spaces that were once crammed, cheek by jowl, with tables. A waiter stretches an arm towards a place in the corner.

'That okay?' Alex seems overly attentive, as if he's trying too hard.

'Good for me.'

We peel off our jackets, sit down facing each other and simultaneously glance down at the daily specials on a chalkboard placed alongside.

'It's a long time since I've eaten out.' Alex keeps his eyes peeled on the choices.

'Me too. I've missed it though.'

Once Alex has ordered the wine and food, he smiles at me. But I don't waiver. 'I could really do with a holiday. Grayson, as I told you, is thinking of moving to Spain and working remotely. I'd love a break away, wouldn't you?'

Alex widens his knife and fork and positions his dessert spoon neatly across the top. 'Yes, you bet. But with the current state of my marriage, I can't see myself going anywhere.' Omission of the word divorce rings in my ears.

'How often have you been to Spain? I really need to get away somewhere really hot.'

Through the opened entrance, whose doors face out onto the street, a continual sheet of rain plays accompaniment to my question.

'A few times. You?'

'Never. Not sure where I'd go. Any suggestions?' My fingers thrum gently on the table, as if I'm warming up for scale practice.

'As I said before, somewhere in the south. Murcia perhaps. You can always guarantee the weather and, as I said before, it's great for golf.'

'I'm still thinking Marbella. If I don't bag a *toy boy*, perhaps I could pull a tycoon.' I force a light-hearted laugh.

Alex's lips close, firm like set jelly. A faint tic settles on his left cheek above the jawbone.

'Yes, I went there once but it's not really my sort of place. It's too in-your-face. The sport's good but I've not much in common with the wheeler-dealer playboys.'

As if on cue, our food arrives. The plates are laden with the special of the day. Pasta Arrabbiata.

'Did you know, Arrabbiata means "angry pasta"?' Alex gently removes a whole chilli perched on top of his loaded plate.

'Looks good,' I say, tentatively picking up my fork.

## 54

Alex pours the full-bodied Chianti into our glasses, which we raise and chink together. Yet a flatness has crept into the atmosphere, which is like bread that hasn't risen, the yeast out of date. The early celebratory mood has drained to the bottom of our glasses, like the sediment from the wine.

I reset the stop clock, eager to probe a bit more before we finish the meal. I steer the conversation back to holidays in Spain, but it's pretty obvious that Alex is as slick as Annabel in changing subject, batting back uncomfortable questions like competing shots in a tennis rally.

'I've toyed with buying an apartment abroad. When my salary goes up, I might take the plunge. It would be an escape route, somewhere to go. Like Grayson, I could do with a few days away from home every so often. You've got to admit, it's tempting.'

Alex wipes his mouth with a wad of paper serviettes and deposits them on top of his empty plate which he pushes aside. 'Do you fancy dessert, or shall we go straight for coffees?'

'Just an espresso, thanks.'

'Yes, I'd best steer clear of dessert too, watch the weight.'

Alex puts his fingers down the waistband of his trousers and jiggles them around. Alex is far too body conscious to overindulge, and his suggestions of lockdown weight gain make me think he's fishing for compliments rather than hoping to be believed.

'Listen to the rain. It's really chucking it down.' Alex looks over my shoulder as he drains his espresso. 'Drink up and I'll go and settle the bill.'

As he walks over to the bar, I feel mentally deflated. It'll take more than a coffee to lift my mood. You see omission of facts isn't lying, but the very act offers up its own clues. By not owning up to his villa in Marbella, Alex has told me plenty.

The train is deserted on the way back to Hitchin. The butterflies have flown from my stomach and the familiar nausea of duplicity has settled in their place. Although Alex is playing some weird sort of game, I'm rapidly losing interest. Whatever he's hiding, I'm no longer certain I want to find out.

I'm lonely, but not so lonely, that trust and self-respect can be discarded in return for a few free meals and the dangled carrot of some future passion. At the moment, what else is he offering me?

A text beeps through as I walk back from the station.

Really enjoyed lunch. Looking forward to tomorrow. Pick you up 7.30? XX

I reply ten minutes later with an emoji *thumbs up* but leave out the kisses.

## 55

As we drive up towards the gates to Annabel and Clifton's house, Alex slows down.

'Is this it? Wow. Not bad,' he says, clapping his palms on the steering wheel.

'Yep. Don't you love the lions?'

A line of bright LED lights, perched atop the towering perimeter brick wall, shine bright and cold and make me think Colditz, *high-security prison*. I recount Annabel's admission that Clifton has carefully secreted cameras all around the property to help protect his castle.

'They're really well-hidden, impossible to spot,' I say.

Annabel, on my last visit, had pointed out the six screens in the hall which display guests' arrival and departure from various angles. Rogue intruders and opportunist burglars don't stand a chance. I tell Alex that, according to Annabel, Clifton watches the recordings like a Netflix crime series.

∽

I dithered about whether to see Alex this evening after the let-down of yesterday, but Annabel helped things along. She phoned around ten o'clock this morning and took me by surprise.

'Why don't you bring Alex round for dinner? See how you get along as part of a proper couple.' Annabel had trilled down the phone. I resisted the temptation to ask for her definition of 'proper'. If her relationship with a two-timing rat of a husband is proper, I'll stick to improper.

'Yes. Okay then. I'll ask him.'

When Alex called to firm up our date, I was attuned for hesitation in his reply when I told him about the dinner invitation. But there wasn't any. He was more than happy to meet my friends.

'I'd like that. Where do they live?'

'Harpenden. West Common.'

'Wow. Expensive area,' he said.

My hat, like the sorting house hat in Harry Potter, now has a purpose. Much as I'd like to forget Barton's murder, it's not possible. I've been thrown into the melting pot of some very strange events and seem to have been handed the role of unwilling sleuth.

If Annabel has been to Alex's house in St Albans, they must have a connection. It's most likely that they knew each other way before the Friday Zoom meet. Perhaps Alex knows Clifton? What I need to find out is why the secrecy? How do they know each other and why all the pretence?

As we stand, side by side, on the expansive porch nestled between four towering greystone columns, Alex rubs his hands together while I clutch the wine.

'Hi, guys. Come in. Great to see you.' Clifton throws wide the doors and ushers us through. The men elbow bump and Annabel flaps her hand at us from a few feet away.

'Come through.' Annabel follows behind her husband, sandwiched between him and us.

When we pass the six security monitors on the way through the marbled foyer, Alex catches my eye and grins.

The dining room is expansive, an open fire at the far end ablaze with logs spitting fiercely behind a fine mesh screen. Two brightly painted ceramic bulldogs are placed one either side of the hearth, indoor sentries reminiscent of the concrete lions. A long impressively laid mahogany table is laden with glassware, chunky silver candleholders and brightly coloured serviettes. On first glance, a full canteen of cutlery seems to have been used to furnish the place settings.

Clifton leads us past the table towards a pair of guests huddled round the fire, champagne flutes tight in their hands.

'Let me introduce you all. This is Bruce Campbell and his wife, Maggie. Bruce works at the bank with me.' Clifton nods towards the couple and back towards Alex and me. As we stand by the hissing furnace, introducing ourselves, Annabel flounces through with a platter of hors d'oeuvres.

'Hi. What fun. A party at last,' she quips and passes round the treats.

## 56

'What do you do for a living, Alex?' Bruce's Scottish brogue slices through the cut-glass-crystal table conversation which has been randomly dipping in and out of vacuous topics. Weather. Lockdown. Vaccinations. Return of spectators to sporting events.

Bruce's voice is deep throat, harsh and heavy like Highland weather. He clutches a bottle of red wine, having discarded the dainty flute and tops himself up every couple of minutes. Meanwhile Clifton skirts the table with a bottle of red in one hand and a bottle of white in the other for the rest of us.

'I'm in computing,' Alex says, his wine lips a vermillion colour, like those painted on a party clown. 'I maintain company systems. Fix operating problems, that sort of thing. But I won't bore you with the details.'

'How do you know this prick?' Bruce's laugh thunders across the table, the plates and cutlery shaking as he bangs down his fists.

'Clifton?' Alex takes his time, but his eyes meet Annabel's, rather than her husband's.

'Who else?'

'I don't really know him. Kristi introduced me to Annabel and Clifton. I met them on a Zoom quiz of all places.' Alex lifts his glass as if preparing a wedding toast.

'You mean you never met these *tossers* until tonight? I'd never have guessed.'

Bruce staggers out of his chair, swaying, and heads for the door.

'Apologies for Bruce,' says Maggie, placing a pale white hand on top of Alex's. 'He's fond of his drink.'

Annabel gets up and fusses around the table, stacking empty plates. 'Coffees, everyone?'

'Here, let me.' Alex helps with the plate piling and carefully arranges dirty cutlery on top. A reminder that he's married, house tamed.

'Thanks.'

Alex follows Annabel to the kitchen, leaving me with Maggie. Clifton has moved away from the table and is talking in important tones into his mobile phone from the farthest corner of the room.

'Excuse me. I'm just popping to the bathroom,' I say to Maggie. 'Won't be long.'

Maggie tops up her glass as I push my chair back and get up.

The kitchen is at the end of a long corridor, with a little recess to the left of the door for coats. Two pairs of heavy-duty walking boots are placed underneath an array of rainwear. I hover and hear muffled voices, but Alex's soon increases in volume as I push further in against the coats.

'Please don't say anything about the villa. Now isn't the time.'

The sound of a knife against plate scrapes in the background.

'Maybe you should tell her. There's no crime in owning a villa, for goodness' sake. It's not as if you're gun running.'

'You know that's not the point. She'll wonder how the hell I can afford a £3 million property.'

'Tell her it was an inheritance. Does it really matter? I doubt she'll be that bothered.'

~

'He's gorgeous. A keeper, that one,' Annabel whispers as she hugs me close, enveloping me against the Arctic blast that sweeps in when Clifton opens the front door for his departing guests.

The government's concerns that too much alcohol can cause amnesia with regard to social distancing have been proved right. Annabel flouts the rules with gay abandon. I break free from her clutches to do up the buttons on my coat, pulling it tight.

'Do you think so?'

'Definitely. Be patient. Call me and let me know how it's going,' she says.

'Thanks, Annabel, Clifton. Great evening,' Alex says as we walk away.

'A pleasure. Good to meet you.' Clifton waves goodbye, legs solidly splayed on the porch.

As Alex and I drive slowly towards the main gates, a small red light flashes on and off to the left of the lion. Alex laughs. 'Big brother is watching you.'

With that he indicates left, rolls down his window and waves his arm back towards our hosts.

I keep my eyes looking straight ahead.

## 57

This morning I'm at the computer by 8am.

When the doorbell suddenly rings, I don't move. But when the noise carries on, I get up to find out what's so urgent. As I've no Amazon parcels due, it's probably a rogue salesman.

I unlock the door, my no-nonsense face prepared, and open up. There's no one in sight but my eyes can't miss the delivery on the doorstep.

A fruit basket piled high with mangoes, bananas, pineapple, kiwis and oranges screams with vibrant colour. I step round it, mosey down the front path and look left and right.

'Boo.'

'Shit. Don't do that!' I scream as Declan appears behind me, popping out from behind the wall.

'Do you like the fruit? I'm allowed to help myself at the end of the day, so voila! This was all left over from the weekend.'

His arm sweeps across the basket. Of course, I can't contain the smile. That's what Declan does, injects Irish enthusiasm with a skilfully manufactured boyish charm.

'Love it. Come in and I'll make you a coffee.'

'Love the footwear.'

My pink panther slippers pad over the gravel back to the front door as Declan crunches along behind. As I bend down to pick up the fruit basket, he nudges me away.

'Here, let me.'

He carries the fruit through and sets it down in the kitchen. While I make the coffees, Declan disappears to the cloakroom and reappears a few minutes later minus his white overalls. A green T-shirt, emblazoned with a golden harp and a black foaming glass of Guinness, fits snugly across his broad chest.

'Were you working?' he asks once we're settled in the lounge.

'Yes. It's non-stop. I've accepted a promotion by the way. It had been earmarked for Barton but...'

'That's great news. Not about Barton, obviously.' Declan blushes, a deep rouge darkening his pallid complexion.

'What about you? Any more news on proper jobs?' I ask him.

'You know what? I like this delivery stuff and am seriously thinking of setting up on my own. There's good money in it, especially now people are ordering much more online.'

Soon an hour has passed, and I look at my watch.

'Listen, I'll let you get on. But I need to talk to you about something first,' Declan says as he sits up straighter. He exhales, puffing his lips and chest out simultaneously and sets the empty mug on the coffee table. 'Do you have time?'

'Go on, but it sounds serious. I'll give you another hour, tops.'

I sit quietly, like a celibate priest in the confessional booth, and begin the pretence that I don't know what's coming.

'I was only eighteen. You've no idea what it was like growing up in Belfast. There's always been "them" and "us". My family have been members of some republican group or another for as long as I can remember. This guy, Sean Ferran, recruited me when I'd no idea how to say "no", walk away. Where the hell would I have gone anyway? Also, Irish catholic brainwashing turned us all into *yes men* robots for the cause.'

'You're answering Barton's question, aren't you?'

'I want you to know the truth. You see the police are sniffing around and I think one of our Friday group has told them about the questions. I've no intention of giving myself up, but it's important that you understand.'

Declan's eyes are dark, intense but with the doleful trustfulness of a child. He needs to talk. Like Rihanna, he doesn't seem to have anyone else or perhaps he wants my backing to keep the whole sorry saga a secret.

'It was so long ago. The New Republican Army roamed the Falls Road with truncheons, hand grenades and automatic rifles, recruiting willing and not-so-willing candidates to their number. There wasn't a choice.' Declan's words roll off his tongue, fast and furious like the gunfire he's describing. 'I didn't know how to get out. Sean told all new recruits that if we didn't follow orders, then we'd better keep an eye on our families. The prospect of our loved ones being kneecapped, or worse, meant we towed the line.'

Fuzzy suddenly screeches from the basket, before a low continuous moan lets me know the babies have latched on.

'Sorry. Feeding time again,' I say, but the interruption doesn't stop Declan's flow.

'When I joined up, or more precisely, was dragged along to sign on the dotted line, Sean had my first job ready. It's like an induction ceremony. If you didn't follow through, you'd end up fearing for your family members. Ma pretended none of it was happening but underneath stood proud that her family was famous in the area, her son carrying the flag for a united Ireland.'

Declan needs to complete the marathon before he can relax. Sweat is working a line, slick across his brow and a pulse in his neck bulges and pulsates.

'Sean hid in the wings, menacing and invisible when I pulled the trigger. Six times. I got two of the sons and the father.'

I don't say anything and wait as Declan gets up, wanders over to the cat world and bends down. His finger, shaking and unsteady, dips in. Fuzzy spits and Declan laughs.

'Feisty old mare, that one.'

'Go on. Finish the story.' I need to hear if it ties up with what Barton told me.

'The father died later in hospital. Complications. Sean held a party, a celebration, and I was given a badge of honour to show the republican world I'd made the grade.'

Declan folds himself down beside the furry family, his head hung low. Silent tears flow down his cheeks. I get up and put my arm round his shaking body as we collapse onto the floor together.

'Crazy, even after all this time I still can't forget. Barton has made it worse, bringing it back up with his fecking stupid questions.'

Fuzzy's purr breaks through like the rumble of comforting thunder once the eye of the feeding storm has passed.

'I met up with Sean when I was over recently in Bangor staying with Ma. He told me my secret was safe, but I could never leave the brotherhood. If I did, he couldn't vouch for my safety. They're bastards, all of them. It's about control, giving their small petty provincial lives importance.'

'Shhh. Listen, Barton's dead. No one's going to care about what you got up to twenty-four years ago. Try to let it go.'

Declan leans across and kisses me gently on the cheek. 'Thanks, Kristi. Sorry, but I wanted you to know.'

An hour later, white overalls back on, and Declan is standing by the front door.

'By the way. I know it's none of my business, but for what it's worth, Alex *whatshisname* is a right prick. Don't waste your time on him. He's married anyway.'

'I know what I'm doing. Don't worry about me,' I say.

'He used to come to the bank, meet up with Clifton for lunch. I always felt there was something shady about him. Call it Irish intuition, always to be trusted.'

As Declan walks towards his van, a renewed swagger in his step, he puts on his starched hat. 'I'll call you,' he yells, before climbing up into the driver's seat and closing the door. He rolls down the window. 'Thanks, honey. See you soon.'

A final wink, and the van rounds the bend and disappears from view.

## 58

P laying hard to get isn't part of any plan but as I've started to cool off, Alex is becoming more persistent. His messages and calls are increasingly intense and the more I delay in responding, the more determined he becomes. If I was out to snare him, I'd be thrilled by my successful game-playing. Headway with a capital H. But I'm not after headway; only answers.

Annabel is the link. While Alex chases me, I'm chasing Annabel. There's a triangle thing going on. After Declan left, I tried her mobile half a dozen times. She'll know it's urgent, as she's the one who usually does the calling. When I do occasionally call, she gets back within five minutes but although she's been on WhatsApp on and off all morning, my messages haven't been opened.

Anger and irritation won't let me rest and trying to work is futile. Instead, I snatch up my car keys and mobile phone and set off back towards Harpenden.

~

I'm soon pulling into West Common but decide to park a couple of houses away from Annabel and Clifton's. If Annabel is ignoring my messages, she might hesitate to let me in, especially if she's forewarned by spotting my car.

I get out, zap the car closed and walk the few yards to their property. I slide behind the perimeter wall and reach out with my left arm to press the bell on the entry pad, far enough along to be hidden from view of camera number four.

'Hello?' Annabel's voice is crisp, curious.

'Annabel. It's me. Kristi. Can I come in?'

'Who's that?' Clifton's voice bellows through from a distance, the orchestra's base drum.

'Of course. It's Kristi.'

As the gate peels back, I hear Clifton's voice again.

'Make some excuse, for fuck's sake.'

Too late. I hurry through and skitter across the gravel to the front door. Annabel, usually snappy, eager for company, takes a moment to appear. She's got the wild lockdown look of unwashed hair, casual clothes and blotchy unmade-up skin. Jeez, she looks completely different from her Friday Zoom portrayal and her Saturday dinner-party hostess appearance. She pulls the door back slowly.

'Kristi. What a surprise? Come in.'

It's midday exactly as I pass by the security screens. An old-fashioned wind-up clock starts a heralding sequence of grating noises before the noon chimes break through, loud and clear.

'Is it that time already?' Annabel screeches, putting her hands over her ears.

Annabel is usually bubbling for company, fizzing at the edges when I arrive, sucking me into her magnetic world of neuroses with a couple of bottles of chilled Prosecco; the first cork already popped. Even when I came round to talk about Barton's demise, she seemed more chipper than today.

'Glass of wine? Excuse the mess. I was a bit late up this morning.'

'Maybe just one. Sorry for barging in but I need to talk.' I'm not sure alcohol is a good idea, but it'll help Annabel relax, loosen her tongue.

'Are you here about Alex?'

'Yes. Sort of.'

I unwind my woolly scarf and set it on a kitchen stool as Annabel gets the wine. She lifts out a half-drunk bottle from the fridge, tries to pull out the stopper and swears when the bottle almost slithers from her grasp.

'Shit.'

'Here. Let me.'

I take the bottle and smoothly release the cork.

We head through to the orangery, my gaze drawn to a newly installed three-tiered water fountain outside in the middle of the recently landscaped patio area. The cascading display makes me shiver. Two pigeons perch on top, playfully rubbing against each other.

We sit down, but the atmosphere is stiff, forced.

'Annabel,' I begin. 'About Alex.'

'What's up? Is he back with his wife?' Her right eyebrow arches.

'Nothing like that.' My glass raps on the table as I set it down. 'You knew Alex before he joined Quiz Night. Didn't you?'

Annabel rakes a hand through her hair.

'Okay. Sort of. He owns a rather plush villa in Spain and lets us use it. That's all.'

'Why didn't you say? I've been spouting on about this new

married man I've met online and all the time you knew him?' My disbelief spits out.

'It's Clifton's fault. Alex doesn't like people to know he owns the villa, and he doesn't generally rent it out. He lets us use it occasionally, but Clifton said I wasn't to let on.'

'Why doesn't he want people to know?' A dog with a bone, I gnaw hard at her words.

'You'd need to ask Clifton. I've no idea.' Annabel's pallor is accentuated by the peach-tinted walls. The thick threaded eyebrows and deep blush-coloured lip-liner tattoo have sucked the colour from her face. She downs her wine in one. 'Top-up?'

Annabel's hand which grips the bottle by the neck, quivers over the rim of my glass.

'No. You're all right. How does Clifton know Alex?'

'Barton. He introduced them.'

Annabel gets up, pokes a small key into a lock and cracks open a window.

'Jeez. It gets bloody hot in here.'

'Have you ever been to Alex's house?'

Annabel draws a hand down her throat, scratching with burgundy-painted nails, the colour faded near the cuticles.

'Sorry?'

Suddenly Clifton appears at the door.

'Hi, ladies? What about a drink for the old man?' He sets a glass down and pours from a new bottle. 'All okay, Kristi?'

Clifton hovers by the open window, his eyes puffy and half-closed. It takes a couple of seconds before he switches on his halogen beam.

'Yes, all's good.' I smile back before I get up.

'You're not going yet, are you?' Clifton asks.

'Some of us have work to do.' I turn to Annabel. 'Thanks for the wine and the heads-up.'

'Any news on Barton's killer yet?' Clifton's voice slots into the awkward silence.

'Not that I've heard.'

'I doubt they'll ever find who did it. Rather random. Probably someone he persecuted in the paper. He could be a right bastard.'

~

I decide to take the longer but straighter route home and drive at speed down the Luton Road, skirting past Airport Way, until I reach the dual carriageway. Concentration on the traffic gives me little respite from the turmoil.

My thoughts roll back and forth, like tumbling dice, with Annabel and Clifton at their core. How well does Clifton know Alex? Does Annabel know Alex separately? Is it possible they've been having an affair? As I press my foot down hard on the accelerator, the car swerves round the roundabout by the Hilton Hotel and careers down the home stretch. The speedometer hits 100mph.

Why is the villa such a secret? Why has Alex not told me? Does his wife own it? How could he afford it? Perhaps his wife is staying there now, not at her parents?

I brake hard outside my house, sweat cascading off my brow like the Niagara Falls. I've survived the speed chase. My breath explodes like an erupting volcano.

'Shit, shit, shit.' I bang the steering wheel till my wrist crunches. A glance at a blank phone screen, and I turn the ignition off and get out. I lock the car, walk slowly up to my front door and slip the key in the lock. I do a swift three-sixty of the neighbourhood but there's not a soul in sight.

The loneliness of self-isolation is back, but this time accompanied by the sharp pointed dagger of fear.

## 59

He's the last person I want to speak to. But it's Joel's third attempt today to connect on Facetime. I've also got several missed messages from Annabel, Alex and Declan which I've ignored. Instead, I've kept my head down, concentrated on work.

Strange, the last six months has given me so much space it felt like I was orbiting the earth, hovering thousands of miles overhead, in a small time capsule built for one. People and reality got sucked down a black hole. I wonder, as I stare at the computer screen, if I'm acclimatising to the solitary way of life.

Fuzzy is thrumming again with increasing rhythm and feeding with gusto, passing on the nourishment to her brood. The deep rumble pauses only when I reach in my hand but restarts on its retreat. The hissed warnings are no longer necessary. Her charges are growing in strength by the day and Declan drools over the regular photoshoots and he's even sneakily posted a few on Instagram.

'Joel. Hi.' A couple of glasses of late afternoon Prosecco encourage me to finally pick up.

'Kristi.' His eyes squint on the screen, tiny rounded pebbles stuck into tired, sunken sockets. Thick black glasses overpower his face, and he looks like Harry Potter in *Harry Potter and the Philosopher's Stone*.

'Do you have five?'

Five. High five? Five minutes?

'Fire,' I prompt. Joel and I have zilch in common. If it wasn't for the Friday quizzes, I'd never be speaking to him one-on-one. Meeting in the pub was a one-off, a desperation to get out.

'It's these bloody questions. The police have just been round, and I wasn't sure what to say.' He's assuming I don't know about his sordid past, albeit an innocent sordidness, if that's not an oxymoron. If accused, Joel would doubtless plead youth and ignorance, unaware at the time of the criminality of his transgression. My thoughts are like those of a barrister for the defence.

'What *did* you say?' I've my sorting hat on again, sorting the truth from the shit. Did he tell the truth?

'The police had a list of all six questions. I told them about Olivia.'

We're back to the bland two-dimensional appearance. A lie in two dimensions doesn't scream as loud as a three-dimensional whopper.

'What about Olivia?' I'm now detective, super snoop and plain curious as to what he'll say.

'That she was my first girlfriend. The first girl I slept with.' Joel shouts across the airwaves, desperate to be heard as if my audio system has broken down. Mayday, Mayday.

'What are you worrying about? Olivia is no secret.'

'Have they been to talk to you?'

'No. Not yet, but I expect they will.'

'Who told them about the questions? That's what I want to know. I thought we all agreed not to say anything.' Joel's fast-paced sentences swerve round and round the racetrack. He can't stop. 'Who do you think murdered Barton? You don't seriously think it was one of our group?'

Joel's forthright outburst is startling. He's such an in-control sort of person. His underlying arrogance is more accustomed to manufacturing phoney silences with a smug resolute expression. He reminds me of a self-serving politician.

*'People who say less are generally listened to'* is Joel's mantra which he spouts ad nauseum in a quiet meaningful tone. While steam billows from everyone else's heated nostrils, Joel watches on with a silent victory smirk.

Joel takes off his glasses, sets them down and rubs his eyes. A droopy fringe, usually neatly gelled, is pushed sideways. Behind Joel is an oven hob with a couple of pans on top, a wooden spoon speared into the larger one. The cream kitchen cupboards have the look of a 1980s MFI range with their large melamine doorknobs and deep-ridged finish. A green kettle sits alongside a black toaster, a slab of Lurpak butter and a pot of jam. His Friday Zoom background is usually spotless, if distinctly bland, from what we can make out as he sits so close up to his screen. The kitchen today looks decidedly lived in.

'I've no idea. It could have been anyone but I'm not sure any of our Friday group would be capable of murder.' I let out a loud puff of disbelief although I'm not convinced by my words.

'Perhaps it was a contract killing.' Joel carries on, glasses back in place, words spurting onto the screen.

'Perhaps. But can you really see Annabel or Rihanna paying some random guy to put a pistol to Barton's head?' I straighten my back and stretch out. 'Listen, it's good to chat but I need to get going. My neighbour needs me to do a shop,' I lie.

'No problem. But would you mind asking round to see who told the police about the questions? I'm a bit embarrassed and you know everyone better than me.' His pebbled eyes do the pleading.

'I'll try. Not sure anyone will own up. Perhaps it was the person with least to hide. Are you sure it wasn't you, Joel?' I can't help myself. He's not going to own up to sleeping with an underage girl, but he's damned that anyone will ever find out.

Who's likely to care? I certainly don't as it all seems so long ago. But, if Joel is still working with young girls, it might be a different story. Perhaps it's not all completely in the past.

'Bye, Kristi, and thanks.'

The screen goes blank.

## 60

THURSDAY 15TH OCTOBER

Alex is waiting for me. Tonight, I'm the one who is fashionably late.

Butterflies are rumbling round my insides, as if I've disturbed their rest. I'm wearing battle armour; close-fitting sheer black dress, pointy heels and a cream pashmina draped round my shoulders. A rare visit to the beauty salon has smoothed over my skin with a sleek light tan.

He stands up, hands in his pockets and smiles. Yes, in appearance he is drop-dead gorgeous and I think Barton. They're two of a kind. Both bastards. But bastards have the passion pull that good guys don't and I still live in hope that the two aren't mutually exclusive.

'Hi. You look gorgeous,' he says, slipping his arms effortlessly round my waist and pulling me close. 'Smell good too.' A dry sniff reminds me of my childhood pet Alsatian, Rocky, whose teeth didn't take long to appear.

'Thanks. You don't look too bad yourself.'

I guessed when, after all the persistence, he only offered up a Thursday night no-expenses-spared date, that Saturday this time round must be earmarked for something else. Or perhaps

227

he's suffering from pre-divorce guilt. Not sure what other reason there might be, as he's been texting constantly.

The Arndale Hotel, bijou but upmarket, is near Hatfield. The restaurant sports a couple of Michelin stars and since its reopening, rocketing prices have added to its exclusivity.

It's nearly a week since Alex and I had dinner with Annabel and Clifton. I finally gave in and called Alex back on Tuesday after his bombardment of messages. It's hard to ditch an attractive guy if the physical pull is strong. But tonight isn't about attraction, it's about sticking to the question sheet. Alex's answers will help me decide whether to give our relationship a last chance and hopefully, tonight's conversation will dilute my more macabre imaginings relating to Barton's death.

'Where have you been all week? You've been ignoring me.' His eyes twinkle as they pierce mine. On the table between us, floating candles drift aimlessly in a designer centrepiece, the pink, white and red buds like exotic pond weed. Classical background piano music turns up the romantic volume.

'I'm busy with work. Once my promotion is finalised, I'll be expected to spend a few days a week back at the office,' I say.

'That's not a proper answer. Come on. Spill.'

It's tempting to go with the flow, enjoy the evening as a one off, a see-where-it-goes type of date but the blatant lies are festering, and I've been a willing doormat once too often. Barton wiped his feet on my thick bristles, trampling the dirt well in. Not this time.

'Okay. There's a few things bothering me,' I begin.

Alex sets his glass down. 'Go on.'

'Why didn't you tell me you knew Annabel and Clifton. Why the pretence?'

'Is that what this is about?' He snorts, think piglet.

I feel as if I'm accusing him of stealing a sweet from my handbag.

'I never said I didn't know them. You never asked. Barton introduced Clifton and me and we'd occasionally go for drinks after work.'

'What about your villa in Spain?' I look in the whites of his eyes.

A waiter appears like a ghost in the half-light and Alex waves him away. 'Ten minutes, please.'

'What about my villa in Spain? Again, you never asked and it's something I don't talk about much. You see, it belongs to Elisa.'

On the plausibility scale, think Richter scale where ten would blow the earth apart, he's riding around four or five. There are definite cracks in the fabrication but it's not clear where they're coming from.

'Oh. I see.'

Alex stretches his hand over mine. 'Shall we order?'

He's managed to swat away the questions like a swarm of irritating flies.

'Yes, but one last question. Sorry, but since Barton's death, things have been bugging me and it's hard to let them go.'

'Should I be scared?' He lifts his hand off, retracting the comforting heat blanket.

'You remember the questions Barton asked. Did you know what they were, and did you mention them to the police?'

Of course, it was Alex who mentioned the questions to the police. Why shouldn't he? But he wasn't able to offer a plausible reason why he had done. None of us told him not to and he tried very hard over dinner to convince me that he had no idea what they were about.

But he was lying, and his parting shot confirmed my suspicions.

'I'd watch that Declan, if I were you. He's got a soft spot for you.'

Back in the car park, after an unsuccessful bid to get me to spend the night in the hotel's honeymoon suite, Alex gave himself away. 'He's a right prick. Is it true he was a member of the IRA? Watch your kneecaps, is all I'd say.'

Healthy jealousy fuels romance, certainly in the early stages. But the throwaway comment about Declan was like a smoking gun. Alex knows about Declan's black past and most likely that it was related to one of the six questions. How much more does he know about the rest of us and how did he find out? Did Barton tell him, or did he do the research himself?

But it doesn't really matter how Alex found out, in as far as it's relevant to my love life. I swore I'd never date another liar and he's given me no choice but to move on. Once a liar, always a liar.

As I snuggle down under the duvet, one last thought takes hold. Alex's deception doesn't help me solve the riddle of Barton's death. I've no idea why Alex is lying or at least omitting to tell me the truth, but I sense a link between the dishonesty and his friend's murder.

It's going to be another long night. I switch off the bedside lamp and pray for a few hours' sleep to put a flimsy lid on the turmoil.

# WEEK 7

# 61

The national newspaper article was tucked away at the bottom of page five, and we all read it after Annabel pinged through the link early this morning.

## BARTON HINTON – MURDERED FOR WHAT HE KNEW?
### Ambrose Kitchener

*Barton Hinton, a reporter at the* London Echo *with a fearsome reputation for digging relentlessly into human interest stories, was found murdered in Durham on Friday 18$^{th}$ September. Shot by a bullet at close range, his body was discovered by a lone walker along the banks of the River Wear shortly after 8 o'clock.*

*In the publishing world, it was no secret that Barton Hinton had enemies. His hard-hitting straight-talking reports earned him notoriety, but little popularity.*

*The police are investigating a possible link between his death and a group of Friday night quizzers, who have been meeting every week since lockdown began. There has been talk of blackmail as a possible motive for murder. However, on the night in question, the quiz took place as usual despite Mr Hinton's absence.*

*The lone gunman may have been someone with a grudge against the victim and there is the possibility that a contract killer, a professional hitman, may have carried out the crime. As yet there have been no arrests.*

*Members of the public are asked to contact the number below if they have any information that they think might be of use to the police in their enquiries.*

We're all punctual tonight, no latecomers. I'm soon fiddling with the screen settings, aiming for clearer definition.

There are seven boxes tonight. Full house. Bingo. Annabel is still the ball caller, having organised the meet and has got her headmistress hat on. Her quiet serious tones suggest the death of a pupil. The seven severed heads, white alabaster faces, could be impaled on death spikes.

Clifton has moved into the orangery tonight, on his laptop, a new fully-fledged member of the *Friday Murder Club*. It would make a great headline, book title. I giggle unintentionally, and all eyes turn.

'Thanks for coming,' Annabel begins, grateful that we all accepted the late-in-the-day invitation. Her drink is fizzing, but the celebratory bottle is nowhere in sight, no doubt in deference to the seriousness of the get-together. She mustn't look as if she's going to enjoy herself.

'You all saw the article. Christ. It's ridiculous that the police might think we're involved.' Annabel takes a large gulp, wiping her tongue over a dribble of foam on her lips.

The silence is awkward. I don't want to speak first, scared of what I might give away. I'm still assuming that I'm the only one who knows the whole story, but I can't be sure.

'The press is parked outside my house.' Rihanna's lips are paler than her face tonight, and her eyebrows quieter in shade. Red circles rim her eyes.

'Same here,' says Joel. 'Bloody nosey bastards.'

I'm scared to look at Alex, surprised that he's turned up at all. It seems a long time since we had dinner, but it's only twenty-four hours. He winks and does a little wave.

'Perhaps someone can fill me in. What were the questions Barton asked you all? I never saw them,' Alex asks.

Fuzzy does a little yelp as she pads across the floor, making a rare escape from the litter. She arches her back. Pilates Angry Cat style, as her claws scratch back and forth on the rug.

'Stop that, Fuzzy.' I don't recognise my own voice but when I look back on screen, smiles abound as light relief floods the party. 'Sorry,' I say. 'It's the cat.'

'Where were we? Sorry, Alex.' Annabel nods, indicating for him to carry on.

'Nothing really. I just wondered what the questions were about that the police seem so interested in. I never saw them.'

'There was nothing about you in them, so you don't need to worry.' Declan's voice slurs, but with a snappy edge. He swills his whisky round, lifts out an ice cube and sucks.

'I think we should agree a plan of action with the police. Let's not pretend that the questions weren't loaded. There was enough ammunition in the answers to give us all a motive for murder.' It's Clifton.

'What the hell are you talking about?' Annabel plonks her glass down and stares at the screen. I assume the angry expression is aimed at Clifton. Who else?

'Come on, darling. Why all the pretence?' Clifton asks.

What a two-faced git. You've got to feel for Annabel as she still has no idea that Rihanna is pregnant. I'm not even sure Clifton knows about his impending offspring.

Barton has definitely stirred up the hornet's nest. The lies are flying, buzzing off in all directions. Any one of us, apart from me, has actually a motive for murder. Clifton is trying to get group approval for us all to say as little as possible, with an agenda of what can and can't be mentioned.

'We need to assume the police have a copy of the questions.' Clifton pauses long enough for the culprit to own up, but the silence urges him on. 'I suggest we agree an answer sheet, simplify the responses and all sing from the same hymn sheet. What do you say?'

Clifton is a wheeler-dealer. He's a banker after all and he's used to lying, cheating, anything to make money and feather his own nest. But he has a point.

'I think it's a good idea,' Declan says. 'Why don't we go through the questions now and agree the answers and put an end to it? If we all agree, then the police will probably leave it there.'

It sounds a sensible suggestion. Problem is, I'll be the only one who knows all the real answers. But I can probably live with that, if the police let this particular line of questioning rest.

'Is that unanimous then?' Clifton checks for the group response.

Annabel disappears off-screen for a minute. When Clifton's head turns away and he starts talking, momentarily with a muted screen, I guess Annabel is facing him. More likely facing him down.

'*Okay.*' '*Yes, sounds like a plan.*' '*If you think so.*' The responses come back thick and fast from the rest of us.

'Alex. You can now hear what the questions are, and the

answers.' Clifton beams, the skilled diplomat, cementing his position as master of ceremonies having knocked his wife sideways.

Master of deceit, more like.

## 62

The house is even quieter than usual when I turn off the screen and cut my lifeline with the outside world. The *Titanic* is going down, the survivors scrabbling for the limited life vests and left me to my fate.

I lift Fuzzy up. It's the first time she's let me hold her since the birthing. Her eyes close as my firm strokes brush down the length of her silken fur. I nuzzle my face close, her pink tongue wetting my nose. Tears stream down my face and she tries to lick them off.

'Shit. What am I going to do?'

I've printed off the answers that we've all agreed to. It's like a confidential NATO pact, signed by all parties. One of the terms and conditions was that we all delete correspondence on our computers which relates to the questions from before this evening and clear our browsing histories. I can't remember whose suggestion this was. Probably the person with most to hide, but at the moment it seems irrelevant.

Tonight's meeting has added fuel to my suspicions that someone in our group did commit murder. They were driven by the real answer to one of the questions, an answer they are desperate to keep hidden. A secret from the past that would most probably send them to prison for a very long time.

The rest of the group have been only too willing to go along with the plan, because of their own skeletons. It's hard to see, from the answers as I read them again, who might have had the greatest motive. Although as I read the agreed manufactured answers, the real ones are what I see.

*Question 1: Who was Joel's first ever serious girlfriend and how long after their first date, did they sleep together. Answer: Olivia. Slept together in freshers' week. Tick.*

*Question 2: What's Annabel's tattoo of, and where exactly is it located?*

*Answer: Eiffel Tower. Near her crotch. Tick.*

*Question 3: What dating site does Kristi use and what's the name of her current mystery single lover? Answer: Suave Singletons. Alex. Tick.*

*Question 4: What was the name of Rihanna's first pet and first fiancé? Answer: Goldie the Goldfish (won at the fair) and Clifton. Tick.*

*Question 5: What secret society does Declan belong to and what does the induction ceremony entail? Answer: Member of the Masons. Secret Oath Ceremony. He can't say anymore. Tick.*

*Question 6: What's my latest scoop and which TV production giant has commissioned the story? Answer: No one has any idea. Just another of his stupid jokes. Tick.*

~

I turn off the bedside lamp and have one final check of my mobile. There's a message from a number I don't recognise. I blink several times.

Stick to the answers. This is a warning. Or you'll be sorry.

# 63

The van rumbles along the motorway, careering as Declan beats his hands on the steering wheel in time to the music. Rock classics all the way. Every bump in the road sends the cargo in the boot reeling, banging out an offbeat accompaniment.

By the time we hit the A23, it's still not even nine.

'We'll be in Brighton before ten. You okay?' Declan turns his head.

'I would be if you'd keep your eyes on the road.'

The sun is high, the sky cloudless. Blinding rays dodge the dirt smears on the windscreen and suddenly blind our vision. Simultaneously, we drop down the visors, laughing in sync at our double act.

'What have you got in the back of the van anyway? Hope it's not precious as it's getting battered.'

'You'll have to wait and see.'

Lockdown has created pockets of life, no continuum. There was only 'home' for a while, then tentative steps back out to restaurants and pubs and a weekly trip into the office to stem the boredom. Nothing links the random places. No spur-of-the-moment popping to clothes shops to browse rails and plan holiday wardrobes, nor little impromptu detours through the park on the way home. It's as if we're living in a vacuum, earning points that allow us a treat, if we're good. And mask wearing compounds the loneliness, random communication with strangers swallowed in mumbled pleasantries.

Declan's insistence that I join him on a trip to the seaside was too tempting, all things considered.

'Go on. It'll do you good. A change of scenery.'

He was right. There's a weird euphoria to joining up the landscape dots, recklessly breaking out of the bubble and stepping back onto the planet.

I crack the window, roll it down a couple of centimetres and let the crisp cold air stream through.

'Can't you just smell that sea air? Not long now.' Declan inhales heartily.

Declan reminds me of being a student, when days were filled with carefree recklessness. He's avoided responsibility ever since. No albatross of a mortgage, the flexibility of renting much more his thing. And marriage hasn't snared him with poisonous promises of a happy ever after.

'Just never met the right girl. But certainly, haven't ruled it out.' Wait and see. Go with the flow. That's Declan.

The seafront finally comes into view. Declan slows down and crawls along parallel to the promenade which is sparsely populated with joggers and dog walkers. He rolls his window right down and puffs out the pent-up tension.

'Smell that freshness. Why the hell do I live in London? I've no idea.'

He points out the beach huts, drives me past the pier,

promising that once we've finished with business, he'll walk me out to the end. Time permitting.

'Some great little seafood restaurants,' he says. 'Or perhaps you'd prefer fish and chips?'

Declan takes a left turn and pulls into a large communal car park at the end of the promenade.

'Here. This'll do nicely.'

'Do nicely for what?'

'Wait and see. You're bloody impatient, Dexter!'

He tucks the van into the corner nearest the sea and hops out.

'Come on. What are you waiting for? You wanted to know what was in the back.'

I climb down and follow him round to the back of the van. He unlocks the doors and throws them wide.

'Hey presto!'

'Oh my God! How much fruit have you got in there?'

There must be a hundred plus fruit boxes, stacked one on top of another. A couple have broken free, their contents rolling randomly around between narrow gaps in the piles.

'Each box contains three types of fruit and three types of veg. £5 a box. What do you think?'

A rainbow array of colour is captured in each box, vibrant edible still-life portraits. Oranges, rosy-red apples, green and plum-coloured grapes mingle with savoy cabbages, freshly uprooted carrots and new potatoes.

The sharp sea breeze, invisible yet cutting, has coloured Declan's cheeks a bright glowing red.

'Brilliant. I love it.'

'Right then. Help me set up. I've got a couple of tables which need unfolding. You see, I used to drive an ice-cream van back in the day, and this was my regular pitch. There's a lack of marshals this end of the shore, so thought it worth taking a chance. Bit like Del Boy. You can be Rodney; my lookout.'

## 64

In the last six months, three hours has never passed by so quickly. The sun has encouraged locals as well as day trippers to the seafront. The food and veg boxes dwindle rapidly in number.

Declan's face mask cups his chin like a smooth black beard but as time passes, he forgets to pull it back up when a new customer appears.

I wander over to a small brick wall, sit down and throw out my legs, decanting coffee from a thermos into two small plastic cups and offer one to Declan.

'Just what the doctor ordered.' He comes close and his icy fingers brush mine as he takes his cup. 'Thanks.' It's hard to imagine not so long ago he was stepping out into the sea, death calling him.

When two o'clock comes around, he suggests it's time to pack up as the car park is steadily emptying. 'What say we go and pick up some fish and chips along the pier. We can leave the van here.' His mask now dangles off one ear, the virus threat temporarily forgotten in the heat of reckless enjoyment.

~

'I got a warning on my phone. *Stick to the answers*, it said.' I rip open the fish and chip wrapping as I speak.

We're sitting on a wooden bench attached to a slatted table which faces out to sea. Tumultuous waves thunder towards us as dark clouds circle overhead. My body quivers.

'Me too,' Declan says as he dips a soggy chip into ketchup and spears a piece of cod with a plastic fork. 'God, this tastes good.' His hair swirls round his face and between mouthfuls his salty fingers push the strands away.

'Who do you think it is?' I ask.

'Sending the messages?' Declan dips another chip and drizzles a sachet of vinegar across his food. 'Who do *you* think?' He turns the question back, emphasis on the 'you'.

'No idea. It could be anyone.'

A small group of seagulls hover, their webbed feet inching closer. A sharp beak suddenly swoops in and devours a fish sliver nestled by Declan's trainers. He sets another chip alongside.

'May as well make it worth his while.' Crinkle lines fan out from the corners of Declan's eyes when he laughs.

'Seriously. Aren't you worried?' I ask.

'What, of the seagull?' He turns and faces me. 'To be honest, I'd prefer to forget the whole bloody thing. You know my secret and that's between you and me. I think we all need to stick to the plan and move on.'

Declan pops a crunchy bit of batter into his mouth, scrunches up the paper and hurls the litter towards a rubbish bin several feet away.

'Bingo,' he whoops, as it hits the target. 'Do you really think one of our group murdered Barton?' he asks.

'It's possible. Everyone seems to have something to hide.'

Declan stands up, shakes out his arms.

'You finished?'

'Yes, I'm totally full thanks.'

He takes my last few chips and tosses them over the sea wall. The seagulls aren't far away and soon cluster noisily round the leftovers. Declan's hands are white, thin frozen icicles. A slight blue tinge colours the tip of his nose, which grazes mine as he pulls me up and into his arms.

'Thanks for your help. Hmm. You smell of sea, salt and vinegar.' He gently brushes his lips against mine. 'Now let's forget all about bloody Barton Hinton and go back to the van and count our ill-gotten gains.'

I tug my bobble hat down over my ears, slip my hands into my pockets and stroll alongside Declan.

Silence, except for the squeal of gulls, is our dimming afternoon companion.

## 65

L *ove and work, work and love... that's all there is.*

Someone has painted the words of Sigmund Freud, an imitation squiggly signature underneath, across a large free-standing placard by the entrance to the railway station. Notices of delays, suicides on the line and faults further on near Peterborough or Cambridge have been consigned to history. It's hard not to smile.

As the train pulls out from Hitchin station on its way into London, Sigmund Freud's summations tease me. Certainly, work and love have been all-consuming since March, in the absence of anything else to occupy my thoughts; but now it feels good to be going to the office, getting away from solitary confinement to mix with humans, face-to-face again.

The simple pleasure of staring out the window at moving countryside needs to be added to Freud's list of things to enthral us. Wonder what he'd have made of murder? No doubt its roots are mired in love or work or sex. Or possibly all three.

The sea air followed by a hot defrosting bath helped me

sleep last night for eight hours straight. First time in ages. My face in the train window peers back as someone I don't recognise. My flowery Italian mask hangs down below my neck, the fashionable accessory an attempt to glamorise the lifesaving necessity. My mother, holed up in Exeter, is constantly warning me of the dangers of impulsive online purchases. As I pull the face covering neatly into place, I'm tempted to take a selfie and taunt her with the extravagance. Although I'll hold back the fact it's come all the way from Milan.

Grayson's office is minimalist, to say the least. 'Make yourself at home,' isn't that easy as there's nothing to welcome me. His heated glass cubicle is spartanly furnished, and he's even removed the very expensive bonsai trees, a collection amassed over the years. At least we'll not have to listen to potted explanations as to origin and cost for a while. The fact they've gone makes me wonder if he'll ever be back.

I swivel round in his leather chair, holding tight to each arm and pause to take in the splendid view over the Thames. Commuters are drifting back but walking with less purpose. The numbers along the riverbank have definitely dwindled. Laptop cases are held tightly, and an occasional briefcase is swung along by an older gent. The worn leather antique bags are from another time.

There's a wall clock behind Grayson's desk. A designer piece made up of large black hands and numbers with no casing. A filtered-water dispenser in the corner tempts me over. I pull out a plastic cup, twist the tap and fill the receptacle to the top. Five minutes to eight. Five minutes to nine in Spain. La Manga Club, with its two resplendent five-star golf courses, is where Grayson is holed up.

I boot up the computer, straighten a paper pad and pull out a couple of pens from the top drawer of the desk. Grayson seems to have cleared out all but the essentials. If working out of La Manga Club is a success, it looks like he'll not be back.

I tuck my feet under the desk, cross my legs at the ankles and make cat doodles on the pad. Fifteen minutes clunk by. Matthew Bolton wanders past, hair oiled down and parted to one side like a Nazi. His macabre appearance is thrown a lifeline by a pink T-shirt and skinny jeans. Dressing down has taken on a whole new look. He gives a mean little wave and mouths 'good luck' as if I'm about to be taken to theatre for open-heart surgery.

Tracy isn't far behind, the short skirt becoming more like a large belt every day. I wonder if Grayson will give me the authority to smarten up the dress code.

At eight twenty exactly, Grayson's face smothers the screen.

'Kristi. Good morning. How the devil are you?' Grayson's face is lit up like a Belisha beacon, his leathery orange skin aglow. A zigzag sunburn mark on his brow is accentuated by a pasty hairline. 'Got a bit of sunburn.' He reads my thoughts and his bleached teeth, up close, seem larger and even whiter than usual.

'All good, boss. How's Spain?'

'Mustn't complain. A bit hot, exhausted from all the golf and hung-over from the Sangria, but hey ho. Life's a bitch.'

His yellow polo shirt suggests he's already been on the golf course or has plans to tee off after our meeting. A thick gold chain is choking his throat.

'Do you want me to get the others in yet? Go through the new working format?'

'Not yet. Just want to tell you first how I see things working for the foreseeable future.'

# 66

While Grayson runs through his plans for the management of the editorial staff, guiding me through a weekly working schedule, my mind wanders as repetition creeps in. Listening to his own voice is still my boss's favourite pastime.

Natalie has popped up on screen a couple of times, obviously having decided to stick by her man for the time being. Once with fresh coffee and once to land an unprofessional kiss on her lover's cheek. 'Off to the supermarket. Bye, Kristi. Take care.' A large wide-brimmed straw hat is held in place with a manicured hand as she floats away. I suspect a new life in the sun was too tempting to turn down.

I think it would be a major miscalculation to suspect that Grayson's sharpness of mind and critical appraisal of his staff's efforts has flown with him to Spain. His small beady eyes are still those of a hawk and he'll not miss much even from hundreds of miles away. His move to Murcia on the south coast must surely rate as the biggest perk of any job and certainly one that puts annual bonuses in the shade.

On the wall behind Grayson are a couple of golfing collages.

*Golf through the ages* is suggested by the array of strangely shaped balls and club heads. To one side is a dark-framed window, stark in contrast to the whitewashed walls. A curved alabaster light fitting is the only other adornment.

Grayson's voice drones on, thick with importance and not a little smugness at having played the virus at its own game.

'There's winners and losers in every war,' he spouted when Covid reared its ugly head like a hovering lighter-than-air Zeppelin, waiting to wreak as much havoc as possible while everyone looked the other way. Grayson's war strategy seems to have worked; sun, sand and sangria the victory spoils.

My heart does a sudden little blip thing. I uncross my legs, perch on my toes and steady the random swivelling. As I take in the Grayson screen set, I realise that could be all it is. He could be anywhere in the world. Perhaps he's in the Caribbean, play-acting he's in Spain so that we're kept on our toes by the meagre two-and-a-half-hour flight back home to check on us. Perhaps he's in Australia? New Zealand? South Africa is a hotspot for golf enthusiasts, or Portugal.

'Okay. So, you've made notes of what I'm expecting? I'll email you later today the weekly itinerary, meeting schedules and so forth and what we've agreed. Perhaps you'd go and get Matthew and the others now, and I'll fill them in next. You're a star, Kristi.'

## 67

A few hours later I say my farewells to the staff, fling on my coat and hurry down the stairs to hail a taxi. On reaching Kings Cross, I rush over to the departure boards and check the times. There's only three minutes until the next fast train to Hitchin.

I race for the platform, sidestepping irate travellers whose trains have been delayed again. My irregular heartbeat pumps erratically but once again I manage to jump through the train doors as the whistle blows.

Beating rush hour has become easier. Before March, catching a train home before six o'clock on a weekday packed with deadlines was unheard of. But as I make my way towards the back of the carriage, my hands pushing off the seats to steady myself, the station clock through the window confirms it's only ten minutes past four.

My designer mask might look good but I'm sweating, both from anxiety and from claustrophobia. When I sit down, I glance round the half-empty carriage and slip it off my nose; like a bank robber after he's checked the coast is clear. I lean my cheek against the window, the glass a cool balm against my scorching skin and count down from sixty.

By the time I reach twenty, nineteen, eighteen... my mind is already scooting this way and that again. If Grayson could have facetimed us from anywhere in the world, then the alibis afforded to the Friday Zoom Quiz group on the night Barton was murdered, must surely be in question. Declan's floral background could have been a room anywhere, Ireland, Scotland or the other side of the world. Rihanna's cottage is pretty twee, the background consisting of a dark bland but forgettable canvas. A few books, a couple of pictures and a large vase of brightly arranged flowers could have been replicated easily enough somewhere else.

Any one of our group, desperate enough to get rid of Barton, could have gone to a lot of trouble arranging their Zoom backdrop. Assuming Clifton as the most likely person to have carried out the shooting has been made easier by the fact that he wasn't at the Zoom meeting on the night Barton died. That said, Annabel's and Clifton's backgrounds would have been harder to reproduce and easier to check out.

Joel's sad bland lounge in his Barnet bachelor pad on the other hand wouldn't have taken much staging.

Then there's Alex. He zoomed in from Barton's flat in Covent Garden, the two times he joined our Friday hangouts. I've been there, seen the cream-walled niche where Alex sat with the brightly lit blue and yellow-flower canvas behind him.

By the time I exit Hitchin station, light rain is falling but it builds quickly and soon becomes a deluge. Hot and bothered from the stuffy heated train carriage, I decide to jog home rather than wait for a taxi. If I push hard, I can do it in half an hour. I dig out trainers from my shoulder bag and put them on in place of my low leather work pumps.

My chest is wheezing as I walk the last a hundred yards to my front door. I turn the key in the lock and the house seems eerily quiet; even Fuzzy and her brood are silent. Closing the door, I swoosh my dripping-wet hair, tear my coat off and shake it down. Without changing out of my wet clothes, I head straight into the kitchen and turn on the computer.

Email messages flood in, Amazon notifications of abortive deliveries, and requests about upgrading BT and energy suppliers. I make a note to read later the one from Rihanna that pops up, marked with a red flag.

I tug my jumper over my head and peel off my socks before opening up my photo gallery. My breath is still ragged.

'Bingo.' I slap my hands either side of the counter, tuck my hair behind my ears, and start to display recent screenshots. Although my initial intent on the first Friday that Alex, known at the time to me as Logan, appeared at the quiz was to capture his picture for personal reasons, I've managed, by pure chance, to screenshot everyone as they sit and work their screens. There are ten screenshots from the first Friday and five from the second, the night Barton was murdered.

Somewhere, if I look hard enough, there may be clues. As I set to the task, the more convinced I become that one of our group wasn't where they said they were on the night Barton Hinton was shot.

It's definitely possible that someone took a trip up to Durham and staged their screen background from another location.

# 68

'Thanks for coming. I needed to talk to someone again.' Rihanna's face tells its own story. Void of make-up, she's barely recognisable. There's not a hint of trademark lip gloss, thick mascara and tinted moisturiser.

'No problem. Always good to get away from the screen for a while,' I say.

I squeeze past her into the cottage which opens out into one large downstairs room. A kitchenette, with oak fixtures and fittings, is tucked neatly into the far corner. A small array of copper pans hangs over an Aga.

'Coffee?' she asks.

'Yes please.' Today Rihanna's stomach looks like mine, the concave firmness replaced by a more rounded mould. The baby is growing.

'I told Clifton.'

'About the baby? What did he say?'

I sit on one of two black bar stools while she froths up milk for my coffee. Her spare hand caresses the bump.

'He says he'll support me, pay maintenance but now isn't a

good time for him to leave Annabel. Kristi, he's no intention of leaving. I've been such a fool.'

Tears trickle down her cheeks and I want to hug her. Until Barton's death I'd only spoken to Rihanna a couple of times in passing and now she's looking to me for comfort. She hands me my coffee and plucks a tissue from a box.

'I'm really sorry. Married men fantasise about leaving their wives, but it's never that simple. I don't think money is Clifton's issue, and I'm sure he loves you.' I find it hard to know what else to say.

Rihanna sits beside me and pulls her slim shapely feet up onto the ring round the bottom of the stool and grips her peppermint tea.

'I thought you'd understand. It's hard to find anyone to talk to. I daren't tell my parents. They'd be furious.' She blows hard to cool her drink. 'How's it going with Alex?'

'Much the same as you and Clifton. Married.'

Rihanna smiles, sniffs the misery up her nose and sips her hot drink.

'Is that where you've been doing the Zoom quiz from?' I nod towards a laptop placed on a table in front of a sparsely adorned pine shelving unit. I recognise the large vase, which is empty, void of the usual Friday bloom arrangement. Half a dozen pictures sit along the unit's length and on the end is one of Rihanna and Clifton, his puckered lips brushing her cheek. From memory, the sparse collection of books is displayed in the same order as in the screenshots which I studied carefully before setting off.

'Yes.' Rihanna suddenly excuses herself and heads upstairs to the bathroom. I take my phone out of my bag, get up quietly and move over towards the table. I take half a dozen pictures of the backdrop. I lift up the photograph of her and Clifton.

'What are you looking at?' Rihanna's voice makes me jump.

'Your pictures. It's a good one of you and Clifton.' I turn it towards her.

'That was taken on a weekend away. He took me to the Lake District in April; all expenses paid.'

I set the frame down and pocket my phone. I don't know if she saw me taking the snaps, but her mind is elsewhere.

'You know Clifton and Alex are good friends,' she begins, sinking down onto the sofa and indicating for me to sit on a recently upholstered Bergère chair. The luxurious feathered upholstery sucks me in.

'I think Barton introduced them but I'm not sure they were that good friends,' I say.

I've an awful sense of foreboding, the heat in the small low-ceilinged room compounding a sense of panic. The strong cappuccino is sweating out through my pores.

'I think they were. Clifton doesn't know but I've listened in to conversations more than once. He and Alex work together and I'm certain it's not all above board.'

'What do you mean? What do they work at together?'

'Alex works on the computing systems of various banks...' Rihanna pauses, undoes her scrunchie, ruffles her hair and hauls it into a wobbling topknot.

'Go on.'

'I can't be certain, but I think Alex passes Clifton insider information from the banks and institutions where he works. Alex has access to confidential communications and, according to Clifton, knows all the tricks of hacking.'

Oh my God. Insider dealing. That's why they pretend not to know each other. They haven't denied the odd drink after work, or a lad's night out with Barton as their leader, but anything else has been veiled.

'Are you certain?'

'Fairly. But please don't say anything. Clifton would be furious if he thought I'd told you.'

～

When I get home, I upload the pictures of Rihanna's backdrop from my phone onto my computer. Comparison with the ones taken before and on the night of the murder is easy. They're virtually identical except for the addition of a couple of photo frames this time round, and the vase today was conspicuously empty.

I can at least tick off one possibility. There is no way Rihanna would have travelled to Durham and been able to recreate the identical backdrop for the night of Barton's murder. I study the two screenshots of her backdrop, confident that the textures, lighting and content were the same on both occasions.

I bring up all the other screenshots and display them all on the computer. I magnify them one at a time and suddenly something catches my eye. I jump from picture to picture and then spot something in the backdrop of one screen that wasn't there in the one taken a week earlier, in supposedly the same location. It's a very small addition to the shot, easy to miss, but I can see it.

Oh my God. Could I be looking at a screenshot of Barton's murderer?

## 69

THURSDAY 22ND OCTOBER

I've decided to take the day off from sleuthing and dealing with what I might have discovered. I've no idea where to go or what to do with my random discovery but need a break from staring at the computer and screenshots. It'll take time to decide the direction to take.

By lunchtime, having made good progress with my column, it was time to text Alex. His reply bounced straight back.

Just say where and when. I'll be there.

I'm now waiting in the Flounder Pub where Alex and I came on our first date. Being first to arrive tonight doesn't bother me and I ignore the waiter's attempts to entice me with something from the wine list. Tonight, it'll be a clear head all the way.

It's been a week since I've seen Alex. But there's been no clock watching or counting the days and hours between meets. I'm here to finish it, the intrigue of future possibilities now buried under heavy muddied soil. Rihanna has reminded me of the loneliness and despair that clings to tawdry affairs as they inch up one-way streets.

'Why don't you do it by phone, or text?' Rihanna suggested when I confided my intentions. 'Or Facetime?'

You see, I'm not only finishing with Alex tonight, but I'm on a mission to ask questions and to gauge his reactions first-hand, when he realises that I already have most of the answers. The physical attraction which teased me with passionate consummation, has been turned off as if by remote control, the flick of a switch. Deceit can turn the most lustful obsession upside down.

'Hi.' His face lights up, his skin drier than usual, hair less neatly styled, as he strides into the bar. The red tie has been loosened, the tight knot sitting unevenly to one side and the top button on his blue work shirt is undone.

'Hi.'

'No drink yet? What'll you have? A bottle of Sauvignon?' Alex clicks his fingers at a hovering waiter and sits down beside me. 'You been here long?'

'No. Just got here,' I lie again, but for different reasons than last time.

'I'm really glad you called. I thought you didn't want to see me again.' He takes both my hands but when I gently slip them away, he moves back.

'Go on. What's up?'

I build slowly, pretending that as a singleton in her thirties, I can't hang around for a married man to get divorced.

'I've been here before and it's not worth the risk,' I say, likening the experience to having only one last roll of a dice, and your life depends on getting the six spots.

'What risk?' He's skilful at turning questions around. I'm tempted to ask what his wife's like and if he plays the same games with her, but I don't. I carry on.

'I know it's none of my business, but you've not been entirely honest with me and after my experiences with Barton, I'm looking for someone I can trust. Completely.'

'When wasn't I honest?'

'You know when. Firstly, you called yourself Logan online. Sorry, but even if you're only after a bit of fun, or even an affair, I don't really get why you didn't use your real name. Not all women who join online dating sites are desperate. They're certainly not all stupid.'

Alex laughs and asks if I'm hungry. 'I'm starving,' he says. 'I haven't eaten since lunchtime, so I'll need sustenance if you're going for the full interrogation.'

'No, not really, but you go ahead. Maybe get an extra portion of chips,' I suggest with a pursed-lip smile.

I yield to small talk until his steak arrives, plate stacked with tomatoes, mushrooms, onion rings and sweet potato chips. I take time to regroup and prepare for the final assault. As I pick at the chips, which Alex has lavishly slathered in vinegar and salt, he slices away with a sharp knife through his blood-red meat.

'There's more, isn't there?' he asks as he nudges a spotlessly clean plate to the edge of the table and wipes ketchup from his lips.

'Why did you lie about knowing Clifton? Well, not telling me that you knew him at all. You've worked with him, haven't you?'

'No. Not really. Where the hell is all this going, Kristi? If you want to call it a day, that's fine by me but you're doing yourself no favours here.' Alex yawns.

'I'm not after favours. I hoped you might come clean, explain what the point of all this has been.'

'I like you, fancy you, that's all. I thought it might go somewhere.' He smiles, his usual soft features set hard as if the laughter lines have been filled in with concrete. 'But happy to call it a day.'

He beckons for the bill. 'Sorry, Kristi. I thought we might have had something special.'

'Did you work with Clifton feeding him insider trading tips?'

'Now you're being plain nosey. Listen, I'll pretend you didn't ask that.'

Alex gets up, shoves his chair under the table and lifts his jacket. 'It's late. I'm going to make a move. To be honest, I can't deal with this shit now. Are you coming?'

'No. You're okay. Is that how you could afford a three-million-pound villa in Marbella? It's not Elisa's, is it?'

Alex pulls cash from his wallet, thumbs through a wad of notes and slaps them on top of the bill.

'And Barton knew, didn't he?'

Alex grips the back of the chair and for one awful moment I think he's going to attack me. His eyes are black.

'Bye, Kristi. Don't worry, I'll not bother you again.'

I watch his ramrod-straight back as he heads for the door. He pauses, glances back over his shoulder and shakes a warning finger in my direction.

The waiter asks if I'd like a drink, on the house. I wonder if he's been watching. Perhaps it's my trembling hands or the fact that he assumes I've been dumped.

'Yes. A large brandy, please.'

# WEEK 8

# 70

FRIDAY 23RD OCTOBER

Head down. For four hours I've been swirling the mouse, adding, deleting, ideas playing me like a trickster. The clock is ticking, lunch break a piece of toast and an apple. The first draft column for *Lies and Lockdown* is to be with Grayson, which he's promised to give measured consideration while he eats his breakfast by the swimming pool, by nine o'clock Monday morning.

It's strange not to have Barton to bounce ideas off. As I scan the final wording a light zephyr of unease skims over me, ruffling my puffed-up feathers.

### *LIES AND LOCKDOWN – Week 1 – Kristi Dexter*
#### *The Backdrop to Deception*

*Ever wonder what the Facetime or Zoom-screen backdrops, the stage sets today for all our lives, can tell us about the people we're talking to.*

*We've all learnt to tinker with screen appearances, like carefully applying make-up to cover up ageing wrinkles or Monday morning alcohol-induced blotchy skin syndrome. False eyelashes are replaced by showcased book displays, designer clothes by sought-after modern art or copies of the old masters.*

*Who hasn't been tempted to display a stag's head, the beast captured in the Highlands of Scotland, shot at close range? Boasting and machismo have been taken to a whole new level. Such trophies must surely have kickstarted many introductory conversations in the online dating world. That said, I'd personally advise against real stuffed animal heads. There are far too many eco warriors and anti-hunt campaigners out there!*

*Depending on the situation, we all tinker with our backgrounds. Des Farnham from Lincoln told his wife, Claire, on a Facetime chat that he was fed up self-isolating with his mother in her dismal bungalow in Yorkshire, when room service knocked, let themselves in and set down the silver tray with burger and chips for one.*

*His wife was horrified. She'd believed Des when he told her he'd painted and redecorated his mother's lounge, the walls in urgent need of a fresh lick of paint.*

*'Got rid of that awful floral wallpaper at last,' he'd bragged. What reason had Claire to disbelieve him?*

*She should have, because Des was holed up in a 5-star hotel, splashing his pension pot on lockdown luxury.*

*You see, Des desperately wanted a break. A break from his wife, a break from life and a break from his mother. A bland screen, and he thought he'd managed the perfect alibi.*

*Then, of course, there is the work set-up. More and more of us are working from home. Mothers all over the country are now thrilled that their grown-up children automatically tidy their rooms in readiness for team meetings with managerial office staff.*

*Even teenagers have started to pull duvets up ready for that Google Hangout party. No more dirty underpants, muddy football socks and lumped up bedding in sight. The bedroom, having been turned into an office, or a selfie lover's paradise, has seen foregrounds and backgrounds benefit from complete makeovers.*

*Finally, on a more macabre note. What about a screen background as an alibi for a murder? Ever thought that your boss might be anywhere in the world when he Team Views with his employees? You all know he's in Australia on holiday, the further away the better. But when his mistress gets murdered, a mile from his home in Surrey, surely someone must suspect that he's not really on the other side of the world. You see, we believe what we've been told. But criminals move with the times, embracing the shock element of new, innovative methods to commit their crimes.*

*Think about where your friends, colleagues and family say they are. Are they telling the truth? Check out backgrounds to their computer or laptop screens. You might find clues of a sneaky deception.*

*I for one, have become Agatha Christie of the digital age.*

The Friday group have all accepted my invitation to tonight's eight o'clock Zoom. My email stressed that I was after feedback for my first column, running in about seven days' time. I assured the guests it wasn't another quiz night.

Barton usually gives me honest opinions. I miss his professional input. Still very sad. Anyway, maybe you'd all help and have a read through. I'd really appreciate feedback. Ideas and criticism welcomed in equal measure. I'll send across the first draft at around seven thirty which should give you plenty of time to read and consider. Cheers. Kristi x

*PS See you at 8.00.*

Alex hasn't replied to the invitation, but I copied him in on the email anyway, attaching the first draft of my column story. Wouldn't want him to feel left out. Also, it's too tempting not to make him squirm.

With that I shut down the computer, tidy my own background and head for a shower.

Not long to go.

# 71

The queue to the online meet is snaking round the ethernet. It's 8.05 and everyone is hovering, spectres nudging at the cables. I take a swig of wine, open the door and let them in.

'Hi, Kristi.' It's Annabel in red. 'I'm on my own. Clifton has gone for beers.'

'Hi, all.' I fiddle with the document in front of me, a nervous rumbling stomach causing cramps. I've hardly eaten all day but a glance at the wine bottle tells me my crutch is nearly half empty.

Declan's smile is broad, like a sunbeam which I guess is especially for me. He's dressed in a green Irish rugby shirt with a white turned-up collar and a gold indecipherable emblem on one side. His beer mug, gripped firmly in both hands, sports a gold harp on the glass. The Irish roots run deep. Confidence in his assurances that he's left the past behind might take time as I still don't know him that well, but a wink makes me blush.

Joel is dressed in black, Rihanna in trademark pink, and as suspected, there's no sign of Alex.

'No Alex?' Declan reads my mind.

'I think he's meeting up with Clifton,' says Annabel.

Alex has probably gone to warn Clifton that I know about their dodgy dealings, but it's all hearsay what they've actually been up to. I've only Rihanna's word for anything untoward. Also, Clifton could be anywhere. I doubt his wife knows the half of what he gets up to and the more I get to know Annabel, the less I suspect she cares. What the two men are at, is also none of my business; but Barton's murder is.

Tonight, I'm after knee-jerk reactions to my article, especially the bit about using background screenshots as alibis. Although I think I've spotted something, maybe worked out from our Friday group who Barton's murderer was, it's still only a hunch. The group's reaction tonight might feed my suspicions, and also might help me decide where to go with what I've come up with.

'Got your article. Certainly interesting.' Joel waves an A4 piece of paper in the air.

'Yes. Well done, Kristi.' It's Rihanna. Her hair hangs loose, and her cleavage is well-covered. I doubt Annabel knows about the baby and will be buoyed by Rihanna's defeated appearance. Annabel is heavily made-up again, false posturing back in place.

'Any thoughts on the article? Improvements maybe?' I begin, my eyes flitting between screens.

'Love Des. What a great idea,' chips in Declan. 'I can see how lockdown would suit some married men. Self-isolating miles away from the wife must be very tempting.' He downs his beer, licks his lips and lifts another bottle, zapping the metal top with an opener.

'What about the murder idea? Clever.' I throw out my bait and dangle the hook.

'Bit far-fetched,' says Joel.

'Any more news on Barton's murder?' Annabel uses an uncomfortable lull in the conversation to get involved. Not sure if it's her lack of digital know-how or unease at Joel's tone that has persuaded her to steer the conversation in another direction. Her voice booms louder than everyone else's.

'The police don't seem to have any concrete leads,' Joel says, his statement having the intonation of a question.

'Have they been asking anymore about the questions? The ones Barton sent us all,' Declan asks.

'I haven't heard from the police again, Declan.' Rihanna's voice crackles through a weak internet connection, and her face flickers in and out. The view of the inside of her cottage is grainy, indistinct this evening, like her expression.

'Grayson told me the police are trawling through recent stories Barton was covering to find someone whom he might have royally pissed off. The police are being thorough, currently questioning a couple of petty gangsters and drug dealers.' Declan's been keeping up to speed and I'm chuffed he's repeating what I told him.

'Barton was a shit though. He never knew when to let it rest.' Joel gets up from the screen and excuses himself. He's wearing checked, what look like pyjama bottoms, red, yellow and green. As if suddenly remembering that his bottom half is visible, he glances back before slipping out of the room.

When he reappears a few minutes later, skinny jeans are back in place.

Half an hour passes in general chit-chat, my article lauded with raised glasses and congratulatory asides. Suddenly there's a bite and the elephant in the room is finally addressed.

'Before we go. Kristi, you're not hinting that a screen-background deceit could have had any part in Barton's murder, are you?'

'Joel, don't be stupid.' Annabel's response to Joel's question is snappy.

'It's not that stupid.' Declan, now with four empty Peroni bottles lined up, jumps in. 'I mean, one of us could have been up in Durham. Who's to say a member of our Friday troupe didn't tinker with their backdrop? It's possible.'

'You mean one of our group murdered Barton? Is that what you're saying? Christ, how ridiculous. Listen, I've got to make a move. Well done, Kristi. Great article.' Joel's screen suddenly goes blank as he disappears from the meet.

'I do think that's a bit far-fetched.' Rihanna keeps her eyes down.

'Yes, totally. Listen, I need to get going too. Great to catch up and, good luck, Kristi.' Annabel waves, both hands taking part. 'Bye. Thanks for organising.'

With the others gone, Declan and I are alone.

'Did you set this up deliberately, Kristi? It wasn't about getting feedback on your column, was it?'

'Perhaps.' My smile confirms his suspicions.

'You really do think one of us murdered Barton and that the killer wasn't where they pretended to be on that Friday night. It would scrap everyone's alibis.'

'It's just a suspicion and probably totally ridiculous.'

'Shit. It's a big suspicion. Listen, are you around at the weekend? I'd like to come and catch up with my baby bundle of fluff, not to mention the kitten.' His Irish eyes twinkle, the throaty laugh resonating through my screen.

'Ha ha. Very funny. Sorry, but I might be going to see Mum,' I lie. 'Can I let you know?'

'Sure. But I'm around.'

'Bye.'

'Bye gorgeous.' As Declan flicks the top off the fifth bottle, I blow him a kiss and disconnect.

## 72

SATURDAY 24TH OCTOBER

*I'd stop digging if I were you. It's none of your business to find out who murdered Barton. Now back the fuck off, or you'll be sorry.*

The windscreen wipers can't keep pace with the lashing rain which is buffeting the car. Lorries cling dangerously close to my tail, their headlights blinding my vision in the mirror.

My hope of a few hours' sleep before I set off were dashed by the threatening text which pinged through around midnight. As I pull into the service station, a couple of hours' drive from Durham, the screen on my phone lights up. I drive at a crawl towards the far end of the car park, slip into a bay surrounded by empty spaces and turn the ignition off. My head throbs, my eyes wide, stuck apart from concentration and anxiety.

*Let me know if you're free anytime. I'm around all weekend.*
*Desperate to see you, and my baby of course X*

It's hard not to smile at the text. Declan's insomnia isn't improving. 4.00am. He's either not been to sleep yet, or he's up ready to start the day. Although he blames *Coronasomnia*, the new term for the nation's inability to sleep, I suspect Declan's sleeplessness goes much further back. I turn my phone off.

The thunder of water smashing against the car competes with the swirling whoosh of the wind. The car shivers. Chip wrappers, milkshake cartons and pieces of random debris whirl around outside, merry dancing mayhem in the dull lighting.

I roll the car seat back, lie down, and pray for sleep.

It was a constant joke that Barton would contact his colleagues from Premier Inns all around the country. Even if he didn't tell us where he was, we could guess from the bland clean crisp surroundings with the cream walls and purple bed throws and cushions. He posted on Instagram, more than once, the logoed golden moon on purple background.

He'd often be lying on the bed, headboard seductively lit behind him, lounging back on a heap of plumped-up pillows, laptop perched on his thighs. Alex told me he occasionally joined his old school friend for a lad's midweek getaway and although Alex would suggest alternative venues to Barton, upmarket hotels with swimming pools and spas, Barton insisted he could only claim expenses if the bill fell under a certain amount. No, Barton liked the Premier Inns. He liked familiarity, routine, although this fact was at odds in someone with such a wild streak.

'A room's only for sleeping in,' he told Alex. Instead, Barton spent money on taking his friend for benders at local pubs and clubs.

Thunder crashes overhead as lighting streaks spear the darkness, buffeting my flimsy car frame. As I drift in and out of consciousness, the thoughts tumble around. I've a big decision to make at the end of the weekend. I've got several choices. If I can't find the proof that the killer was in Durham or Newcastle on the night Barton got murdered, I can try to put it all behind me, let the police carry on down their dead ends. This might mean the case never gets solved, even though I'm privy to a wad of evidence. I'd have to learn to live with a guilty conscience, but not sure how.

Or I could go to the police on Monday morning with the answers to Barton's questions, the ones he emailed me, and hand across half a dozen possible suspects to his murder. By doing this, I would be selling long-buried sinister secrets in the lives of my friends. Criminal charges could lead to prison terms, if evidence was unearthed. I'd be grassing up the only people I've been in contact with for the past six months, my lockdown lifeline. Then, there's my growing attachment to Declan and I'm not sure I could save him, if I took this route.

The best outcome is if I can find the proof that the killer was staying in the north-east, near enough to get to Barton, murder him and get back to their hotel and set up the stage-set alibi backdrop in time for the eight o'clock Zoom quiz. Then I can go to the police, hand over the evidence and keep everyone else's secrets intact. There'll be no need for any of us to stray from our recently agreed answer sheet. If the culprit tries to turn the tables, it will be too late for the police to be interested. They're after Barton's murderer, not those with suspect shady pasts.

It's a long shot, but I have to try. Finding evidence needed to get a conviction is the only real solution; for me and the Friday group.

Finally, my eyelids flicker and the shutters go down.

∿

When I wake up it's nearly seven and the wind and rain have abated, replaced by a ghostly calm early morning light. I rewind the car seat, drag a brush through my tangled hair and scrabble around in my bag for a mask. The service station is quiet with only a smattering of people gripping cardboard coffee containers, walking to and from their vehicles.

I get out, lock the car and hurry inside to pick up a large cappuccino and croissant. After a quick stop in the ladies, I'm back in the car resetting the satnav. According to the display, I should be in Durham by nine. I key in the address of the Premier Inn in the city centre, wend my way out of the car park and slip back onto the motorway heading north.

As I gather speed, pushing the accelerator up to over a hundred, I pray it won't be a wasted trip.

One thing's for certain, it's going to be a very long day.

# 73

MONDAY 26TH OCTOBER

I set off early for the office, the old Monday morning feeling welcoming me like a long-lost friend. Station parking spaces, once a rare luxury, are plentiful and it's only a few yards walk to the ticket machines.

Inside the half-empty train carriage, straining face masks and subdued commuter voices remind me that we're still in the middle of a pandemic. There's a guilty pleasure in forgetting the nightmare, even briefly but the hospital-ward hush lingering in the air, brings it back. Mobile phones are on mute.

Quiet has joined the ever-growing list of 'new normal' expectations, but first thing Monday morning the unusual quietness is strangely welcoming. Anxious irritability, relayed over the airwaves in important voices, has been replaced by thoughtful introspection. I close my eyes and sink into the journey.

As the train rolls into Kings Cross, I wonder at our ability to adapt. The label of 'new normal' has been attached to us all, like tags on suitcases notifying the authorities of some far-flung destination.

Stepping out onto the platform, I know I'll be the first to tear the tag off, bin the suitcase and roam free once the madness has ended. I've pencilled in the summer of 2021 as the date for a return to the 'old normal'. A long-dreamt of trip to America, east to west coast by Greyhound bus, is my planned coming-out treat for when the war is over.

Twenty minutes later I reach the office, where things are starting to feel a bit more familiar with staff filtering back for a couple of days a week. It's odd though, not hearing Grayson's foghorn of a voice before his face appears. He may be small in stature but he's big in character and his personality used to fill the space.

It's a quarter to eight by the time I'm sitting at my boss's desk, computer fired up and ready to go. I stare out across London, the sky above the concrete towers a hazy red glow. A momentary rush of excitement flows through me, the bright halo on the horizon a beacon of hope for the future.

'Kristi. You're on time. What a pleasant surprise.' Grayson's face appears on screen, like a huge golden sovereign. The usual puckered forehead has been ironed flat; the Spanish lifestyle has covered up the stress fractures.

'Good to see you too. How's life in the sun?'

'Can't complain. Listen, can we get started? I've a busy day ahead.'

'You're not golfing again, boss. It must be tough living there.'

'You can say that again. Anyway. Your column.'

I hold my breath. 'What do you think?'

'An honest opinion?'

My stomach churns.

'Bloody brilliant. Yes, *Lies and Lockdown* will debut this week.'

'That's great news. Thanks. You'll not regret it.'

'A question though. Was I the inspiration for the screenshot murder theme? I promise I'm in Spain. And I definitely didn't murder that rat Barton.' Grayson laughs, slapping his hands up and down on his desk.

'Sort of. Thing is, Grayson, I might have a really big scoop for next week.'

'Go on.'

'Catching a murderer by screenshot is not that far-fetched. You see, I think I've solved the mystery of Barton's murder by using that very method.'

Barton spent his life trying to beat all the other hacks to the biggest scoop but always lagged a step or two behind. He never asked for help, hoping to hog the limelight, but his egotism slowed him down.

His failure to share has taught me a lesson, and today I tell Grayson everything, all about my theory and carefully secreted evidence.

'Bloody hell, Kristi. Send over the pictures. What a story!'

'You can't tell anyone until I've been to the police. Promise me you won't.'

'My lips are sealed but you be sure to get your draft to me asap. What a headline. It can accompany your *Lies and Lockdown* angle. Brilliant work. Barton will be turning in his grave.'

When I log off, I head for Matthew's office to delegate responsibilities for the next few days. He's still definitely peeved that I jumped over him for promotion, but he'll make a good right-hand man going forward and this is his chance to prove himself.

As I prepare to knock on Matthew's door, Barton's philosophical approach to life rings in my ears.

'Life is changing,' he said. 'We need to learn to go with the flow, lose the tunnel vision. It's a new flow, not the new normal,' was how he put it. 'Kristi, you need to embrace change, grab chances when they come along and avoid life in a rut.'

I wipe away a stray tear and remember something else he'd said. 'Life's far too short.'

# 74

Clifton turned up unannounced at Rihanna's cottage a few days after she told him about the baby. Rihanna had clung to the hope that once he'd had time to think it over, he'd mellow, consider other options. He'd told her often enough he loved her, that they'd be together soon. But Rihanna was wrong. Clifton's initial measured response when he'd heard about the pregnancy had been replaced by anger and frustration.

'I thought you were on the pill?' Clifton spat.

'I was. But I had that stomach upset for a couple of days. Remember?' Rihanna's tears dribbled silently down her cheeks. She swooshed the back of her hand across her face. 'Please sit down. We need to talk it through.'

Clifton stomped around the cottage like a caged lion. He lifted up photo frames, set them down again and ran his fingers along books lining the shelves.

'Listen. How far gone are you?'

Rihanna stared in horror at her lover. She looked down at her stomach and set a protective hand on top.

'I've already told you. Twelve weeks.'

Clifton stretched out his hands. 'Come here.'

Rihanna tentatively leant into his chest before slumping against him, her hands gripping as if to the edge of a crumbling rock face. She was scared to speak, even more scared to listen.

Clifton gently nudged her away, wiping her face with a stubby finger and pulled her down beside him on to the sofa.

'It's not too late for an abortion.'

'What?'

'An abortion. I can pay. You don't want to be tied down by a kid, do you? The timing's all wrong.'

'For you maybe.' Rihanna shoved him off, got up and shouted at him. 'I'm in my late twenties and I'm keeping this child. If you don't want to be involved, I'll do it myself.'

'You're crazy, and what about Annabel? She can't know. How the hell are we going to keep this a secret? She's already all over the place.'

Rihanna walked slowly towards the door, undid the latch and threw it wide.

'Bye, Clifton.'

'I'm not leaving.'

'You are and it'll be the last time. And, don't worry. I'll not say a word to Annabel. That's your job.'

Rihanna lay down and didn't move for a couple of hours after Clifton left. Cold air seeped through gaps in the old wooden window frames and caused a numbness in her hands and feet.

She finally got up, went and twisted the thermostat on the heating. Flashbacks of Clifton lifting up her cat, swinging it by the tail until the squealing stopped, had come crashing through her thoughts again. Although it was years ago, it seemed like yesterday. *Bobbles* had been the name of her first pet.

'Oh my God. I didn't mean for that to happen. Shit.' Clifton had gingerly laid down the dead animal. 'It was only meant to be a bit of fun. You shouldn't have given me an ultimatum. Again.'

It was always Rihanna's fault. Every time Clifton walked away, she blamed herself. She'd even apologised for pushing him to kill the cat. But there'd be no apology this time.

As the kettle boiled on the hob, whistling with untimely melody, she made up her mind. This was the end of the road for her and Clifton. More importantly, it was also going to be the end of Clifton.

As she picked up the phone, she knew it was time to share what she knew. She'd given her lover one chance too many, but he'd had his last.

# 75

Annabel didn't like surprise callers at the house, and it was hard to hide her irritation when Kristi suddenly appeared. But curiosity mingled with irritation as Annabel led her guest back through to the conservatory.

'No Clifton today?' Kristi asked.

'No. No idea where he is. To be honest, it's good not having him under my feet.'

'Everything okay?'

It was far from okay but sharing her problems with Kristi would be like holding up a white flag of surrender. Everyone was playing a game. Annabel knew Clifton was seeing Rihanna again, but didn't really care. It suited her not to have him in the bedroom. Annabel and Clifton, to the outside world, were the perfect couple. Big house, plenty of money, holidays in the sun and champagne on tap. Keeping up appearances had become a way of life and one that suited Annabel.

'Yes. All's good. You? How's Alex?'

'Actually, Annabel. That's why I'm here.'

'Sounds ominous. Make yourself at home and I'll get the drinks.'

'Thanks. But no alcohol. I've got a busy few days ahead.'

Annabel glanced at the clock before disappearing to the kitchen. It was still only midday, but Christ did she need a drink.

~

The first time Annabel had seen Kristi was in Sorrento, at her own wedding to Clifton. She hated Kristi on sight for no other reason than she was with Barton.

Barton had been Annabel's life for as long as she could remember. He was the passion she couldn't forget, the sex that filled her being and no one had ever come close. Marriage to Clifton had brought her acceptance, an enviable lifestyle but Barton had brought her alive.

She lifted out a cut-glass pitcher and filled it with lime and soda, popping ice cubes on top which floated like broken off pieces of glacier; larger chunks lurked below the surface. She plucked a few mint leaves from a fresh plant on the windowsill, sucked on one before adding the rest on top.

With Barton dead, Annabel's simmering jealousy of Kristi had begun to abate. In many ways, Kristi reminded Annabel of Barton. They were both hard to dislike, but with impenetrable armour. It was the confidence, tinged with smugness, that irked Annabel.

As she wandered through with the drinks, Annabel guessed why Kristi was here. She guessed that Kristi had found out about her and Clifton's relationship with Alex and Elisa.

Alex and his wife Elisa had been introduced to Annabel and Clifton by Barton. Alex, an old school friend of Barton's, had hit it off straight away with Clifton. Their friendship was soon sealed by a mutual distrust of Barton.

Elisa and Annabel became close, their bond glued by their relationships with similar types of husband, arrogant liars with roving eyes. The villa in Spain had been a blessing for everyone, but especially the wives. Lounging by the pool, hunky tennis pros for company, Annabel and Elisa sunbathed and enjoyed life's finer pleasures while their husbands worked from home.

Kristi, shoulders bunched forward, sat on the edge of the seat. 'I need to ask you something.'

'Fire away.' Annabel coughed on the mint and let the ice cube, which she'd been sucking, pop back into her glass.

'How well do you know Alex? We're finished by the way.'

'Not that well. Why?'

'I'll come clean, Annabel. I'm fed up with lies and now that Alex and I are over, I may as well ask. You see, I saw you at his house in St Albans not so long ago. You never told me you knew him.'

Annabel sat down, sipped the cold drink and let it burn the back of her throat.

'Hands up. Clifton and Alex are good friends and I get together with Elisa now and then. It didn't seem like my place to tell you, especially once you'd already started seeing Alex.'

'Are they really getting a divorce?'

'I doubt it. I'm sorry, but Alex plays around, and Elisa turns a blind eye. She's too in love with him, petrified he might leave.'

'Why the hell didn't you tell me?'

'It wasn't really up to me. I did warn you about getting involved with married men.'

'What were you doing at Alex's house? Were you visiting Elisa or Alex?'

Annabel couldn't remember. She would either have been popping round for a coffee with Elisa, or to pick up the keys to the villa from Alex. Kristi's angry slit eyes bored into her.

'Don't worry. I wasn't sleeping with Alex, if that's what you're thinking.'

Kristi set her glass down and stood. She zipped up her hoodie and took her mobile and keys off the coffee table.

'I'll make a move. But thanks. And I wasn't worried that you were sleeping with Alex, I just wanted to know.'

Kristi hovered, as if making a decision about what to say next.

'Seeing as we're being honest, I may as well tell you what I know. Clifton is still seeing Rihanna.'

Annabel lifted the glasses and empty pitcher, balancing them precariously in her hands, and carried them through to the kitchen. When she came back into the hall, Kristi was already standing by the front door, slipping her trainers on.

'I do know. Clifton's bad at keeping secrets but thanks for your honesty.' Annabel pulled the front door open, leaning against the wall as Kristi went out. 'Bye. Thanks for coming,' she said.

Kristi got into her car, wound down the window and revved the engine.

'Thanks for the drinks. Take care and hope things work out with you and Clifton.'

'Don't worry about us.' Annabel smiled, full gritted teeth and stretched-back lips. She lifted her arm, shook the Rolex into place and prepared to wave.

'I assume you know that Rihanna's pregnant?' Kristi's voice was crisp and clear.

As Kristi drove off down the drive, Annabel's head spun, and her legs turned to jelly. As the gates closed, she gripped the door frame before slithering to the ground.

# 76

Barton's murder has been like a giant jigsaw puzzle, thrown up in the air and the pieces scattering into corners and dark recesses. Putting it together, bit by bit, has been a challenge but I'm getting there. If I can complete the last couple of sections, then I'll be ready to go to the police.

My hand hovers over the brass door knocker. I take a deep breath and give a gentle rap.

'Coming.' Rihanna's foggy voice calls out straight away.

'Come in.' She opens the door and snaps it shut when I'm inside, pulling a safety chain across.

The cottage is dimly lit, wall lights emitting an eerie glow. I peel off my coat and hang it on a hook by the door.

'Wine? Tea? Coffee?' she asks.

'Whatever you're having. Tea's fine. How are you? You don't look so good,' I say.

'I'm fine but can't sleep properly. Not surprising, really.' Rihanna's smile is weak, insipid like the mug of milky tea she hands me. We sit down together.

'I'm assuming Clifton hasn't mellowed. Is he still intent on an abortion?'

'Yes, but he's more worried that Annabel will find out about the pregnancy.'

'Oh.' I set my mug down. 'I might have let the cat out of the bag.'

'You told Annabel?'

'Yes. I'm really sorry but she's such a bitch, it sort of slipped out. She's known Alex all along and is good friends with Elisa, his wife. She's been lying to me the whole time.'

Rihanna bends down and switches on a floor lamp, the light forming a soft halo around her head which dissipates when she straightens.

'Don't worry. It would have come out soon enough and she deserves to know. Maybe she'll finally kick him out. Funny, I seem to have been waiting my whole life for Clifton and it's taken this long for me to see what a shit he really is.' Rihanna's voice races.

'When you phoned, you said you'd something to tell me. About Clifton and Alex,' I say.

Rihanna unfolds her legs and stretches them out in front of her, reminding me of Fuzzy with her silent posturing. Rihanna straightens a couple of girly magazines on the table before continuing.

'The night Barton was murdered, Clifton came here. We'd just finished the quiz. He told Annabel he was going to the pub, but on his way home he popped by.'

'Go on,' I coax.

'I'd just got into the bath, so came down, let him in and went back upstairs saying I'd be about ten or fifteen minutes.' Rihanna puts her hands together, palms flat, pulling them in towards her face, as if she's offering up a silent prayer.

'Anyway, I didn't bother getting into the bath but threw on a dressing gown instead and headed straight down again. Clifton was on the phone, in the kitchen, talking in a low voice. He didn't hear me, but I listened in and managed to creep upstairs before he realised.'

'Who was he talking to?' I don't really need to ask as it's all starting to slot into place.

'Alex. He was in Durham that night.' Rihanna's face has the guilty look of a child as her tongue runs around her pale lips. 'I heard Clifton's side of the conversation. *Okay. We'll talk when you get home. Don't forget to bring the gun back.* Clifton snapped shut the phone as I walked more noisily down the stairs.'

My hand clasps over my mouth. 'Shit. You mean he knew Alex had shot Barton?'

'Yes. I didn't tell you before because I was still hoping to stay with Clifton. I thought my being pregnant would be the catalyst for him to leave Annabel. If Alex shot Barton, Clifton had an alibi as he was here with me.'

'He'd have let Alex take the blame, is that what you're saying?'

'Yes. I think that was and still is his plan. Barton was blackmailing them both because of what he knew about their insider dealing arrangement. Both Clifton and Alex had plenty of reason to have it in for Barton, but I think it was Clifton's idea to use the Zoom backdrop stage set to keep them both clear from suspicion.'

'But if Alex was found out, then Clifton had an alibi. Also, Clifton wasn't the one to pull the trigger. I have proof through screenshots I took during the Zoom quizzes that Alex's backdrop was different on the two times he joined the group. That's why I went up to Durham. I found out where he was staying and how he did it.' I let out a loud sigh, puffing out my lips.

We both sit for a few seconds in stunned silence as if a bomb has exploded and rendered us speechless in the aftermath.

Rihanna is the first to speak again. 'Listen, do you fancy a proper drink? I might have a small one. My nerves are in shreds.'

'Yes please.' I nod, lips pursed in a weak smile.

Rihanna gets up and picks up a half-drunk bottle of red wine from the sideboard, lifts down a couple of glasses and pours herself a half measure and fills mine to the brim.

'I definitely need this,' she says.

'Me too. Thanks.'

Once we've drunk the wine, talked about what to do next, I finally get up to leave. Rihanna watches from her doorstep as I head down the small flight of stone steps to the road. I glance round at her dark stone cottage, quaint and homely by day, but lonely and isolated by night.

'Thursday morning. I'll come and pick you up. Nine sharp.'

'I'll be waiting,' Rihanna replies. Her arms cross her chest as she hugs herself for warmth and comfort.

The country lanes home are dark, the twisting roads gnarled like my thoughts. A muntjac deer, drawn to my headlights suddenly appears in the road and the car swerves, skidding on the damp surface. When the animal finally jerks to the other side, I slow the car down and pull into a passing place in the road. My heart is thumping, my palms and neck damp.

The near miss with the animal hardens my resolve. Life's too short not to do the right thing. Rihanna and I will go to the police station on Thursday morning and tell them everything.

I drive off again, reminding myself that tomorrow I have one last thing to do.

# 77

At five in the morning, I decide to get up. Nightmares, shot with bloodied battle scenes and macabre distorted images of our Friday Zoom group, have tugged me back and forth from fitful sleep. Annabel's head appeared like Medusa; snakes coiling round her crown. Clifton was pointing at the writhing reptiles with a handgun. Alex held out a thorny bunch of red roses, the petals wilting and falling like drops of blood. Joel was in a circle, holding hands with two small girls with Rihanna in the centre pointing an admonishing finger.

I throw cold water over my face to shock away the images. My eyeballs, cold and glassy in their sockets, look as if they've come from an ocularist's set. I tug a brush through my hair, knot it in a ponytail and go downstairs.

Fuzzy has picked up on my mood and stares at me from the corner of the living room. Her eyes are wide, the drunkenness of contented sleep replaced by nervous tension. Her head moves slowly, her soft tongue caressing her babies, but her eyes follow me.

I put a hand down to reassure her, then pull on my trainers. I dig out a woolly hat and tug it over my ears, noticing that the thermostat by the front door is showing only six degrees.

'Won't be long,' I whisper and wait for Fuzzy to lower her head before I leave. 'Go back to sleep.'

The early morning sky is bright and clear as dawn seeps through. I look up and say a silent prayer before I set off at a light jog around the estate towards the path that skirts the back roads into town. Five minutes in, I build up speed, pounding faster and faster until my brain concedes defeat to my body, and conscious thought gets buried under the pain of aching limbs and physical exhaustion.

An hour later, as I walk home up the hill with my hair flowing loose, hat stuffed into my tracksuit bottoms, I gently dissect everything that's happened.

Six months ago, getting through the days was a challenge, fear, loneliness and anxiety attacking everyone in different ways. Quiz nights became a pastime which kept the nation connected. If Covid-19 has been a random pandemic, a sinister twist of fate, then our Friday Zoom meets have followed a similar path with a likewise unexpected turn of events.

It's hard to work out though, if Barton hadn't set the ridiculous questions, whether Alex and Clifton would have gone ahead and murdered him. They might have found another way to deal with him, but the quiz set-up gave them a chance to create an alibi for murder, which was meant to be solid, if not entirely foolproof. Alex and Clifton would never have guessed that I was going to take screenshots, but they would have assumed the group members would remember the bright yellow canvas hung behind Alex on the night of the murder. The gaudiness of the painting would have been hard to forget.

Clifton has a separate, solid alibi, having been seen in his pub, at least four hours' drive from the scene of the crime, around eight on the night of the murder and Alex had the five other members of the quiz group to confirm the illusion that he had been taking part from Barton's flat in Covent Garden.

We only see what we expect, or what we want to see. If I hadn't taken the screenshots, I'd never have suspected Alex capable of murder. No one else in our Friday group was looking properly at the screens, each of us with our own motives for being present.

But then, how well do we know anyone? There's the problem with Joel's history, for one. I know the questions will definitely come out when the police learn the whole story. Joel could have made one simple mistake, as a teenage boy by sleeping with an underage girl, but it might be more than that. It's up to him to deal with it though. My loyalty is now to the truth as I can no longer protect him.

My main concern is Declan. Warmth trickles through my body when I think of him. Together we might be able to help each other over the next few months and who knows? Maybe there's a chance of a future together. I've saved his life once this year and now want to do everything I can to keep him safe. But he needs to know the truth about what happened to Barton.

When the sun breaks through and the birds are in full song, I'll phone him.

As I turn the last corner and head up the path towards home, I laugh out loud. Fuzzy's head is poking out through the cat flap. My outburst cracks the silence and lets the darkness join in the mirth.

## 78

'Declan. It's me.'

'Jeez. You know how to keep a guy waiting. Where are you?'

'I'm home again. It's a long story. Are you still there?'

Background interference gurgles over his voice.

'Yep, I'm here. Sorry, it's a cheap phone. It'll work better if I park up and take it off loudspeaker.'

'Where are you?'

'Hemel Hempstead, not that far from you and my round finishes in Stevenage. Shall I come over when I'm done?'

'Yes please. Declan, I'd like to talk. There's things you need to know.'

A horn blasts and Declan yells down the handset. 'Bloody idiot. Hang on, Kristi. Road rage is back.'

I smile, not sure if Declan's talking about himself or another driver.

'Fire away. Sounds ominous,' he says.

'It's a long story. I'll wait till you get here.'

'Right. I can be there around six. If you need a shoulder to cry on, I'm your man.' His tone, light and breezy is Declan's barrier against the world. Perhaps it'll fence us both in and keep us safe.

~

I dig around in the freezer and find a batch of chicken jalfrezi curry, neatly labelled and dated. My mother was certain that rationing was about to be introduced in March and spent a couple of weeks cooking all my favourite meals. October's here and the freezer is still full, the inevitable shortages never having materialised.

Last night Mum phoned to check if I was prepared for the second wave of the virus, but I assured her I'd still plenty in reserve.

'Who's this new man, then?' She can read me like a dog-eared book.

'He's not a new man, Mum. He's a friend who delivers fruit and veg, and is dropping by later with a couple of boxes.'

'Whatever you say.' I haven't given her Declan's name, having learnt the hard way that a name given means grandchildren are on the horizon.

'I'll come down at the weekend, I promise, and bring you a box. There's plenty,' I say as Mum blows loudly down the line. By this weekend, once I've dealt with the evidence I've gathered about Barton's murder, my life should hopefully start getting back to normal. Whatever normal now means. At least my nightmares will be confined to pandemic issues, rather than cold-blooded murder.

# 79

I find a couple of half-used candles, uncork a bottle of Merlot and put Ed Sheeran on in the background. It's already six o'clock.

It's been six months, give or take, since I regularly wore dresses. My mother's parting shot was, 'Tidy yourself up, Kristi. Even if he is only the delivery boy, you really shouldn't let yourself go.'

I smooth down the sides of the black dress, straighten the gold clunky necklace and listen to the sound of footsteps on the drive. When the doorbell rings, my stomach flips as I unlatch the door.

'Hi. Come in.'

'My God! You look gorgeous. Can I pocket my face mask and ask for a kiss? Here, I picked this up on the way.' Declan hands me a bottle of Prosecco, puckers his lips and brushes mine, before he bends down and picks up the two large fruit and veg boxes which he'd set on the porch.

'Something smells good.'

'Chicken curry. Mum's recipe.'

~

The eerie glow from the candles and the romantic background melodies weave a calming magic. Declan pours the wine and holds his glass up, clinking it against mine.

'Cheers, and thanks. It's been a long time since anyone cooked for me.'

'It's good to have someone to cook for.'

'What was it you wanted to talk about?' Declan takes a large glug of his wine.

'I'm not sure if you'll believe what I'm about to tell you, but here goes.'

I set my glass down and push my empty plate to one side.

'You remember I said I was with my mother at the weekend?'

'Yes, I remember.'

'I wasn't. I was in Durham, and Newcastle.'

'What the heck were you doing up there?' Declan fills his mouth with the last of his rice, straightens his knife and fork then nods a 'go on'.

'Why don't we sit on the sofa and I'll tell you. We can have apple crumble later, if you've still got an appetite.'

As I clear away the dishes, Declan pops to the cat basket and gently lifts out his baby.

'Can I?'

'He's yours.'

'He'll keep me calm, especially as I'm expecting some sort of bombshell.'

We sit on either ends of the sofa, Declan lounging against a cushion with his eyes stuck to the small bundle of squirming fluff. Through Declan's slim fingers, rogue glimpses of dark kitten fur poke through. His forefinger moves continuously backwards and forwards across his charge.

'Listen to that.' He puts a finger to his lips and tilts his ear.

'What?'

'He's purring. God he's so cute. Right. Where were we?'

## 80

'I know who murdered Barton.'

'What?' Declan's crystal-blue eyes widen.

'After Barton got murdered, everyone started acting strangely. Barton's questions rattled quite a few cages. The fact that nobody in our Friday group wanted to tell the police about the questions had me wondering if one of us could have had anything to do with his death.'

'Ouch.' Declan shakes his finger as the kitten's mouth takes hold. A faint hiss escapes. 'I did wonder, but as the police haven't been too interested in our Zoom group, I didn't give it much thought.'

I get up and puff out the candles which are in their death throes, flickering through a choking smoke.

'Look.' I go to the table where my laptop sits and lift up a series of printed out photos. I sit down again and spread out the images between us, turning them towards Declan.

'I captured an anomaly in screenshots I took on two consecutive Friday nights. The Friday before the murder and the night of the murder. Here.' I point alternately at two pictures.

'What am I looking at?' Declan peers in the half light.

'Can you see what's different in the backgrounds of Alex's screenshots?'

'It's like "Where's Wally?" for fuck's sake.'

'Look again.'

'Ah, there.' He points a finger.

'Exactly. You see, Alex said he was in Barton's flat both times. The large yellow canvas in the background, in both screenshots, would lead anyone who wasn't looking closely, to assume he was in the same place on both occasions. Alex even took me round to Barton's flat and showed me where he was staying, and where he sat on Zoom nights. The canvas was impossible to miss.'

'I'm not really sure I want to hear any more.' Declan raises his eyebrows. 'But go on, I'm listening.'

'The lighting on both the screenshots is dim, the only glow coming from the light above the canvas. Although it's definitely a bit brighter on the second week. If you look closely, you can see that the light fitting is attached to the frame itself, not to the wall. Where your finger is, there's a small flush plug socket in the wall. It's not that easy to pick out in the hazy definition but it's definitely there.'

'Yes, just below the bottom right edge of the sunflower canvas.'

'On week one, same layout, same framed canvas but no socket.'

'Shit. You're saying he wasn't in the same place on both nights?'

'Exactly. The second one, the night Barton was murdered, has been staged. Although the lighting is slightly brighter, that on its own proves nothing.'

'Hardly enough proof that Alex murdered him though, is it? What was the motive?'

'Alex wasn't on the bombshell list of questions, but he

certainly had motive. You see, Barton was blackmailing him. And Clifton.'

'Why?'

'Rihanna told me. She's pregnant, by the way, and Clifton wants nothing to do with the baby. So, she was more than happy to land him in it.'

'Christ. What else is to come?'

Declan lies horizontal as I scrape together the images, and lets his baby waltz up and down his chest.

'Rihanna heard Clifton and Alex talking on the phone, on more than one occasion. Alex works on the maintenance of computer systems at large financial companies where he's able to hack into internal communications and pick up insider information. He then passes on some very hot tips to Clifton at the bank. Together they've made a hell of a lot of illegal money.'

'Jesus.' *Periwinkle* falls down onto the sofa, but a faint purr can be heard when Declan plops him back down onto his stomach, resting a firm hand on top.

'Alex owns a £3 million villa in Marbella, which Annabel and Clifton regularly use.'

'How do you know Barton was blackmailing them?'

'Rihanna and I assume so. She heard Clifton on the phone the night Barton was killed. He was telling Alex to bring the gun back. With Rihanna's testimony and my evidence, I think the police will have enough to bring them in.'

Declan gently pulls himself off the sofa and lays the bundle of fluff alongside its siblings. He wipes his palms up and down on his T-shirt and collapses into the hard chair by the table.

'Do you think Barton was going to blackmail us all about his bloody questions and what he knew? It was this thought that sent me over the edge.' Declan's eyes glaze over.

'Personally, I doubt it. The questions were just Barton being shitty. He thought he was so funny and, I don't think he liked any of us that much. Apart from yours truly, of course.'

'That doesn't explain why you were in Durham.'

'I guessed the police wouldn't be overly excited by the screenshot theory in isolation, so I spent the weekend trawling Premier Inns around Durham and Newcastle to see if anyone remembered Alex. You see, Barton stayed at Premier Inns when he moved around the country and I guessed Alex might do the same. The pair met up regularly when Barton travelled. It was a long shot, I know, but a hunch that paid off. Alex knew that the rooms are all pretty bland, with clean cream walls. Rihanna hadn't, by this stage, told me what she'd heard the night Barton was murdered.'

'And?'

'Bingo. I was exhausted, about to give up and come back when I tried one last hotel, near Newcastle airport, and struck lucky.'

## 81

Declan has moved back onto the sofa and pulled me in to lie against him. He smells fresh, with hints of lemon and oranges. I joke it's a tangy aftershave, but he assures me it's a clinging aroma from the fruit deliveries.

'No one on any of the hotel receptions I visited remembered Alex from the photo I showed them, and there was, of course, no record of an Alex Allard staying anywhere. But at the last hotel, I'd about given up when a chambermaid asked to have a look at the photo.

'She remembered Alex, because after he left, she was cleaning the room and noticed the paint had peeled away where it looked as if someone had stuck a self-adhesive hook on the wall. To hang something on. Look, I took a picture of the wall and there's nothing there, other than the damage.' I turn my phone screen towards Declan.

'Alex most likely hung the canvas up there, it's about the right height, and you can see there's a small flush plug socket on the wall. Alex was definitely in Durham the night Barton was murdered.'

'Will the chambermaid testify to having seen him?'

'Yes. I've got her details and she's tracking down the guy who was working on reception that night as it's likely he'll be able to identify Alex also, even though Alex probably used a different name to check in. I suspect he paid cash and travelled by train so there'll be no CCTV images of number plates.'

'And with Rihanna's evidence, it looks as if you might be able to nail both Alex and Clifton.'

~

Declan strokes my hair, and we giggle when he says I'll have to do as a substitute for his fluffy friend. Then, all of a sudden, I start to cry.

'Jesus. What have I done now?' Declan's face is a picture of horror.

'Nothing. It's all been so stressful and...' I hesitate. 'Lonely. Lockdown and murder. It's a lot to deal with at the same time.'

'Shhh. I'm here now. We'll have fun with our new family when this is all over.'

'Thanks, Declan.'

His kiss is gentle and as he holds my face between his hands, I cry again.

~

It's almost nine o'clock when Declan finally pulls himself up.

'Thanks for supper.'

'Thanks for listening.'

Declan shoves his hands in his jeans and hovers like a nervous schoolboy. 'You'll not need to mention the questions Barton sent us when you give your statement to the police, will you?'

'No. We've all agreed answers anyway, and even if Clifton

and Alex try to put any of our group in the shit, I doubt the police will be that interested. They're trying to solve a murder and won't have time, I suspect, for ancient history.'

'Clifton will go down for insider dealing as well as conspiracy to murder. Serves him right. Never could stand him, and Rihanna's well shot.' Declan takes my hands, before he wraps his arms round my tense shoulders. He's like an anchor tethering me to reality.

'And you'll be well rid of that other prick, Alex. Smarmy git. You really know how to pick 'em.' Declan's lips are soft, encouraging and as I close my eyes, it's as if the life raft has arrived, ready to keep me buoyed till I get to shore.

'Listen, do you want me to stay? I can sleep down here.' His eyes shine.

'Not tonight. I need a few hours' sleep. Rihanna and I are going to the police station first thing in the morning. Maybe you can meet us afterwards?'

Outside there's a sudden rattle and thunderous bang. We jump in unison.

'Shit. What was that?'

'The bins. The wind must have picked up and tossed one aside.'

'If you're sure you don't want me to stay, I'll make a move. Text me what time you want me to come over tomorrow, and I'll pull another sickie.'

'Will do. I'll let you know when we're done but it could take time.'

'Okay. I'll be there. You can count on me.'

With that, Declan is gone.

## 82

How many times had Rihanna tucked herself away in the cottage and waited for the phone to ring? Hovering for crumbs, the stale broken-off bits of hope. She had finished with Clifton more times than she could remember, but his contrite smile, soft promises and strong arms tugged her back and she had lapped up the promises. 2020 lockdown had made the loneliness worse.

The wind howled through invisible gaps. She turned the heat up and drew the curtains. When tomorrow was over, she'd put the cottage on the market. Cambridge would be a starting point and she'd work north until she found her next home, putting distance between herself and the last fifteen years. She patted her stomach, looking down at the miniscule bump. They'd start afresh, her and the baby.

A sudden loud rap at the door made her jump. She fell sideways and grazed her head on the edge of the bookshelf. She sat down and held her breath. But it was too late to turn off the lights.

'I know you're in there. Let me in. I'm sorry, Rihanna. Please.' Clifton's voice hammered through the walls.

Clifton wasn't a beggar, apologies getting choked down like rancid bile. He was good at turning blame away from himself with slick words and white lies to cover his tracks. How many times had Rihanna blamed herself for him not leaving Annabel? Rihanna had been too clingy, too needy, too desperate. Too in love. Getting pregnant had awoken a part of her that she'd smothered with her insecurities. The growing baby was feeding a new determination and Clifton had run out of chances.

The rap of the door knocker got louder, banging like a distant jungle drum roll. Then silence. Rihanna listened for retreating steps down the path and a few minutes lapsed before she dared inch the curtains apart. Clifton's car was still parked down below on the street.

She swung round as the handle on the back door jiggled up and down.

'Rihanna. I've told you to keep the door locked. You never know who could get in.'

Clifton's face appeared before the rest of him. He wiped his feet, slipped off his shoes and laid them neatly inside by the door.

Rihanna's hands shot to her face.

'Rihanna, I just want to explain. Apologise. Listen, I'm really sorry and I can't live without you. I'm going to leave Annabel and will tell her this weekend. This time I promise.'

Clifton tottered forward with baby steps, arms outstretched like a child looking for help.

Rihanna reached instead for the edge of the table. 'It's too late, Clifton. We're over.'

'You can't mean that.'

Rihanna inched backwards, pushing her arms out, palms flattened towards him. 'I do.'

Clifton slapped his hand on the kitchen worktop, the thunderous crack reverberating through the silence. 'I can't let you, Rihanna. It's always been you and me. But you shouldn't have told Annabel about the baby. You promised not to.' His fingers jittered up and down hard on the counter.

'I didn't tell her. When would I have seen her? I don't even have her phone number.'

Clifton's eyes narrowed. Seconds passed.

'Well, if you didn't tell her, then who did?'

The tunnelling wind suddenly gripped the back door which Clifton had left ajar. The bang shook the walls, and an empty glass was catapulted from the draining board, smashing to smithereens at Clifton's feet.

Rihanna knew the sequence. Her ex-lover's default behaviour moved from begging to blame to anger. She thought of her kid brother's transformer toys. From machine to monster in several twists.

'Leave it. I'll clear it up,' Rihanna said.

Clifton lifted up a large broken-off shard of glass, holding it between his thumb and forefinger. Slowly, deliberately, he opened the bin and threw it in.

'Problem is that people don't know when to keep their noses out of other people's business.' Clifton moved up close to Rihanna and put his hands firmly on her shoulders.

'How much more does Kristi know? What have you been telling her? She's the only other person who would have told Annabel about the baby.'

Rihanna winced as his fingers dug into her skin.

'Know about what?' Rihanna asked, eyes wide.

'Don't play the innocent with me. I can read you too well. Kristi's been stirring things up with all her *Lockdown Lies* shit. She'd better not be planning on sharing with the police what she thinks she knows. All that bullshit about screenshot set-ups. I mean, I ask you.'

Clifton dropped his hands to his side, prowled round the room, his chin jutting forward, and his mouth clamped shut.

'She thinks Alex might have killed Barton,' Rihanna whispered.

'What? Why, for God's sake?' Clifton's response was accompanied by a blast of spittle.

Rihanna moved very slowly back towards the front door.

'I don't know. Listen, it's nothing to do with me. I haven't said anything, you know I wouldn't.' She glanced down and patted her stomach.

Clifton stepped forward and stubbed a finger hard against her chest. His eyes were black.

'I'm warning you. You open your mouth and I'll be back,' he hissed.

Rihanna felt her face drain of colour and, not daring to move, she hovered until Clifton stepped away and pushed her to one side.

He pulled the chain back and opened the front door. The wind caught and catapulted it against the inside wall with a thud.

'I was never really going to leave Annabel,' he said. 'I think you got the wrong end of the stick.' Clifton's laugh got swallowed up by the ferociousness of the gale. 'Anyway, I've got another visit to make tonight. Bye for now.' He yelled over his shoulder and marched down the stone steps towards his car.

The phone kept going to voicemail. After six attempts, Rihanna left a message.

'*Kristi. Kristi. Please call me back. It's Rihanna. I think Clifton's on his way round to yours and he's furious, murderous. I've never seen him so mad.*'

Rihanna picked up the phone again, scrolled through contacts and then pressed 'call'. There was only one other person who might be able to help.

## 83

It's five minutes past nine when I wave Declan goodbye, lock the front door and pull the chain across. Sweat, salty and glistening, coats my limbs but my tongue runs over parched lips trying to irrigate an arid landscape. The anxiety kicks in moments after he's disappeared from view.

The full moon, a bright golden globe, beams its brilliance through the living room window. Fuzzy is alert, eyes like black tourmaline gemstones, opaque and resinous as she arches and pulls herself up.

'Shhh. Go back to sleep.' I run a palm firmly along my cat's back, soothing the white lustrous coat. Her lids, sharp knife-edged slits, battle closure. Her four babies are knitted together; one large dark ball, the rich edging to her ermine fur.

I no longer have a choice. When the dawn chorus breaks, I'll be waiting outside the police station with the evidence. It's time to come clean. Of course, I should have owned up sooner. But what are friendships, if they don't include loyalty? I've been trying to protect people I hardly even know, letting them hold close their darkest secrets. But tomorrow, it'll all be over.

Rihanna will be with me, her testimony the icing on the cake of proof.

I bend down and open the small drinks cabinet. The whisky bottle calls to me like the Drink Me Bottle in *Alice in Wonderland*. I half-fill a glass, crack my lips and swallow. A burning flame ignites my throat, like an out-of-control forest fire and tears sting my eyes. I collapse onto the sofa, plump up the cushions and close my eyes. I feel my body shrink as I slither through the rabbit hole and tumble towards oblivion. Not long to go.

A swaying tree branch raps against the window and rattles the glass. As the whisky tumbler slides from my slackened fingers and smashes to the floor, I'm shocked awake. The tapping is persistent, rhythmical and through a foggy brain, I hear a ghostly voice calling my name.

'Kristi. Kristi. Are you there? Can I come in?' A sharp bang rounds off the persistence.

The golden moon circle has dipped sideways, sunk low on its jet-black canvas. The outline of a person, face pressed tight up to the window, is shadowy, indistinct. But I know who it is. What the hell does he want so late? Shit. The curtains are too wide apart for me to feign sleep.

The beat of knuckles moves from the window to the door and the voice gets louder.

I drag myself up, my head thick and pounding. It crosses my mind it was odd that he didn't phone first but then remember I've turned my phone on silent.

'Okay. I'm coming,' I yell. As I unchain the door again, I check the time. It's still only nine forty.

'Christ it's cold out here.' Clifton rubs his hands, blows into cupped palms and steps inside, pushing the door firmly shut.

Annabel must have told him she knows about Rihanna's baby. My mind is slow, my head muzzy as it ratchets up the thoughts. Yet, Clifton is surprisingly calm. Maybe Annabel hasn't thrown my name to the wolf. Otherwise, why is he here? He has no idea that I've pieced together the murder jigsaw and doesn't know that I'm going to the police tomorrow.

'We need to talk, Kristi.' Clifton sets his car keys on the table and looks at me. A vein throbs in his neck which is red and hardened from alcohol. Smoking has helped raise his blood pressure, but Annabel has, more than once, assured me that pills have it under control. I think she tries to put her own mind at ease.

I move towards the kitchen.

'I'll put the kettle on.' My voice is hoarse. 'Is it about Annabel? Rihanna? Yes, I know about the affair and–' I rattle with the mugs, but Clifton cuts me off mid-sentence.

'You told Annabel, didn't you? About the baby as well.' His face is blank, his mood calm or perhaps the pot is simmering, on the way to the boil. Hard to tell. My head is thick from nightmares and whisky.

Fuzzy's sudden squeal makes me turn. She's frightened.

'What have you got in there?'

Clifton moves back into the lounge and hovers over the cat bed.

'Would you look at those?' His voice brightens as he peers down.

I try to push in between Clifton and the cat bed, but he stands firm. Images of what he did to Rihanna's cat all those years ago flash up. He stares down at the animals.

'Oh, that's my cat; and her litter.'

'You know Rihanna once had a cat. Met a sad end.'

'Let me make the tea and we can talk.' I turn away, willing him to follow.

In the kitchen, I grip the sink to steady the shake in my hands. I put a tea bag in each mug and pour over the boiling water. I need time to think. I squish the tea bags round and round.

'Milk, no sugar, please.' As Clifton's voice booms in my ear, I lose my grip on a mug and watch it smash to the floor, china shards scattering everywhere.

'Shit. You scared me.' My voice is shaky.

'I can see that. Now come and tell me why I frighten you. I'm not in any hurry.'

I dig out a dustpan and brush from under the sink. 'Let me clear up first.'

'Leave it. I'm not that thirsty.' Clifton puts a hand firm against my bottom and slaps me back in the direction of the living room.

I collapse into the hard chair while Clifton looms over me.

'Listen, Clifton, I'm really sorry about telling Annabel but there's been so many secrets lately it sort of slipped out. She deserves to know.'

'Don't you think that was up to me to decide?' He bends down on hunkers in front of me. 'You see, Kristi,' he hisses, 'you need to keep your nose out of other people's business.' His breath, rancid and stale, wafts up my nose but fear keeps me silent.

'I saw the ideas for your column. You think you're so bloody clever. You and Barton deserved each other. Go on, tell me. Who murdered him?'

As Clifton straightens up, his knee creaks like an unoiled hinge. He wrings his hands together.

'I've no idea. Why are you asking me?' My vibrato voice quavers. Clifton needs to believe that I've no idea and that I've let it go.

Suddenly I spot the screenshots which Declan tidied up

before he left. They're in a neat pile but perched on the edge of the table.

'I'm interested in your theories. I've a good idea myself who killed the bastard, but I'll tell the police what I know, not you. The questions Barton asked gave a few people in the Friday group good reason to finish him off. There's Joel, and of course, your precious Declan. Did you know he's murdered before?'

The room spins on its axis, round and round. I'm scared I'll not be able to stand up.

Clifton takes a step towards the table and picks up the screenshots. He licks his thumb and works through them. He pauses at the one where I've ringed the plug socket with a dark felt-tip pen. His eyes flick back to me.

'What the hell's this?'

'What?'

'Don't you fucking play with me.' He throws the picture my way but suddenly his hand appears and shoves my head hard down towards the ground as I bend to pick it up. 'What is this?'

My grandmother's cuckoo clock gears up for the ten o'clock chorus, the wind-up clunky and laboured. When the bird appears and begins the Koo-Koo chorus, Clifton's voice momentarily gets swallowed up.

## 84

The kittens are shuffling about in the basket, scratching, meowing, and Fuzzy is stiffly upright like a painted ornament. Low intermittent squealing noises tells me she senses danger, but her body is rigid. Suddenly I let rip.

'Alex murdered Barton, but you know that. Were you too scared to do it yourself? Did you think if Alex got caught, you'd walk? Did you give him the gun? And was it your idea to stage the backdrop as his alibi?' My voice speeds up, the accelerator teasing me to lose control as my words get louder. A band of perspiration has collected on my forehead and on my neck, but I carry on, fear making me reckless.

'Alex hacked the computers, passed the information on to you and you used it to make money. Is that how Alex paid for his palace in Marbella?' I sit motionless, cemented to the chair.

Clifton moves away, wanders round the room. His right hand slips inside his jacket.

'I'll not say anything, I promise. As you say, it's none of my business.' My voice pleads as my eyes follow his hand, but instead of a gun, he pulls out a stiff white handkerchief, wraps it round his flattened nose and honks into it like a foghorn. Wind howls through a crack in the kitchen window, and hairs stand up on my neck.

Clifton moves back towards the cat bed and looks down at Fuzzy.

'This is what we're going to do, Kristi.' He puts his hand down, grabs Fuzzy by the scruff of the neck and hoists her up.

'Leave her alone!' I scream, catapulted from the chair. I grab his arm, but this encourages him more, as he kicks out with his shoe, catching my shin before he swings the cat round in the air. Fuzzy's howling mingles with the wind. Claws widen, but without a target her shrieks get louder. Clifton holds her squirming body off to one side.

'A vicious little madam. Reminds me of someone.' He smirks.

'Please. Please. Put her back.' As I rub my bruised shin, Fuzzy's puckered face makes me cry.

Clifton drops the cat on top of the litter.

'You bastard.' I lunge towards the basket, but Clifton grips my wrists.

'I'm warning you,' he hisses in my face. 'One word to the police and you'll be sorry. Keep your mouth shut, or I'll shut it for you and your precious cats.'

Clifton slams the door when he leaves, the bang like a kettle drum hammering out a finale. I collapse onto the floor, shoulders heaving with silent sobs. But the sight of Fuzzy hobbling tentatively towards me bursts the dams and I can't control the flood.

Fuzzy crawls onto my lap, nudges her head close into my chest. Her body is stiff, but warm.

The screen on my mobile suddenly lights up. It's on the table by the photographs and I remember I forgot to turn the volume back on. It must be nearly ten thirty. Who the hell is ringing me now?

## 85

After Clifton left, I managed a bout of fitful sleep. Fuzzy reluctantly crawled back to her babies while I collapsed onto the sofa. I remember looking at the clock at one, two and three before I finally gave in.

My alarm pierces my slumber at eight sharp and unlocks the day ahead. I get up, tidy the lounge and down three strong coffees before showering. The hot water scalds my body as I try to cleanse away last night's events, Clifton's threats still ringing in my ears.

Fuzzy follows me aimlessly around, expectant but unsure of what. I ring Rihanna to see if she can be ready any earlier and laugh when she tells me her coat is already on. Before I lock up and leave the house, I try Declan's number, but it doesn't connect. I send him a text telling him we're on the way, earlier than planned, to the police station and I'll call him when we're done.

~

An hour later and Rihanna and I are sitting patiently in the police interrogation room, my head thick from lack of sleep and fear but my mood buoyed by sense of purpose. It's as if I'm nearing the end of a marathon, the finishing line in sight. The stone-grey walls lend sombre comfort.

'I rang Declan after Clifton stormed out. I left a voicemail, telling Declan I was worried you might be in danger. Did he get back?' Rihanna's voice shivers.

'Thanks. He rang me around ten thirty, but I told him I was fine. I didn't tell him about Clifton's visit as I didn't want to worry him anymore.'

'Does Declan know we're at the police station?'

'Yes. I told him we were coming in.'

Rihanna stares down at her feet. She's unusually subdued, but then it's a big ask to hand over the father of her unborn baby on a plate to the police. Clifton is looking at a long stretch for insider dealing, as well as conspiracy to murder. I put a hand over hers.

'It'll be okay. We're doing the right thing.'

As we wait to give our statements, I check my mobile for messages, having switched it to silent. There's none from Declan. He hasn't read my WhatsApp messages either; strange as he usually responds quickly. I get up and turn to Rihanna.

'Give me five minutes. I'm popping out to call Declan.'

On the way, I pass the detective and explain I won't be long.

Outside, the sun is bright, fiercely piercing the chill cloudless sky. My fingers are moist, the phone slippery in my grasp.

*'Declan. It's me. We're at the police station. Haven't heard from you. Please call. We're about to give our statements. It's ten thirty. Bye.'*

Once I've left the voicemail, I take a deep breath, leave the phone on vibrate and head back inside.

## 86

It's exactly midday when Rihanna rounds off her statement. Her words exploded into the recording machine like an eruption of bottled-up fizz. Her eyes are streaming, a heavy downpour of tears, now that she's finished.

'Well done. I know that can't have been easy,' DCI Arbuthnot says, handing Rihanna a tissue box. Rihanna left nothing out, giving her testimony credence by recounting her relationship history with Clifton in detail. The detective then turns to me.

'Right, Miss Dexter. Perhaps you'd like to give us your version of events.'

The detective runs a palm over his silver-grey pate, and clasps his hands behind his neck, his bony elbows pointing east and west. 'In your own time.'

Arbuthnot clicks the recording machine back on.

The telling is harder than I imagined. I display the screenshots, embarrassed at recounting my short pathetic dating history with Alex. I relay details of my trip to Durham, proudly presenting particulars of the hotel where he stayed along with the name and mobile number of the chambermaid who remembered seeing him. I show the detective pictures of the wall in the hotel where Alex must have hung the canvas and subsequently damaged the paintwork, pointing out the small plug socket.

Finally, I round off my statement by recounting Clifton's threatening visit last night.

'Most impressive. Well done, Miss Dexter.' Arbuthnot clicks the machine off, reels his elbows in and sets his arms down on the table.

I turn to Rihanna, whose pale face is blotchy round the eyes from crying and rubbing. She looks at me. Something doesn't feel right, and she senses it too. I lean forward.

'Ladies, I now need to tell you both something. I've been keeping it until I got your full statements as you've certainly given the police plenty to think about.' Arbuthnot blinks hard, eyelids flickering open and closed, and rubs his thumb and fingers up and down his chin. He blasts out a pent-up steam of air before he continues.

'We arrested someone this morning for the murder of Mr Barton Hinton and have them already in custody.'

'What? Who?' Rihanna and I speak together, our eyes locked on the detective.

'Unfortunately, I can't release that information yet. Suffice to say, fresh evidence has given us enough to make an arrest and charge someone with the crime.'

'Is it Alex. Mr Allard?'

'Clifton? It can't be Clifton.' Rihanna grips the table end.

'I'm really sorry, ladies, but I'm not in a position to say anything further at this stage. But rest assured, we will thoroughly look into everything you've told us. Insider trading and hacking with intent can carry lengthy prison sentences. Your detective work won't have been in vain.'

The silver fox stands, pulls back his shoulders and extends his hand. 'Thank you, both. We'll definitely be in touch.'

# 87

## The night of the murder

Maybe lockdown had addled Alex's brain, logical thought killed off by the pandemic that swept the nation. A madness had taken hold and his brain had become like a shrivelled walnut in a hard crenellated casing as he lost touch with reality. When Clifton talked about murder, producing a handgun from his private collection, Alex at first assumed it was some sort of a joke. A Wild West spoof.

'Ha ha. That's a good one. No seriously, what the hell are we going to do? Should we just pay Barton off?' Clifton's unsmiling face was stony like a weathered rock.

'I'm not joking. We need to silence him. You do realise, if our insider dealing gets out, we're looking at prison time.' Clifton drew breath as Alex digested his words. 'And I'm certainly not going to buckle to Barton's blackmailing demands. Never. Over my dead body.' Clifton strutted around the room like a bull teasing the matador with sharp horns and restless hooves.

'Bloody hell. I mean a bit of insider dealing is one thing, but murder? You're crazy.'

Alex's pulse raced, his life passing before his eyes, as if he himself was looking down the gunman's barrel.

'What are you suggesting? Pistols at dawn?' Alex rubbed his eyes and ran palms across his cheeks. His fingers trembled over the stubble on his chin.

'I've given it plenty of thought,' Clifton said. 'It's time to finish the bastard off for good. At least listen to my plan.'

Clifton's plan, flimsily brushed aside at first, soon festered like an angry spot. As events in Alex's life spiralled out of control, the scheme looked like the only solution.

When Alex's suitcase, raggedly packed with the zip half closed, had landed in the hall, and Elisa had slammed shut the bedroom door, the only person Alex could think of going to for help was Clifton. Usually, Barton would have been his first port of call, but since the blackmailing had started, Alex headed straight for his partner-in-crime.

The plan to murder Barton wasn't a spur of the moment decision, based on a single moment of madness, or pent-up fury, but rather a hotchpotch of ingredients that came to the boil with Alex at the centre of the overheating cauldron.

Elisa threw him out after she learnt of his online dates with Kristi, but his wife's discovery wasn't coincidence. Barton must have told Elisa because no one else knew at that stage.

A few days later, when Barton suggested with a wide boyish grin that he'd always fancied a villa in Marbella, Alex realised it wasn't a joke. Barton was turning the screw.

'Perhaps an early Christmas present?' Barton had laughed and slapped his hands together, the sharp smack loaded with threat. Barton promised, a finger held up over closed lips, that the insider dealing would never surface if he got the Spanish villa keys this side of Christmas. The gift would buy his silence.

Then, of course, there was Clifton. Alex's business buddy harboured a long-seated hatred of Barton which had been seriously fuelled by the quiz questions. Barton had given Clifton plenty of reason to take him out when the latter's engagement to Rihanna came to light. But it was Clifton's small-man insecurity that had taken the major blow when he realised Barton had slept with Annabel shortly before their wedding. It hadn't taken him long to work out the reasons for the Annabel tattoo questions. Barton was taunting him, letting him know that he'd had sex with his wife.

Clifton wanted Barton dead, and together, he and Alex could get away with murder. Clifton had planned the whole thing.

~

'How, for fuck's sake?' Alex's hands had developed a steady tremble, like a tremor building in the wake of an approaching earthquake. 'You can't just go up to a guy and shoot him. I'd rather go to prison for playing the financial system than for murder.'

'What if you had a cast-iron alibi?'

'Go on.'

'Your fancy piece, Kristi, took screenshots when you suddenly appeared at quiz night.'

'And?'

'She emailed them to Annabel. There's a couple of you in Barton's flat, with that ridiculous overpriced yellow and blue canvas in the background. I've seen them.'

'So? What are you on about?'

'Hear me out. If you followed Barton up to Durham, met up

with him this coming Friday before the Zoom meet, pulled the trigger then you could turn up to the quiz as usual at eight. All you need to do is take the painting with you, hook it up and use the same backdrop as before. A blank wall, such as those in all the Premier Inns Barton has stayed at over the years with the bright memorable canvas hung up behind, would be your alibi. Everyone would assume you were in Barton's flat in Covent Garden. Who would know otherwise?'

Like a migrant, desperate to cross the Channel, it felt to Alex as if Clifton was trafficking a flimsy rubber craft.

'Firstly, someone would need to have screenshots this Friday for comparison. Who's going to take them? You can't rely on Kristi taking them again.' Alex went through the questioning motions.

'Don't worry. Annabel will take them. I'll make sure. I'll think of some reason, leave her to me.'

Of course, Clifton had come up with a pre-meditated murder plan, where he got someone bumped off without having to pull the trigger himself. All Alex had to do was work out how to lure Barton to some desolate location and blow his brains out.

## 88

'*Nearly there. See you soon.*'

Alex used a cheap pay-as-you-go burner phone to call Barton that morning and to text him throughout the day confirming location and time of meeting up. Old friends. Alex told Barton he had a job in Newcastle, and it seemed a shame not to get together for a catch up, a few beers. He could be with him around six.

Alex found himself in a pub by the river, knocking back shot after shot, as six o'clock came and went. He had dialled Barton's number several times since five, left a message but the last call made ten minutes earlier hadn't connected.

The Premier Inn where Barton was staying was only five minutes away, so after Alex downed the last glass, he got up, wound his scarf tight before buttoning up his dark raincoat and throwing the hood over his head.

The thunderstorm was at full force as he hurried across the small, deserted precinct and down the stone steps that led to the hotel. When he reached the foyer, as luck would have it, the receptionist had her back turned and he was able to head unnoticed straight up the stairwell by the entrance. Room number 10 was on the first floor. Glancing up and down the empty corridor first, he rapped hard on the door.

'Barton. Barton. Are you there? It's me, Alex.' He put his ear tight to the wood and listened. He kept knocking at regular intervals for several minutes before he tried Barton's mobile again, but there was still no connection.

Barton had disappeared or else had deliberately given Alex the slip.

~

As Alex jumped onto the train back to Newcastle, getting into an empty carriage, he shivered. Water dripped from his forehead into his eyes and his fingers were numb. He pulled off his soggy trainers and settled his feet on the heat vent under the window as the train pulled out of Durham station.

He took out his phone, noting three messages from Clifton, but still nothing from Barton. As the train rattled through the darkened countryside, Alex's head throbbed. A steady flow of relief began to warm his body when he realised that instead of 'getting away with murder', he'd got away 'without murdering'. What the hell had he been thinking? Barton's no-show had brought him to his senses and saved both their lives.

By the time he arrived in Newcastle, his head was clearing, the fuzziness dissipating, and he realised he'd had a lucky escape. Turning off the phone, he headed for the taxi rank. He'd be back at the hotel where he was staying overnight in plenty of time to join the quiz.

He took the stairs up to his room two at a time, whistling gently as he slipped the key card into the slot. Once inside, the sight of the staging, with the bright yellow and blue canvas hanging on the wall behind the desk which held his laptop, made him smile. What the hell had he been thinking? He went across and straightened the canvas which he'd hung on a white plastic hook, and then clicked on the small battery-powered light attached to the frame. He'd leave it there, seeing no reason to let on where he really was. Everyone would assume he was at Barton's flat again. Why tell them otherwise?

He had forty minutes to spare before the quiz was due to start, so stripped off and headed for the bathroom where he swivelled the shower setting to full power. Closing his eyes against the scalding assault, he stepped under the cascade and scrubbed hard to remove all traces of evil intent.

With five minutes to spare, he dimmed the lights in the bedroom and sat down with his back to the canvas and switched on his laptop. He turned his burner phone back on before he clicked 'join meeting' and saw there were another three missed calls from Clifton. He got up again, went back to the bathroom and smashed the mobile screen with the shower head, over and over, until it went blank.

At one minute to eight, he was ready to rejoin the real, but virtual world.

## 89

Two hours later, exhausted not only from the washout in Durham waiting for Barton, but also the play-acting on screen, Alex finally switched off the computer. As he lifted the canvas off the wall, yanking when it got stuck, he cursed as the plastic hook dislodged, and flakes of paint drizzled to the floor like accusatory dandruff.

He undressed, flung his clothes over the chair and pulled on a clean white bathrobe which he found in the wardrobe. He slumped on the edge of the bed, the evening's events having left him feeling like a stage actor might, anticlimactic, as he came down from a theatrical high. The earlier alcohol shots, their potency weakening by the minute, had left him dehydrated, and the battle back to soberness was only beginning.

With his hands over his face, head bent forward, he began to cry. Heaving sobs, like those from a five-year-old on the naughty step, wracked his body and silent rivulets dribbled down to his chin. He reached for the remote control and switched on the television. In the corridor outside the bedroom, new arrivals' voices carried through the flimsy walls. The clunk of luggage, excited chatter and heavy footsteps set his nerves jangling.

The local news was running, devastation caused by the storm already having led to tragedy. Powerlines were down in Sunderland and a fallen tree on some remote coastal road had caused what looked like a fatal accident.

Then a picture of Durham, the brightly lit cathedral filling the screen as it towered over the River Wear near Prebend's Bridge, appeared above a red strapline of breaking news.

*Early reports are coming in of a shooting near Prebend's Bridge in Durham. A body has been discovered on the towpath beneath the cathedral. Local police are asking for witnesses to come forward. If you were in the area at any time this evening, please call the number below.*

Alex was a sceptic, humouring Elisa when she talked about sixth sense, ghosts and the afterlife. But as his eyes bore through the screen, he knew that instinct and sixth sense were one and the same thing. He guessed instantly who had been killed and what might have happened. A glance across at the discarded canvas told him it might have been a wise decision to stage his backdrop.

But who the hell had pulled the trigger?

# 90

Emotionally drained like blood donors' arms, Rihanna and I don't talk much on the way back from the police station. I drop her off and wait until she's reached her front door.

'Bye. Speak later,' I call through the open car window. Her wave is limp, hand flapping like wet lettuce.

Although Detective Arbuthnot didn't tell us who had been arrested, he did shake his head in a conspiratorial manner when Rihanna pushed for confirmation that it wasn't Clifton or Alex. If it had been Alex, Clifton would be in the frame for conspiracy to murder. I assume Rihanna's history with Clifton and their impending baby was the reason she had cried heavy sodden tears of relief.

I pull out into the empty High Street and head for home. My car skitters in sync with my brain, swerving this way and that. I career round a fallen tree branch and narrowly miss a lone cyclist. He shakes an angry finger, a gloved spoke, as I honk my impatience.

I slip my mobile into the side pocket of the door, secreting the temptation to keep checking for messages. The silence from the device speaks volumes, but I'm not sure what it's telling me.

Lack of communication from Declan has set my nerves on edge.

As I park up outside my house, I notice the paint peeling off the white facia boards, small black rotting patches spread through like a contagion. The paving slabs which lead to the front door are cracked and uneven, rogue slithers of green slime dotting their surface.

I turn my face towards the watery October sun with its beaming icy smirk. Perhaps I'll browse summer holidays later, pick out a special half-price deal and make plans for a future which beckons on the horizon.

My key grinds in the lock as rusting flakes float to the ground. Declan promised to fit a new lock and as I look back at the slippery slabs, I remember him telling me he'd ordered a pressure washer on Amazon.

'It'll clean those slabs in no time,' he'd said.

I feed the cats and turn the heat up, the chill amplified by the quietness. My stomach rumbles, but I can't eat. A heavy unease has settled, like cold pasta, in the pit of my gut and blocks out the hunger. I dig out a rogue Green Tea tea bag from the back of the cupboard, rinse through last night's mug and pour over the boiling water. The harsh aroma stings my nostrils.

While I wait for the computer to boot up, I head upstairs and change into leggings and a warm sweatshirt. The blanket which Declan tucked in under Fuzzy as she went into labour, is hanging loose over the side of the wardrobe. The room seems smaller than usual, the walls closer together.

Five minutes later I'm back downstairs and have all the screenshots displayed on my computer in gallery view. Apart from Alex's backdrop, which I know was staged, nothing looks out of the ordinary. On a notepad I scribble. I think of my childhood Cluedo obsession. Solving a murder by linking together three things: the murderer, the weapon and the room where the crime was committed.

The kitchen, the ballroom, the conservatory, the hall, the billiards room, the study, the lounge, the library and the dining room. It takes a minute or two but I'm bizarrely chuffed that I don't have to google the combinations. The characters don't come to memory so easily but like our Zoom quiz, there were six people in the frame. My old, tattered set, once my mother's, was complete with Miss Scarlett, Professor Plum, Mrs Peacock, the Reverend Green, Colonel Mustard and Mrs White.

On the screen in front of me, I stare at the pictures of the Friday night Zoom guests and their backgrounds. I doodle a picture of a gun at the top of my notepad and circle it. There is no doubt about the weapon of choice. I then write down the names of each person and where they were on the week when I took the screenshots for the first time and the following week when the murder took place.

I have only one aim, to convince myself that Declan didn't kill Barton with a single shot, or alternatively, hire a hitman to carry out the crime for him. Declan has contacts who know how to aim guns and evade capture.

Suddenly my future happiness seems to depend on Declan being innocent.

# 91

My eyes are soon dried out like shrivelled prunes from staring at the computer screen. I've scribbled over several pages of the notepad, letting my mind roam wild with various computations. Although there is the possibility that some random member of the public, or someone holding a deep dark grudge could have murdered Barton, I keep coming back to our Zoom group.

The questions Barton sent still drive me in that direction. Alex and Clifton might have planned to kill Barton but perhaps Alex got cold feet? He doesn't seem like a pre-meditating murderer, but then I never really got to know him. Clifton would never have done the deed himself. He's a coward with a capital C. Little dog syndrome. Big bark, nasty bite but small and gutless. I put a huge line through the duo, certain now that they're not suspects, fuelled by the detective's insinuations.

Rihanna's screenshots are dark, romantic lighting smothered by the heaviness of the cottage's ancient beams. A small table light has bathed her head and shoulders in a film of brightness. But there's no variation from the week before the murder and the night of the murder. She sat in the same position on both nights. I draw the black felt tip through her name. She's definitely the Miss Scarlett of the group, a femme fatale in bright seductive clothing, but no killer.

I lean forward as I stare at Declan's screen. A picture tells a thousand stories. His mother's hovering hand as she passes him a cup of tea has been captured in one shot. A veined white claw dotted with deepening liver spots. The heavy rain beating relentlessly behind Declan wasn't staged. Sad, but I've even checked the weather report for the days in question.

It's hard to imagine Declan walking into the sea in a suicide bid, having just instructed someone to carry out a murder on his behalf. He's not a coward, but my felt tip hovers.

The last two screenshots are of Joel. They've seemed so insignificant, a bit like Joel, that I haven't really studied them properly. He's my Reverend Green of the group. Pious, holier-than-thou. Joel always knows best, and he views everyone, apart from himself, as a fool.

I stare at his bland backgrounds. The first one looks as if it was taken in a lounge, but he's so close up to the screen that there's not much detail and it's hard to be certain. To the right of one shoulder is the square edge of an insipid beige curtain. The walls are painted a nondescript sickly cream. Think days of magnolia décor, when it was the interior designer's dream choice of colour. But on closer inspection, the cream has more of a milky coffee hue.

In the second shot, the night of the murder, Joel's face is still very close up to the screen, but he's in a kitchen. I've never been to his flat, but the kettle gives a distinct clue. Somewhere in the recesses of my mind, I remember a green kettle. Of course, I facetimed Joel recently and although I've no screenshot of that occasion, it's in my mind.

I look at my watch again. It's five, and still no word from Declan.

## 92

The square cube of the holding cell, walls newly slathered in a brown slimy paint wash, made him think of an oubliette; a dungeon where prisoners were thrown in medieval times and left to rot.

Perched on the hard slatted bench, the silence screamed admonishment. Isolation was following him like a wily fox sniffing out a chicken fenced in by weak, poorly erected, wire.

Bottling up all the growing-up shit, he soon became a loner by choice, preferring to pick and choose his interactions. Strange how the last six months of isolation had made him question this selective lifestyle when the choices were suddenly denied, snatched back like sweets from a spoilt child. Lockdown had killed off people's illusory control over life, leaving a blind panic in its wake.

When the police arrived, read him his rights and bundled him into the car with the accusatory flashing light, he didn't resist. At first, he thought it was all a bad dream and that he'd soon wake up, but perhaps he'd been asleep for years. He'd never owned up to his past, the reasons for all the shit, brushing the rancid dirt away into the recesses of his mind. Every so often the filth would throw up a new maggot which squirmed to uncover the rot. Barton had been one of those maggots.

He gazed up at the barred window by the ceiling, the sunlight knocking gently to be let in. He conjured up her soft bright smile with the clear blue eyes and gently curling lashes, her natural easy beauty. Thoughts wafted over him like a warm breeze until he drew his eyes back down to the blackened concrete floor.

Falling in love hadn't been part of any plan. Murdering Barton Hinton had. The gun had been a long-held secret possession, smuggled in from the States, which he knew how to use and lovingly cleaned from time to time. Perhaps lockdown had exacerbated his anger, the fury dripping steadily from a leaky framework as the weeks passed. The questions about his life had sent him over the edge. A bullet to the quizmaster's head had been the only option. The River Wear had gobbled up the weapon. The perfect murder, or so he'd thought until she told the police what she knew, even with no idea of what he'd done.

He'd googled prison cells a few months ago, their spartan fittings luxury for the poor in third world countries. Three meals a day, fresh water and a television room to chill. But he'd increased the screen size on the images, not to check out the décor more closely, rather looking for overhead bars where he could attach a cord with a large enough gap to thread his neck through and high enough off the ground so that he could dangle as the breath left his body. As backup, he had secreted a razor blade into one of the soles of his shoes.

He didn't think of suicide as cowardly, rather a way to cheat the system and move on to a better life.

## 93

I manage to hold off until seven o'clock before I lift the half-empty wine bottle from the fridge. Yesterday, it would have seemed half-full but as I peer through the opaque thick-green glass, I'm already wondering if there's another bottle in the cupboard. A drink is all I've got left to cling to.

I poke through the remnants of cheese, cold chicken and a damp unopened bag of salad on the shelf. The smell from the fridge reminds me that everything has a sell-by date and most of the contents are well past. I rip open the bag and sniff the wet rancid leaves with their sad reminder of my good intentions to lose the lockdown pounds. I throw them in the bin and instead go to the larder and dig out a rogue emergency bag of roasted peanuts which I pour into a bowl. It's like a last supper, the final meal before surrender.

Fuzzy joins me on the sofa, leaving her snug brood for a rare visit. She's not purring, spookily quiet, as she pushes her head hard up under my hand for assurance. Her body is battling against relaxation and as I crunch the nuts in my teeth, her nose pokes into the salty container. Her milk and supper in the corner haven't been touched.

EastEnders' theme music begins to roll and as I lie back, I pray that my mind will give in and allow me to get lost in other people's tragedies.

～

At first when my mobile rings I think the noise is coming from the television; a production device to suggest background action in a spartan socially distanced screen set. I nudge Fuzzy to one side and lean down and pick up my phone, but she squeals when I pull up sharply.

'Hi, gorgeous. How are you? Sorry I didn't phone earlier but I've been delivering in Bournemouth and forgot my bloody phone. The traffic back was a nightmare.'

My voice is hoarse, the words faintly choking.

'Are you okay?' Declan asks.

'I'm fine thanks. It's so good to hear your voice.' Relief floods over me like a tsunami, the force causing instant devastation to my fears and doubts.

'Hey. Are you crying? Have you missed me that much?' I can hear the smile in Declan's voice with its shaky edge. 'How did you get on at the police station?'

'Rihanna and I gave our statements, but...'

'You don't need to tell me. I've already heard.'

'Yes, they've arrested someone, but they wouldn't tell us who,' I say.

'Oh. Haven't you heard? Annabel phoned me.'

'Annabel? Why? It's not Clifton, is it?'

'Christ, no. I think she's phoning round, spreading the gossip so that there's no doubt of Clifton's innocence. Well, innocent in as far as murder goes.'

'Who's been arrested?'

'Can't you guess? Joel. Who else?'

# WEEK 9

## 94

Harpenden Common is peppered with walkers, joggers and a small fitness group doing star jumps led by a man in combat gear booming out instructions.

Annabel is being pulled along by a determined Jack Russell terrier, a long-promised gift to herself and now a feisty house companion. The puppy arrived only a couple of days ago, and I bite back a smirk noting the obvious resemblance to her husband, but I keep the thought to myself.

'Where's Clifton staying?'

'With his mother, of course. I sent him packing last night. He'll be telling her the accusations are all lies, unfounded conjecture, and she'll believe him.'

Annabel's hair is flying wildly in the wind, wispy unlacquered strands swirling with gay abandon. Without make-up, her face is fresh, youthful even and today the faint lines around her eyes hint at maturity rather than age. Attempts to fill in the cracks with expensive make-up and chemical fillers have been replaced by fresh air, and copious amounts of bottled water apparently.

'Has he been charged with anything?' I ask.

'The police arrived yesterday afternoon to begin questioning and a full enquiry is being set up. I doubt he'll be able to cover his tracks on the insider trading. He's been cautioned and not allowed to leave the country. I'll plead ignorance and Clifton has agreed to keep my name out of it. It's the least he can do.'

'And Alex?' My voice chases after her as the puppy skids ahead through the sodden turf.

'Elisa has already left him. I think it might have been on the cards all along, even before this all happened. I didn't realise how fed up she was, but I honestly thought she'd never leave him.'

'I think I had a lucky escape.'

'I spoke to her first thing this morning and the investigation into Alex and Clifton has been the last straw. Elisa is now keener than ever to distance herself from all the dirt that's going to come out.'

'Has Alex been charged with anything?' I jog to keep up.

'They're being investigated together, Alex for hacking finance companies' computer systems and Clifton for insider trading. The police are dealing with it as a single crime orchestrated by both men. The police aren't interested in the surmise that the pair were plotting to murder Barton.'

When I don't reply, Annabel continues, 'Clifton is *all talk* but not much else. Could you really imagine him as a cold-blooded murderer?' Her derisive snort gets swallowed up when a large black Labrador bounds towards the terrier which yaps and snaps at the larger animal's heels. The Labrador's hackles rise and when he bares his teeth Annabel frantically tugs on the lead to reel in her pet.

'Come here, Tiger. That'll be your name,' she croons, lifting up the shaking bundle. 'Tiger. Cute but fierce.' The Labrador bounds away, after a mighty whack on the backside with a stick from its owner.

'Tiger's a bit like Clifton.' Okay, it's too tempting not to share the observation. I can't help myself and our laughs clap together and relieve the tension.

'What are your plans?' I ask.

'It depends. I suspect they'll both do time, although Clifton will fight and defend his innocence to the bitter end.'

'I mean will you stay with him?'

'It's early days.' Annabel sets Tiger gently down, and then scoots off after him across the fields. 'Let's wait and see!' she yells over her shoulder.

When we get back to Annabel's house, she uncorks the customary champagne. It seems odd to be celebrating, but she assures me it's purely her preferred choice of drink. Yet I sense an element of celebration. Perhaps she's relieved her husband's not a murderer but more likely because she's got the house to herself. Either way, Annabel's pretty impressive in her resolve. It's true. Money makes misery easier to bear.

Today the orangery has a strange smell of puppy breath mingled with vanilla-scented candle. A strange pairing. Tiger is Annabel's first sign of rebellion against Clifton's dictatorship which banned house pets, although I'm amazed at her speed of moving forward. Perhaps, like Elisa, she's been planning the future for some time. Tiger's arrival has been serendipitous.

'So, what was the story with Joel?' I curl my legs up under me and sip the chilled nectar. Annabel rolls down a section of blinds to block out a streak of sunlight and sits alongside.

'It was one of his pupils. Pippa Carter. Poor girl was devastated when her parents went to the police. Apparently, Joel had been giving her extra tuition during lockdown. When the school closed, she would go to his flat.'

'How old was she?'

'Fifteen.'

'Shit.'

'She's convinced they're in love and says she's prepared to wait for him. Anyway, it came out during questioning, that she mentioned Joel had gone up to Durham for a few days around 18<sup>th</sup> September. Joel was staying with an elderly aunt who lives in a small coal mining village on the outskirts of the city. I suspect the police had been keeping tabs on our Zoom group after Barton's questions came to their attention.'

'So, some sharp DI probably made a connection,' I say.

'It hasn't come out yet how the police got proof that it was Joel who killed Barton, but I suspect we'll hear soon enough. They must be pretty certain as he's being locked up until the hearing.' Annabel lifts a pleading Tiger onto her lap before continuing. 'I think Joel may have done it before.'

'What? Murder?' I open my eyes wide.

'No. Don't be stupid.' Annabel chuckles. 'Lured young girls back to his flat. He left his last teaching job under a cloud.'

'Did you know that Joel's first girlfriend wasn't Olivia?' I set my drink down on the bevelled-glass side table.

'No. That was the obvious answer to Joel's question. We all agreed.'

'Well, it wasn't. It was a fifteen-year-old called Josie.'

'You're joking. How do you know?'

'I'm a great nosey dirt-raking journalist, remember. Barton taught me well. And, by the way, Declan will be with me for our Zoom tonight.' I blush.

'Will he indeed? You're a dark horse.' Annabel's unmanicured nails scrape down Tiger's soft coat as his pink-stippled tongue laps furiously across the back of her other hand. She bends down and gives him a little kiss on his head.

~

An hour later I'm back in my car, crunching over the Cotswold pebbles of Annabel and Clifton's driveway towards the main road. In my rear mirror I watch Annabel, standing on the porch with her head sunk low into Tiger's body, wave after me. So much for an ivory tower.

It's hard not to compare my rotting facia boards and dirty slabbed pathway with all that money can buy. But as I drive away, I realise I wouldn't in a million years swap my life for Annabel's.

My future is bright, with my very own knight in shining armour waiting in the wings.

## 95

### Zoom meet

Declan arrived last night with an overnight bag. A toothbrush and disposable razor on the bathroom shelf this morning offered weird comfort. A small travel aftershave perches on the bedside table.

Lockdown and the last six months have given me a glimpse into a singleton future. The joy of peace and quiet at home, after a daily frantic commute, has lost its thrill. Working from home has made me desperate for real company. Virtual meetings and remote socialising are no longer a novelty. Grayson, in a rare act of magnanimity, has offered all the newspaper staff £12 towards drinks and takeaway for a fortnightly Thursday online social.

'You can flirt and get drunk together without the worry of sexual harassment lawsuits!' He thinks he's hilarious, but more pertinently likes to think he's keeping up with the times.

When I got back from Annabel's, Declan was stirring vigorously at a casserole sizzling on the hob.

'Something smells good.'

'Irish stew.' He held out a spoon for me to taste. 'My mother's recipe. Plenty of potatoes.'

'Hope you're not feeding it to Fuzzy?' The cat was rubbing against his calves, weaving in and out. Her noisy contentment had the whirring timbre of distant rumbling thunder.

'Would I do that? Here. I've uncorked the wine.' Declan opened the fridge and pulled out a cold bottle of Sauvignon. 'Your favourite.'

'Thanks, Declan.' I went up and put my arms round his waist.

'What's this for? You haven't tasted the food yet.' He laughed. That's his way, his barrier against the world. Keep it light. Make jokes. But it feels good to have company filling my solitude with noise and banter.

When Declan suggested we do a final Friday night Zoom, it didn't feel right.

'Why not? It'll give me a chance to be question master. I've always dodged the responsibility, but I've googled some great teasers. And I thought it would be fun if we joined from separate rooms. Let's see who twigs that we're in the same house.' A mischievous twinkle was all it took to persuade me. Why not indeed?

～

'Hurry up. Invite them in. It's nearly eight.' Declan yells through from the kitchen and I can hear the swill of ice cubes from where I'm sitting in the lounge.

'I don't know why you're in such a hurry. You're usually the last. Where's Fuzzy by the way?' I ask.

'On my lap,' he says. I smile back at myself on screen.

At eight on the dot, I click the Invite link and open the virtual doors to the guests.

Annabel and Declan appear first. Alcohol is already working its magic, like oil on bicycle wheels, loosening the conversation and building the atmospheric momentum. The gears will soon ratchet up.

Annabel's lack of make-up is a token gesture to sombreness, but I know otherwise. She'll pretend that she's devastated, grieving, duped, and double-crossed. She'll try to hide from the rest of us that she's moving on pretty quickly from Clifton's crimes. She's pretending that she knew nothing about what was going on, but no one will believe her. The Shakespeare tomes have already been removed in preparation for tonight's gathering and replaced by Jackie Collins and Jeffrey Archer novels.

'I've ditched the Shakespeare,' is her opening gambit, a sharp chess player making the first attack.

'Good idea,' Declan says. 'Did you really think we'd fallen for all that literary shite.'

Rihanna's flaky face pops up next. A whiter shade of pale. She's like the inspiration for Procul Harum's famous hit.

'Hi.' The squeak is higher pitched than usual. A light-blue blouse is buttoned to the throat and her topknot is wobbling to the side.

'Hi, Rihanna. How the hell are you?' Declan is in control. If I didn't know he was in the next room, I'd be wondering why he's so jovial, upbeat.

A fifth screen pops to life, looking like a bright and breezy advert for summer holidays. Flamenco music can be heard in the background, low but unmistakable.

'Who the hell's that?' Declan yells at the screen, but the question is for my benefit.

'Who the hell are you, more to the point?' Grayson's voice

booms, whereas Declan's is a shout. Grayson's tanned face and arms commandeer the eye. His orange shirt conjures up images of satsuma season and his trademark thick gold chain chokes his neck.

'Hi, Grayson. Glad you could join us,' I interject. 'That's Declan yelling at you.'

The laugh from all the screens is muffled, but unanimous. Even Annabel sniggers. A yappy bark tops up the chorus. 'Shhh,' Annabel says to something invisible on her lap. I frown when I think of Fuzzy next door with Declan.

'Thanks, doll,' Grayson mumbles, as a slim shapely hand with shiny pink nails hands him a long-stemmed glass crammed with ice cubes, pale green liquid and a stripy straw. 'Hm, delicious.' Grayson slurps. 'That's Natalie, by the way. My significant other.' The manicured hand waves in front of his face.

'Is that everyone?' Annabel's voice is low-pitched, and as she hoists Tiger up, his pert tail flaps in her face.

'I think some members of our usual group have been otherwise detained,' says Declan. 'Not sure Pentonville Prison allows Zoom meets.'

'Can we get on with it?' Rihanna's voice is shaky, sounding like an old 45 record being played by a scratchy needle.

At this point I take a few screenshots. For the album. They'll be for the start of the new memories catalogue. When Declan begins to talk and fills centre screen, I take several shots. They're for the future. Who knows? Perhaps one day our little group will view them together, or separately. But today is a step towards a brighter tomorrow.

'Right. Pen and paper ready? Let's get started,' commands the quizmaster.

$\sim$

You learn a lot about a person by the type of questions they ask on quiz nights. I'm intrigued by the mix that Declan's come up with. He's kept them all general knowledge, varying the intellect and content level to include everyone. He's definitely a charmer, knows how to win favour. There's even a question about Pilates poses for Rihanna. One about Jack Russell terriers for Annabel. *Where did the name Jack Russell come from?* Annabel is delighted that she knew. The Reverend Jack Russell, a famous early breeder.

A rogue question about the number of golf clubs in Southern Spain tells me that Declan knew all along that Grayson would be joining us.

'Final question for the night. What did Barton Hinton die from?'

The screens freeze, the faces in each frame motionless. No one speaks. What the hell is Declan thinking of?

'Okay. If none of you can answer me, I'll tell you about the cause of death. Apparently, according to the coroner, Barton Hinton's death has been recorded as due to Covid-19.'

**2021**

# WEEK 53

## 96

### Zoom Meet

W hy the hell is Declan wearing his painting overalls? His side profile is to his screen, but I can see him rubbing in between his fingers with a cloth.

'Glad to see you dressed for the occasion,' I say.

'Jesus, Kristi. Give me a break. It was you who wanted me to strip the wallpaper. I'm covered in paint and I'm not going to dress up for some poxy quiz.'

I screenshot my fiancé as he curses when his finger gets stuck in the zip of his boiler suit.

Rihanna appears next. It's been nearly a year since I've seen her, and my mouth drops open at the change in her appearance. Her hair has been shorn like a springtime sheep, gentle woolly waves rippling over her scalp. Blonde has turned to a natural copper beech.

'Hi. Hope we're not late.' She whispers in deference to the body cocooned in what looks like a huge bandage across her cleavage. Motherhood has so transformed her appearance that she might need a new passport.

'How the hell are you, Rihanna?' Declan shouts at the screen, having uncovered a 'Welcome to Bangor' T-shirt with a paint splatter on the shoulder. 'Christ. Is that you?' Declan unceremoniously sticks his nose up against his computer, popping his eyes wide for effect.

'Hi, Declan. Meet Marty.' Rihanna gently peels back the bandage to reveal a small round sleeping face. Her voice is so quiet that Declan checks that she didn't say Arty.

A pair of arms are roped, think noose to restrain a heifer, around Annabel's neck when she appears at the party. My eyes move from the strong, tanned and muscled arms to the perfectly coiffed head tilted against a bicep.

The Dom Perignon label is back, but unlike Annabel's listing head it's positioned with the label perfectly square to the middle of her screen. It's like a TV advert, the perfect couple nothing more than a marketing ploy to sell something expensive and completely useless to an unsuspecting public. Annabel's desperate for us all to buy into the pose.

'Hi, guys.' Annabel's right hand moves over her shoulder and lands on the bicep not already occupied by her head. 'This is Santiago.' Santiago's thick curly locks straggle across Annabel's forehead before he throws his head back and sweeps his mane away with flick of a wrist.

'Hola.' His voice has the thickness of treacle. I note Declan's raised eyebrow and am imagining his sarcastic mutterings. He raises his Guinness which is overflowing with foam.

'Hola, Santiago. I thought that was the name of a place. A pilgrimage site.' Declan slurps his drink and makes a lip-smacking noise.

'Santiago is my personal trainer.' Annabel's doe eyes turn

upwards and thick Spanish lips caress them, flitting back and forth as if playing a harmonica.

I want to burst out laughing and know Declan's struggling to contain his mirth. He winks.

Marty gurgles, and Rihanna's repeated use of 'shhh' is louder than her words. The loving mother reminds Santiago what can happen in a careless moment of passion. When the crying starts and the bandage gets pulled farther back, I notice Santiago leaves the screen.

'Is Grayson coming or not?' Declan turns his watch towards us.

'It's only ten past,' I say. 'Give him another five minutes.'

I notice Rihanna and Annabel have muted their screens. Declan and I have nothing to hide, so we carry on the small talk.

No one knows we've got engaged. They'll assume, from our screen backgrounds, that I'm at home in Hitchin and Declan is back in Bangor with his mother. They don't know yet that she died in early summer. A heart attack. But according to her son, sole beneficiary of his mother's estate after she'd fallen out with her daughter, Máiréad, the cause wasn't purely down to hardened arteries and old age. Years of bigotry, cynicism and agitated discontent would have led the strongest constitution to an early grave.

Declan was eager to clear out her possessions and get on with his life. A coat or two of paint and the profits from the house will go towards our joint home together.

'We'll need somewhere with a large garden and well away from London.' It's not just that Declan wants us to grow our own fruit and veg to help with his burgeoning business (four vans now and two employees) but 'we're not giving any of the cats away'.

Fuzzy is stretched out along the bookshelf and her crazy four are skittering around the place. John, Paul, George and

Ringo. The names were Declan's idea. When we decided to keep all four, the name *Periwinkle* got binned.

The final screen pops up.

'Grayson.' Declan seems to know it's Grayson but I'm not sure how. My boss is completely bald, having forgone the wispy ageing look for a slicker, more virile statement. Although I catch up with my boss on screen every few days, it's been months since Declan's seen him.

'Declan, Kristi. Great to see you.' Grayson runs his stubby fingers across his head, teasing the hairs that are already battling back. 'Who the hell's that with Annabel? Is that her son?'

Good old Grayson. He can't help himself.

'Hi, Rihanna.' When there's no reply, he repeats himself in a much louder voice.

'She's on mute, Grayson. The baby's yelling. I think it's feeding time.'

Rihanna disappears for a few minutes while we all make small talk, catch up on the past year.

## 97

Gaps in conversations often tell us more than the conversations themselves.

While we prepare for one last quiz, small talk is like a hoe skirting round the edges of a garden of weeds, fiddling with the borders but ignoring the ugly stubborn stragglers that lie at the centre.

Joel finally hanged himself in March. But tonight, our chat doesn't venture towards the macabre. The future is why we've all turned up. Together our little troupe of survivors has got through the Covid war, and more poignantly survived personal struggles as the pandemic raged.

Clifton has gone to prison for three years, although Annabel is confident that he'll get out after a maximum of eighteen months. Apparently, he's capable of good behaviour when he puts his mind to it.

Alex was given a two-year suspended sentence and a few hundred hours of community service to make up for his hacking crimes. The villa in Spain has been sold to pay for all the fines and legal fees that he and Clifton have amassed. Elisa eventually came back to stand by her man, but Annabel has no idea why.

She'll not be standing by Clifton and the divorce papers have already been presented to her husband's lawyer.

Although as Santiago's sneaky eyes slither through the screen like a snake's tongue, I decide it's not my place to warn Annabel. She's a poor judge of character, but I have to laugh when I remember her warning me off married men.

Rihanna is a natural mother. Clifton, Marty's father, has been banned by Rihanna from seeing his son but I suspect she'll weaken as the months go by. I will remind her, when Clifton presents the first bunch of conciliatory flowers, what a shit he was and that she mustn't ever have him back. But something tells me, this time she'll not need a warning.

Finally, Grayson is on his own again. Natalie came back to England, but my boss has already got his eye on a young Spanish chica who has taken his fancy. Thank goodness he's not coming back.

Remote working benefits us all. I've finally moved my stuff into Grayson's old office and the three-day-a-week commute for the staff suits me fine. The new working normal has now had the 'new' dropped out of the saying. Normal now is just different to what it was twelve months ago.

'Okay. Here we go. First round. General Knowledge.' Declan bangs a spoon against his glass to get our attention.

I burst out laughing when I realise the only person holding up a pen is Santiago.

THE END

# ACKNOWLEDGEMENTS

Writing is frequently a solitary, lonely task but it is the people along the way who keep you going with their unwavering encouragement and belief.

I would like to thank my friends, my family and all those who read my books and ask me every day how work is progressing. A special thanks to my enthusiastic reviewers who take time out to give honest opinions.

*The Six Guests* was written during Lockdown 2020, and I need to give special thanks to hubby, Neil, and our son, James, who made the summer pass so quickly. In between cooking and playing 'mini' tennis in the garden, I was given time and peace to write, and regular online quizzing provided inspiration for this particular work.

I am, as always, indebted to my publishers, Bloodhound Books, who work tirelessly to get our books out there. Betsy's astute insight into my manuscripts has been brilliant, both in terms of content and marketing, and along with Fred, they run a tight ship.

Morgen Bailey, as an editor, is second to none. Her attention to detail is amazing and when my books go to print, they have been polished to perfection.

Again, a huge thanks to Tara Lyons, whose prompt response to so many queries marks her out as a true professional. Also, thank you to Maria Slocombe for her fabulous marketing of Bloodhound books. Her riveting trailers have helped so many novels gain media attention and rise up the rankings.

Finally, I would like to thank the NHS again, for their unwavering commitment to duty, along with our wonderful scientists who brought us the Covid vaccine. Without hope that the pandemic would be over, writing would have held little pleasure and *The Six Guests* might never have happened.

Thank you all.

# A NOTE FROM THE PUBLISHER

**Thank you for reading this book.** If you enjoyed it please do consider leaving a review on Amazon to help others find it too.

**We hate typos.** All of our books have been rigorously edited and proofread, but sometimes mistakes do slip through. If you have spotted a typo, please do let us know and we can get it amended within hours.

info@bloodhoundbooks.com

# ABOUT THE AUTHOR

Diana Wilkinson (née Kennett) graduated from Durham University with a degree in geography then after a short spell in teaching, spent most of her working life in the business of tennis development.

A former Irish international player, Diana finally stepped off the court to become a full-time writer. The inspiration for much of her work has come from the ladies she coached through the years and from confidences shared over coffee.

Diana's debut novel and her first psychological thriller, *4 Riverside Close*, quickly became an international best seller. Her second and third books, *You Are Mine* and *The Girl Who Turned A Blind Eye*, are also set in North London, in areas where Diana lived and worked for many years. *The Six Guests* is her fourth psychological thriller, set during the Lockdown of 2020.

Born and bred in Belfast, Northern Ireland during the height of the civil unrest, she now lives in Hertfordshire, England, with her husband Neil and son James.

CPSIA information can be obtained
at www.ICGtesting.com
Printed in the USA
FSHW012352110721
83142FS

9 781913 942915